WINDS OF CHANGE

Alisa Allan

Alisa Allan (signature)

Bon Voyage Books
An Imprint of Travel Time Press

Bon Voyage Books
An Imprint of Travel Time Press

Winds Of Change
Copyright © 2005 by Alisa Allan

ISBN: 0-9761480-0-5

The reproduction or utilization of this work is strictly prohibited. This includes not only photocopying and recording but by any electronic, mechanical, storage and retrieval system or any other means hereafter invented, in whole or in part without the written permission of our editorial office, Travel Time Press/Bon Voyage Books, 163 Mitchells Chance Rd., Edgewater, MD 21037 U.S.A.

This is a work of fiction. Any names, characters, places or incidents are products of the author's imagination or are used in a fictitious manner. Anyone bearing the same name or names is not to be construed as real. Any resemblance is entirely coincidental.

Visit us at www.TravelTimePress.com

Travel Time Press: SAN# 2 5 6 – 5 7 9 X

PRINTED IN THE UNITED STATES OF AMERICA
First Printing: June 2005
10 9 8 7 6 5 4 3 2

Dedicated to:
Elizabeth 'Granny' Oswald
April 10, 1899 – April 2, 2002
MAY SHE DANCE WITH THE ANGELS

It all began with Granny as she created a world for not only her family, but those pulled in and made to feel a part of it. A family of unity, a family of lifelong bonds to cherish. Perhaps an art to create such a thing, if so, Granny was master at it. She led a full life, traveled extensively as her family grew and dispersed in different directions, from California to Canada and even Europe. Healthy and vibrant she danced at her 100th birthday celebration and commented that she could have done better had she had her tennis shoes on. On her 102nd birthday she did the Charleston and the December before her passing found her 'holding court' at a Christmas party of more than 200 people.

Elizabeth Miller Oswald didn't have the riches of a material world, she wasn't wrapped in expensive furs and diamonds nor have mansions filled with cars she'd never drive anyway. She spoke the truth when she told you she never wanted for those things, for she knew what truly mattered most and she passed this on to each and every one of us. A sense of family, the very meaning of it, and the value of being blessed with loved ones.

Granny had a way of drawing people in. Of making you feel a part of her life, making you feel 'at home' wherever you were. As a granddaughter, I have vivid memories to cherish, yet more memories that aren't in vivid detail. The times our family simply gathered together for occasions or for no reason at all in a small white house that seemed to overflow with people. Full of tales and laughter, yet I can't recall details of what we laughed about or the stories that were told, only the sense of being there, and being a part of it all.

Blessed and lucky to have their great-grandmother for many years of their lives, my children learned this the same way. I simply sat them in a room full of people, full of laughter, immersed them in it, and they too were drawn in, absorbed it all. Although indefinable in words, whatever it was, you knew, and you understood.

Granny, I thank you for this silent legacy. This silent gift you've given me. I thank you for all the memories we've shared that I can vividly recall, but especially for the memories I can't recall in detail. For I now understand it's from these memories, you passed on this silent gift without saying a word.

PART ONE

The Dividing Line

CHAPTER 1

It was Christmas in New York City. Somewhere in the distance of the large penthouse, sounds of carols filtered in and she wanted to close the door to drown out the noise. She was always so overly sentimental during the holiday. It began when the first decorations appeared just after Thanksgiving that a slow ache began to build and grow stronger day by day, it quietly ate away piece by piece through the layers of indifference she'd developed over the years.

Indifference that most times let her successfully push away the old memories that tried to filter through, but that time of year it was much more difficult to master. She would get a stirring from a certain scent as she passed the tree stand on the corner. The smell of pine, of burning wood as people warmed themselves from an open fire in a metal barrel. As she walked down the sidewalk to a meeting or to her office she'd catch a quick scent of something baking, any other time of year she wouldn't notice she passed a bakery every day. At that time of year she'd change her route to avoid it until after the New Year came.

The other day she found herself with the slightest hint of tears in her eyes for no apparent reason as she stood on the sidewalk and waited for a cab, looked out to a busy city of shoppers and holiday cheer. It was an odd moment to be caught so vulnerable and she often wondered if the memories would forever plague her, or if a time would come those long ago memories would not be so easily retrieved from her mind, eventually weaken and disappear to non-existence. Such a treasured part of her past, but she would easily let them slip away if they tried. There was pain in knowing it all went on without her.

People traveled from far to see a city famous for its glorious display's, they reveled in its splendor, but Samantha just wanted to disappear. Before Trenton, she would disappear. Go away to an island or some other place that didn't go to extremes to celebrate the season with such flair as America did. She'd make her excuses to her friends that invited her to join in their festivities and escape on a solitary trip that always helped, when she returned in January she was much stronger.

Now that Trenton was in her life she ignored everything around her as best she could and got through it somehow. Pulled reserves from somewhere deep and moved through the season in a trance with an inner strength she'd honed to perfection over the years. A strength that faltered at times and weakened her, but it was now Christmas Eve, and it was almost over. She would get through the night before her, and Christmas day tomorrow, she always did. Then she would move forward with the path she'd chosen, one that continued to take her far from the banks of New England and what she'd left behind.

Trenton stepped into the room and stood for a moment before she noticed him. When she looked up, whatever he'd seen in her eyes a moment ago was gone. That same far away look he'd see sometimes when she didn't notice he was looking at her, and although he never asked, he often wondered where she went to in the deep of her mind. It wasn't with him, of that he was sure. And it always left quickly, making him wonder if he'd seen it at all.

"We should leave soon, Samantha, are you almost ready?"

Trenton pulled her back to where she needed to be, in the present. Without turning, she watched him from the mirror of the vanity table as he rooted around in the safe, it didn't get past her he seemed anxious to go that evening and she commented on it.

"I've never seen you in such a hurry to get to one of your mother's parties."

"Tonight is different." He caught himself and continued so she wouldn't question his meaning. "You know how she is about her Christmas Eve party, and traffic is going to be impossible. We're already late."

"I don't even think Spalding is home yet, I'm sure if he's late, we'll be excused if we're late. Or don't you hold as much clout as your father?"

"If you asked mother she'd say I had more, but that's because I'm her favorite son."

"You're her only son."

"And I reap the benefits of being an only child, but that still won't excuse us for being so late for her Christmas party. It's her biggest one of the year, she starts planning for the following year the day after." He found what he searched for, a pair of Cartier diamond cufflinks, very particular double cufflinks with enamel and linen centers. Alongside them was a pair of earrings he now held out to her. "You haven't worn these yet, have you?"

She glanced at them quickly. "No, I haven't. They're not exactly appropriate for the office and that's the only place I've been lately."

"You could wear them tonight."

"I could." She answered with hesitation and hoped he hadn't noticed.

It wasn't the type of jewelry she preferred. It was the type of jewelry reserved for the elite few, people like her mother, his mother, and many others who used it as a benchmark of wealth. The kind of people who draped themselves with expensive jewels to wear like shiny beacons to announce prosperity, but that type of thing never suited her. Though others would wear them proud, she tried to think of an excuse not to.

Trenton waited beside her. "Put them on, let me see."

With no excuse not to pacify him she put the earrings on. They were a birthday present he'd given her this past year, her thirty fifth. So proud he was when he'd first presented them to her, and even now as he looked at her in anticipation. They matched her outfit perfectly and she had no excuse to deny him, she wondered why she couldn't have chosen something purple to wear instead.

Flawless large rubies circled by brilliant diamonds on her ears, matched impeccably to her red ankle length Valentino skirt topped with black silk. With her dark hair pulled up loosely, wispy tendrils of curls around her face, the earrings were pronounced even more. They were beautiful. Even if it wasn't something she felt suited her in particular, they fit her life now.

Trenton leaned down and kissed her neck. "They look great."

Samantha paid little attention to his words, in her mind she was planning a shopping trip to buy something purple, there was little in the safe that would go with purple. Other women would be envious of the jewels, but she felt like a Christmas tree with shiny red baubles hanging from her head. Was thankful he hadn't bought her a diamond tiara to look like the top star.

"All I need are my shoes and I'll be ready."

"I don't know if I want to go out or not." Trenton leaned down and kissed her again, her skin soft, her smell sweet.

"We can stay in, just say the word."

There couldn't have been anything better on that Christmas Eve if he'd just agree and they could forget about his parent's annual party. It was an explosion of holiday cheer in his mother's home, at least in Trenton's city penthouse there wasn't even a decorated tree, not so much as a card displayed and they received many. It had been the cleaning lady to put the carols on the sound system before she'd left that day, and though she wanted to turn them off, Trenton had been in good spirits and refused. It was easier for her when there were no reminders of what time of year it was, easier to push aside her sentimental instincts.

"You know that's impossible, we have to go, but we'll come home early. Will that suffice?" He kissed her again, wanted to please her, wanted to stay in, but he had plans to carry out.

"How early?"

"Early enough, we have some celebrating to do."

"It sounds like you mean something other than Christmas Eve." She cocked her head to the side with suspicious question in her eyes.

"I might," was all he said and gave her no indication of more.

"What do you have up your tailored sleeve, Trenton Edwards?" She looked at his handsome face reflected behind her in the mirror. He was so suited for his tailor made tuxedo, as if he could have been born in it.

Trenton changed the subject instead of answering. "When are you going to move your stuff in?"

"I've moved my stuff in. I've been living with you for months now, haven't you noticed?"

"Some things, but not everything, if you were moved in you'd put your personal things in the drawer and not in that ratty old bag."

"I keep the bag in the drawer, doesn't that count as moved in?"

The case he spoke of was anything but stylish, stood out in the grandeur of his penthouse like a weed in a perfectly manicured garden of roses. The jewels that hung from her ears were obvious signs of her present and future, the tattered blue and yellow case her past. They clashed in their differences. Maybe it was something she should have let go a long time ago. It was just a bag, wasn't it? The phone sounded and saved her from further discussion of it as he left the bedroom.

"I'm sure that's the car, do I have to tell him to drive around the city a few times until you're ready?"

"I just have to put my shoes on," she assured him as he disappeared from the room.

But he was gone and couldn't see she made no attempt to do so. Subconsciously, her hand lingered on the softness of the bag he spoke of, fingers pulled slightly at a frayed piece of thread, the print of blue and yellow now worn and faded. As she looked up into the mirror she caught a glimpse of similarity in her own eyes. Once intensely vivid, once flickered with light like the ruby and diamond earrings that flashed their brilliance on her ears, there was no shine evident in her eyes now. Deep blue eyes that used to absorb every moment of excitement life had to offer now looked just as worn and faded as the special bag she held onto.

Lifeless, they stared back at her in the mirror as if they were a stranger's eyes, so unfamiliar. When had they changed? How long ago had they lost their life, and why hadn't she noticed when it happened? Casualty of age, she told herself. Stress and tension from long days at the office worked its weary spell, lines had begun to form, not pronounced and distinct just yet, but it was only a matter of time.

Maybe she should start taking better care of herself. Look into skin products that touted youth in a bottle, but she barely had time for anything but a quick wash of her face with soap and water. Wasn't disciplined or vain enough to worry about more, now wondered if she should as Samantha touched her face lightly, felt a tinge of melancholy still as she realized how quickly the years were slipping by.

****

When they arrived at his parents immense home, they handed over their coats to the tuxedo clad Butler at the door.

"Good evening Mr. Edwards, your mother's been waiting for you. Ms. Durham." He nodded to Samantha who smiled warmly.

"Did father make it back to town?" Trenton took an experienced quick survey of the growing crowd.

"I'm afraid his plane was delayed, but he will arrive this evening."

Extremely wealthy people used holidays and occasions as part celebration and part business networking, they used it as opportunity. More than two hundred people milled about on that Christmas Eve in a home professional decorator's had worked into a showcase. A magnificent display, one that rivaled Times Square and Rockefeller Center, complete with live carolers dressed in old fashioned costumes hired to entertain. Their melodious singing transmitted to every room by hidden speakers.

Before they mingled they made their way to Trenton's mother who didn't mingle, Trenton's mother held court and waited for people to come to her. He received warm affection, Samantha the distant politeness they always exchanged.

"Trenton, darling, you're late."

"How do you know we haven't been here for an hour?" He countered playfully as he kissed her on the cheek. "Evening, mother."

"Because you would have come to see me the moment you got here." It was a statement made of fact, what she expected from her only child, nothing less would have been acceptable. She turned her attention to Samantha with a smile as she openly surveyed her outfit. "Samantha, you look festive this evening. This ensemble suits you so much better than your normal boring wardrobe. You ought to wear things like this more often."

"It would be difficult to conduct business in something such as this. I don't think I'd be taken too seriously."

"Ah, business." Harriet swooshed her hand through the air to dismiss the thought.

Samantha's relationship with his mother was minimal. Each of them kept their distance, a mutual understanding and respect for the other with the knowledge they had little in common other than the man who stood between them. Samantha wrapped up completely in business, his mother in the social scene her wealth entitled her to. The two of them ventured off through the room and left his mother to play her role as she 'received' other guests.

"Trenton, no one ever told me you had a much more attractive side to you." The man walked up to them and looked to Sam with a coy smile.

"Jonathan, this is Samantha Durham."

"Nice to meet you." She shook his hand politely but wanted to find a napkin immediately to wipe away the feel of his sweaty palm.

"Durham, I know that name."

"Her family owned Durham Glass among many other things, our companies merged several years ago."

"Ah, that Durham. I was thinking of a Durham I talked to from your firm today."

"The same." Samantha admitted. "Jonathan Turner from Cedis Enterprises, correct? We're negotiating the contract for the overseas distributors."

"You? You work for..." He didn't complete his sentence and looked confused. He hadn't put the name together that day, she'd been heir to a fortune, and he never suspected she worked for a living, not even with her own company. And if he had suspected, he would have thought in the capacity of another position, one not so active.

It always took people by surprise and it could be avoided if Trenton simply introduced her as Samantha and said she was a corporate attorney other than what her family was. Or rather, had been.

"Well, I pictured the Edwards Chief Corporate Attorney a little more conservative. You know, the gray hair, the mousy glasses. Had I known you looked this good I may have been a little easier on you."

She could feel Trenton's arm tense as she laughed sardonically. It was always a man's mistake to take her lightly. "Please don't mistake a big set of tits for a small brain and think you have to go easier on me. But if that's a mistake you wish to make I'll have my little ole' contract over on your desk in one hour and all you'll have to do is sign on that little dotted line. I'll even use one of those pretty highlighter's and color it pink for you."

"Why do you have to do that?" Trenton said when he'd quickly made their escape.

"What? Defend myself? There are few men in this room who would admit I have a brain and its unfortunate it has to happen at parties, but at times they have to be reminded."

"We need that ratified contract and..."

She stopped him in mid sentence. "Not that it would stop me, but it isn't as if it's in jeopardy no matter what I say to Jonathan Turner, and we both know it."

"Your optimism sounds promising, but there's no need to take chances."

"I don't take chances. While we're on the subject, when I was going over the final..."

This time it was Trenton who interrupted. "You're not doing this. You're trying to pull me in and I won't let it happen. I'm not talking business tonight. For once, we won't discuss anything business. Can we do that?"

"Since when do you not want to discuss business, you're taking all the fun out of the evening." There wasn't much else there to keep her attention.

Another incident came about when she was introduced again. So much could be avoided if he introduced her by her first name, if he didn't care that people knew who she was.

"Gary Bunch, this is Samantha Durham." Trenton smiled proudly.

"Durham Corporation, a name I'll never forget. I lost my ass in the stock market when..." Gary tried to catch himself but it was too late.

Samantha's eyes were her normal stone reserve as she finished his sentence. "When my father was killed. Yeah, so did I." She said dryly.

"I'm sorry... I didn't mean..."

"To be so insensitive? Of course you didn't." She said with a cynical tone. She knew who he was and what type of person he was whether she'd ever been formally introduced or not. She made it her business to know about many people.

Samantha smiled broadly but the others were uncomfortable, everyone but the man's wife who hadn't been paying attention. The woman openly continued to adjust her dress at the bosom to show off her new purchase of breasts to best advantage. Samantha looked to the woman, shook her head and walked away.

Bored with ladies conversations of their latest purchases, including body parts, she found little to keep her entertained as she moved away from Trenton and off on her own. She surveyed the beautiful crowd from a discreet distance and thought about all the silicone and plastic implanted for all kinds of artificial body parts, wondered if there was a 'real' person in the room. In the back of her mind she thought that if there were a fire, there would be nothing humanly distinguishable left, they would all have melted into a puddle.

She wasn't like them. She didn't get into talk of the latest fashions, the best, most exclusive places to vacation, or anything else they thought interesting and worthy for words. Once conversation started it continued in a circle. Someone mentioned something, but the next lady had one even better, and the next, and the next. The same when they talked of children. Another thing along with everything else she didn't have in common with them.

They discussed them like possessions. Didn't talk about sweet little things their children did, funny little stories, a first tooth, accomplishments such as their first step or they'd learned to ride a bike. Instead, little Bradley was accepted into Carver Academy, an exclusive private school, or they'd just purchased little Amelia her first horse. Never mind the fact she was six months old and terrified of the thing. But they wouldn't have known that, it was the nanny's job to make sure Amelia spent time with the horse.

And she didn't fit into the men groups either, intimidated them, scarred egos. When Samantha blasted through their world she did so with a drive and determination that frightened most. Had she been a man she would have been strong, assertive and powerful, instead, she had other names. None anyone would dare reveal to her face, but she knew what they were. She'd had to fight hard for respect, but she'd earned it from those who were secure in themselves to not let their ego be affected. For the others, Samantha didn't care. She wasn't there to make friends.

As she looked around the room she couldn't help but think of them all as clones. No diversity. Nothing to distinguish them apart. She had to note with the exception of Trenton, he stood out among them with an air of power that seemed to be like a tangible mist that surrounded him.

He was extremely handsome, that was the obvious, but her main attraction to him was that they were equals. Their work habits were the same and he never threatened to interfere with that, it was because of their constant work habits and working so closely together, that the relationship evolved. Then somehow moved from a casual thing to a constant and Samantha wasn't even sure how it happened but it worked well for both of them.

Unlike his mother, who would have preferred her son be with someone more like herself, his father couldn't have been happier. When he finally arrived to his own party, Samantha was excited to see him because he brought with him her chance to discuss business. Everything else was a bore.

"How's my favorite opponent?" Spalding asked as he kissed her on the cheek with affection.

"I'm not your adversary anymore, Spalding, remember? We're on the same team now."

"You're still my favorite. I've often thought of taking back the merger just so we could fight about it longer."

She smiled. He was a kind fatherly man she'd come to know well, worked with side by side over the years and learned a great deal. "We could always do it over again, just for kicks."

"Just for kicks?" he huffed and continued, "And have you rake me over the coals again? I said longer, not the entire thing over, I barely made it out alive." Like Trenton, Spalding was well trained to scan the room quickly to survey the people there. "Have you been keeping everyone in line? Including Trenton?"

"That isn't my job. We both know if it were, there would be far fewer employees. I don't make a nice people person, so many of them frustrate me."

"So many of them fear you," he laughed at the truth.

Spalding considered one of his most successful days in business was not only the merge with her fathers company, but more important, that she came with it. Samantha Durham had not only surprised him but the entire business world when she took such a strong position, the role vacated by her father. Over the years she'd earned great respect and fear for doing something that seemed to naturally be in her genes.

Just as she was about to ask about the trip, Trenton approached them with a look to both that he, for once, was not interested in business that evening. He had other things on his mind and told his father they'd meet him in the grand living room in thirty minutes.

After Spalding left, he saw the disappointment in Samantha's eyes, and also a growing suspicion as he pulled her close to him. She was on the verge of asking about what he had planned but he stopped her.

"You can wait a while longer. If I told you now it wouldn't be a surprise."

"I don't like surprises," she said.

"This is the season for surprises, and everyone likes surprises."

"I'm not everyone. I like to be prepared, I don't like to be caught off guard, it leaves me with a feeling of no control."

"I'm the last one on earth that has to be reminded that you're not everyone, certainly not your typical woman who would be delighted at the thought of a surprise on Christmas Eve." Trenton stared into intense eyes that held a hard edge, a guard she never let down.

"I hope you're not planning anything foolish."

"Me? A foolish man? I pride myself on my intelligence." He pulled her closer and felt the tension of her body. For an instant he second guessed himself, but knew if he didn't do it this way she would easily dismiss the idea he had in mind.

When he felt it time, Trenton took Samantha by the hand and led her to where most of the group gathered, in front of his parents. Then he got down on one knee, offered a gigantic four-caret diamond ring as he proposed marriage, and then everything after that was a blur.

No one waited for an answer as instantaneous celebration broke out and Champagne was distributed all around. People smiled, laughed, and congratulated them. Standing in the center of the melee of more than two hundred people that surrounded her, smothered her, Sam watched the activity as if she floated above it. Watched it all take place as if she were engulfed in someone else's foggy dream.

****

As Trenton slept that evening, she reached into the drawer and retrieved her blue and yellow bag before going into the massive, quiet living room that overlooked the city. Samantha placed the soft material against her cheek, tried to find the smell of it that was lost now, but she could still remember it well. As if it hadn't disappeared, from memory, she could distinctly recall the smell of sweet lavender mixed with sea air, a freshness that soothed and calmed her. Even the memory conjured up a peace for her, but in the next instant when she opened her eyes to her reality, it brought turmoil.

She sat alone in the room curled up in a chenille chair and stared at lights of the city beyond the floor to ceiling windows. She wondered about all the people behind all the windows waiting for Christmas in the morning, so many others around the world doing the same thing. Families gathered in celebrated joy, crossed countries and continents to be with loved ones. And she sat alone.

For a moment she allowed herself to close her eyes and remember. Could smell the scent of cookies and cinnamon, see the lights of the boats on parade in the harbor, even feel the warmth not only from a roaring fire but also from the people she shared it all with. When she allowed herself, Samantha could even hear the voices, the laughter. But it had been so long now, the sound of the laugher was faint and she couldn't clearly distinguish it. Not who it belonged to anyway, because there were many that used to gather on Christmas at the Inn by the sea.

Then she had to tell herself they still gathered, they were all there Samantha, it was only you that wasn't among them. Only you with a mere thought to connect you, while they were all there in person. To try and stop herself from thinking anymore she stepped to the window and placed her cheek on the cold pane of the glass.

She wanted desperately to tear her thoughts away from the direction they wanted to go, but she couldn't. She prided herself in her strength, so strong most times but it was the worst time of year for her, the season that always made her so sentimental and vulnerable. The marriage proposal from Trenton only made her feel more emotionally unbalanced and for a quick moment she looked to the telephone. Don't pick it up Samantha, she had to tell herself. You've never faltered before, never called in moments of weakness, never when you felt so defenseless and exposed.

Carter should have been the last person to think about but he was the first, always the one that crossed her mind when she felt lonely and in need. Isolated like the lonely child she used to be. Alone, she felt the kind of terror that made her feel the entire world was falling upon her shoulders, and in lost abandonment needed to turn to the one person who always made the world seem right. But he wasn't there. Carter and her life on the banks of New England had been lost to her long ago.

Not only did she feel like a twister was ripping through her insides, she felt confused as she looked to the large stone that now adorned her hand. Shouldn't this be where she should feel satisfied? Isn't this what they always wanted for her? As in all the other times she'd asked herself that question, she felt the same. Nothing. No different than she did yesterday, no different than ten years previous when she began this quest. Every step of the way she waited for a feeling that never came. When could she stop? When would she ever be fulfilled? She knew the answer, not until that desperate little girl inside stopped crying out to her.

She'd made her choices long ago and could only look ahead now. The engagement to Trenton would be an official close to her past and a commitment to moving forward to find what she needed even though it split her heart in two. One side of her lonely heart told her she had to keep going forward, while the other side of her lonely heart had to stop her from going back.

She looked up to the dark sky and concentrated on a star that shone bright, thought of Carter one last time before she locked the thoughts away again. In the moment of question she'd lost her focus, lost her way, but even as confused as she was, Samantha knew she couldn't go back. That lonely little girl inside wouldn't let her. A soft cry broke the silence.

CHAPTER 2

She was attracted to Carter the moment he sat down next to her in Professor Derring's lecture hall. It was her freshman year of college.

"Am I late? Did I miss much?" He inquired in a whisper as he silently slid into the seat next to her.

She glanced up at him without interest and glanced away. A few moments later looked up again when she felt his eyes still on her, he merely smiled and waited for an answer.

"Did you miss much?" She raised her eyebrows and spoke sarcastically. "This lecture will be over in five minutes, you only missed the first fifty five minutes. I'm sure you can catch up."

He smiled with confidence, sure of himself. "That's okay, we'll go over your notes at lunch today."

"We will?"

"You don't want me to fail do you?"

"What do I care?" She turned her attention back to the book and flipped a page.

"If I fail this class it might send me into a tailspin. I'll become depressed, fail my other classes, drop out of school. I'll end up homeless and living in a train station. You wouldn't want that on your conscious would you?"

"No need to worry about my conscious. I'll be fine."

He leaned in closer. "Think if I took up the guitar, I could make enough for a hot meal once a day?"

"I'll be sure to drop a dollar or two in your can when I pass by. The subway is a good spot." All of a sudden the words she tried to read didn't make sense anymore.

She didn't tell him he didn't need to play the guitar, all he had to do was smile and he'd make a fortune. It wasn't like her to be so instantly attracted to someone, she always distanced herself, but maybe it was because he didn't look like the guys from her elite private school she'd grown up in. Instead, he looked like everything her parents would disagree with.

Dressed in worn jeans and a navy blue sweatshirt with the sleeves slightly pulled up, one could distinguish muscles because of his build. Even if they weren't clearly visible, you sensed them. With his dark tousled hair and just the slightest hint of dark shadow stubble on his face, it gave him a boyish charm.

"I have another class after this so I won't be able to meet you until probably one or so," he continued talking as if there were no question.

"How disappointing." She said dryly but didn't look at him again.

"It is disappointing. I know you wanted to meet me right after this, but I can't miss my next one. It's a killer professor and he's giving us our fourth test in four weeks of school."

She laughed on the inside, but her outward appearance was still one of disinterest, didn't want to give him any encouragement. She pretended not to listen to him but every word he said filtered through and he didn't give up. As soon as the bell sounded she gathered her books and made her way to the door but even that didn't put him off, he was right next to her.

"Slow down, don't you want to know where to meet me?"

"I'm not meeting you, you're going to amount to no more than a homeless guitar player and I won't support you."

She walked faster and as hard as he tried, Carter got stuck in the middle of the crowd and had to yell across the throng of people. "Hey wait!"

He watched and felt helpless as she walked faster and faster and more and more people came between them. Short of knocking people over to get to her there was nothing he could do, so he shouted as loudly as he could so she would hear above the growing noise.

"One o'clock at Casey's Brew House on Buchanan Street."

She never turned around and he could only watch her disappear around the corner not knowing if she heard.

By twelve thirty Carter was waiting at the designated spot. One came, then one thirty, and two o'clock passed but he still sat patiently reading. It was almost three before she arrived.

"Right on time." His grin was large as he stood when she approached the table.

"Didn't you say one o'clock?"

"One o'clock, three o'clock..." he shrugged his shoulders. "I knew you'd come."

"How is that possible when I didn't even know myself until five minutes ago?" She herself grinned, he made it impossible not to. And she was surprised by the feeling in the pit of her stomach.

"You didn't want to come, tried to talk yourself out of it ever since I asked. You even went back to your dorm and pulled out all your books, settled in for the afternoon to study. But you couldn't concentrate."

"Don't think I'll ever admit to it." She sat down in the chair he pulled out for her, impressed by his manners.

"As long as I don't have to admit I'd been in that lecture hall for the first fifty five minutes. Nor will I admit to the fact that it isn't even one of my classes."

"Now I know you'll end up a homeless guitar player, you can't even make it to the right class."

"But I take opportunity when I see it. I've been trying for two weeks but you've been walking around campus preoccupied with your head in a book and I could never catch up to you. You seemed to vanish into thin air around every corner. When I saw you walk into the lecture hall I knew I had to take my chances."

"Okay, so maybe you have potential since you at least must have found the class interesting since you paid attention the first fifty five minutes, even if it wasn't your class."

"I never heard a word he said. By the time I got inside, I didn't know where you'd gone and I had to take a seat as quick as possible. Unfortunately, not only was it closer to the back of the room, but on the other side. So every time the professor turned around I had to move from empty seat to empty seat. It took me fifty five minutes to reach you."

She smiled. Curious about this stranger who not only had impressive manners, but she liked his pure honesty. Immediately sensed there would be no pretenses, no guesses or games. And of course his physical attributes didn't go unnoticed, when he smiled at her he pulled her in with a charm she felt he didn't use lightly. Intuition told her he wasn't the type to go to so much trouble for every girl he might find attractive.

"So," he said. "I wouldn't blame you if you thought I was a stalker after I just told you everything. If that's the case, I wouldn't even blame you if you lied to me. But now that you're finally within a few feet, before you disappear again, I have to have a name to go with the face."

"Samantha. Samantha Durham."

She looked in his eyes for any recognition and saw none. It was habit. Habit for her to try and distinguish if someone would be interested in her or what her name was because that's how it was in the atmosphere she'd grown up in. It was why she'd chosen the small school versus a bigger name college her father wanted her to attend. This was a different atmosphere and no one knew or cared who she was. And though it hadn't been planned, she decided at that moment she would postpone any disclosure as long as possible.

Carter smiled with satisfaction to finally know. Liked the way she wanted to look distant, but he could tell she was interested even though she fought it. "Well, Sam, I've decided to help you. Now I'll be busy with all my guitar lessons, but I'll fit you in. You're taking this much too seriously, it doesn't have to be all work." He spoke as if it were a serious discussion. "Fun is a very important aspect of survival, and I don't think you've caught on to that."

"And I suspect you have a solution for me?"

"It will take some time but I'll work with you. I've appointed myself your liberator."

She didn't know then, how true his words would be. In the few moments of actual time they'd spent together, she already had the nickname 'Sam' and they already had the private joke between them of him being a homeless guitar player. There was a connection to him she couldn't explain. He drew her in with ease, made her feel a contentment just to sit next to him.

The ease of their conversation flowed well into the night and from that day on they became a constant in each other's lives. He an architect major, she corporate law, they didn't have any classes together, but before class, in between and after classes found them together for the rest of the school year.

When summer came and he had to return home to Cape Cod, he suggested she join him. She debated for a long while. Tried to use the excuse she had to work for the summer and he made the argument his mother always needed extra help at their bed and breakfast Inn. So while her parents had 'holiday' as her mother called it, as if she were European royalty, Sam would move into the Inn by the sea.

Her father was more accepting of her choice, though a little disappointed she wouldn't be working at his offices as he hoped, but he would be back and forth to Europe with her mother anyway. He understood and told her to have fun, enjoy her young college years. Though her father understood, her mother reacted just as Sam thought she would.

"Does his family summer at Martha's Vineyard?"

"No, they don't 'summer', they live there. And it isn't Martha's Vineyard."

"Hyannis Port dear? Cartwright who? What is his last name?" Then excitement lifted Joan's voice. "It's a Kennedy? Oh Samantha, is it a Kennedy?"

"Stevens mother, his name is Carter Stevens."

"The name doesn't sound familiar." Joan tried to think of all the people she knew in that area and didn't recognize his at all.

"You don't know them."

"Is he studying law? Business?"

"He's taking architectural classes. Likes working with houses, building, remodeling, that sort of thing." Sam knew it wouldn't please her mother to know he wasn't into business or finance or anything else that would be acceptable to her.

"Who are his parents? What do they do?"

"Why does everything revolve around that for you? Isn't it enough that I want to be here with him because he's a great guy?" Sam knew it was enough for her, but would never be for her mother.

"You're my daughter, I just want to know who you're spending the summer with."

"You just want to know what their bank statement says."

"That's not true." Joan sounded hurt although they both knew it was the truth.

"Why does it matter, you'll be in Europe." Sam sighed but finally relented and told her what she wanted to know. Knowing full well it wouldn't please her. "His parents run a bed and breakfast."

"You mean like one of those houses people basically rent out their bedrooms?"

"It's a bed and breakfast Inn."

"They call it an Inn, it doesn't make it so. Are they that poor they have to rent out their bedrooms? Is this some sort of school project Samantha?" The tone of her voice was indication enough she wasn't pleased.

"Sure, if it makes you feel better to think that."

"What am I to tell our friends? I can't tell them you're working at some cheap motel. I don't know what's come over you, if you want to summer at the Cape we have friends in Martha's Vineyard. Surely you can stay there in much more suitable arrangements."

"No mother, it isn't the point of staying in Martha's Vineyard, I'm not even going there. I just called to let you know where I'd be. Just understand this for me, will you? Send me a postcard from one of those beautiful places you love in Europe." Sam hadn't called for approval. Though she'd been on her own much of her life, she had still been under their wing. It surprised her how independent she felt after a short year away and she wouldn't listen to her mother's arguments no matter how hard she tried.

When her mother argued and complained that she wouldn't see her for weeks, Sam promised to visit after her classes were over. Told her she would take a few days before going to Cape Cod and that seemed to make her happy. Then it was Carter she thought about. Carter had come to sense not to question her, instinctively had come to understand quickly her parents weren't something she revealed much about. She was always vague in answers and never went into details so he understood when she told him he would have to initially go without her and she would meet him there.

"This isn't a ploy to get out of this, is it?" he asked.

"Of course not, I don't even want to do this, but I promised her I'd visit before I spent the summer away."

"A few days?"

"A week or two."

Carter raised his eyebrows, wanted it more pinpointed than that but wouldn't get it. The thought of two weeks made him panic. "A week?"

"Or two, I'm not sure. But after that we'll have the summer."

"I'm already missing you and you're not even gone."

Because their departure would coincide with the end of her school year, Sam scheduled to spend two weeks at their place in New York instead of their home in Virginia. But when she got there she had to wait three days for them to show up even after she was assured they would be there by the time she arrived.

It happened often. It was something she dealt with her whole life. From a very young child till then, she'd grown up with broken promises as she waited patiently for her mother to come. But this time Sam wasn't as patient as she normally was. This time aggravated. Felt it a wasted three days when she now had a life outside of her mother and it waited for her elsewhere.

As angry as she was, when her mother showed up she was pulled into guilt. The guilt of a young child who had compassion for a mother she couldn't understand, but loved regardless. She could tell it had been a difficult few days for her mother just by her appearance, something else she'd been through all her life.

Joan hugged her quickly out of courtesy. "I'm so sorry dear, I think I got the flu, I just couldn't get out of bed."

When was her mother going to realize that Sam was old enough to know she was an alcoholic? She'd never put a name on it as a child, all she'd wanted to do was help, even if she didn't understand her moods. But as an adult she knew she wasn't the one who could help her mother.

"Where's father?"

"He had to go straight to the office, something about a crisis. You can have offices all over the world and I can't understand why there isn't anyone else who can deal with things." Joan immediately walked over to the bar. "It's too much for me, I need a drink."

"Why don't we go out?" Sam asked quickly before she could pour.

"Not now honey." Her mother sighed as if she'd just run a marathon. "I need a drink and I need to relax."

Sam knew she'd probably been drinking for a few days, and then she hadn't maybe one or two days. Not that she didn't want to, only because after a binge she had good intentions, but they didn't last long in her state of denial.

"What time will dad be home, will we be going out to dinner?" Sam watched her pour. It was only slight relief to see her mother picked up the gin bottle instead of the whiskey.

"Maybe I'll feel better by the time he gets here."

In a much better mood that was induced by alcohol, Joan was ready for dinner when the time came. The three of them went out and enjoyed the time together as much as they could before they had to return home as Joan's intoxication grew. And she seemed fine the next day when she insisted Sam go shopping with her. Sam tried to talk her into doing something else but the spending spree left Joan more satisfied as they came back with bags and bags of things.

When they left earlier than planned the next day, a few weeks ahead of schedule, Sam left all the purchases in her New York bedroom where her immense closet was already overstuffed with designer things. Things she didn't want or care about. She looked at all the bags as her consolation prize for them leaving early. It was to relieve her parents of any guilt they might have been feeling, although Sam was unsure they'd ever felt any.

****

Sam's mind was on her mother the entire trip to the Cape. She hadn't realized how much she actually missed Carter until she pulled up to the Inn and knew how close he was. It was then her feelings grew in intensity. The simple thought that he was so near sent a strange emotion through her and thoughts of her mother disappeared. Carter was all she thought about as she stepped up onto the porch and the anticipation of seeing him was enough to frighten her.

Waterside Inn was a long gone whaling captain's summer home that had been updated and remodeled over the years, along with two smaller guest houses. It now stood stately and dignified along the banks of the narrow spit of land of Cape Cod. Although large, the wraparound porch gave a sense of welcome to all, and once you stepped inside it was just as warm and inviting there.

The very moment she entered its doors, she knew she'd come to a special place. Not only because of the comfortable furnishings, the large windows that offered expansive panoramic vistas of the water all around, and the smell of cinnamon and muffins. But Carter's parents were more than gracious as they welcomed her with open arms.

His mother hugged her with sincere tenderness, gave her an overwhelming sense of belonging just by her touch. Any nervous hesitations she had about being there were immediately dispelled.

"You're early, I didn't expect you so soon." Grace said.

Sam felt bad for being unexpected but hadn't been able to get hold of Carter on his cell phone and didn't know the number to the Inn. "I'm sorry, if it's a problem I could..."

"Oh gracious, please child. I'm excited you're here early, I've been waiting to meet you for so long." Grace touched her face gingerly and Sam found herself blushing. "You're even lovelier than I imagined."

"Grace, you're embarrassing her." Carter's father, Robert, came from across the room. He was a large man, the hug he gave engulfed her but it was just as sincere and kind as Grace's had been.

"Carter went fishing, and he's going to be so disappointed he wasn't here to meet you but that just means we'll have some uninterrupted time together." Grace put her arm around her and led the way as Robert carried her small suitcase.

Samantha was given a room decorated in blue and white that overlooked the water. Soft white gauze curtains floated at the window and the view was magnificent when she stepped over to see the ocean. It spread before her as if it too received her lovingly into this strange and wonderful world Carter called home.

Grace then showed her around the Inn. Talked and chatted the entire time and after the tour they finally settled on the deck that faced the bay. Sam liked her tremendously, as if an instant bond had been preformed in some earlier universe, the kind woman felt far from a stranger. If she thought it odd Sam didn't talk of her parent's much when asked about them, the woman didn't say anything. She simply moved on to another subject.

"I am so glad you're early, I was counting the days and they seemed to be getting longer. Carter has had a little company though. A friend of his you probably know from school. Michael?"

"Oh, I hadn't realized he was coming." Sam had met Michael several times and liked him, they'd become friends themselves.

"I don't think he was planning on it, I think Carter begged him. He's only able to stay for a few days. I'm pleased Carter is home and I'm more than pleased he invited you. I had visions of him calling and telling me he wasn't coming home for the summer."

"I don't think you have to worry about that, he loves it here, I can tell when he talks about it. It would take an awful lot to pull him away."

"A mother's worries." Grace sighed. "His first year away, gaining some independence, and I had a feeling home was the last place he'd want to be. I'm glad I'm wrong."

It wasn't long after that Grace saw the small boat coming into the bay. It was then she realized what time it was and she had a few things to do. "I've got dinner to finish yet and I'm sitting here like its Sunday."

"Can I help with something?" She asked.

"Absolutely not, it isn't a working day for you, you just wait for Carter."

When Grace left, Sam walked down the steps and stood on the board walkway. Several boats at one time all crowded around the pier and they had to wait to dock. Sam watched Carter and Michael and when Carter looked up and she waved to him, it took him only seconds to realize who it was. So intent on getting to her, and not being able to wait, in one smooth quick movement he dove overboard and swam to shore.

Sam was laughing hysterically by the time he reached her. Wet and dripping he scooped her up in his arms and held tight as he buried his face deep in her neck and held his lips there. The warmth of his touch was the remedy to feeling cold without him.

Carter held her in mid air. "I didn't expect to see you here."

"A change of plans and I couldn't reach you on your cell phone." Her heart raced to finally be in his arms, she felt so secure even if she was in mid air.

"Do you know how good you look? Almost a week is much too long, I've been dying. And I was sure you were going to torture me and make me wait another week."

"I take it you missed me?"

"No, I always take an afternoon swim fully clothed, and that water is freezing the beginning of the summer. Do you know how cold that water is?" He began to walk towards it as if he planned to throw her in.

"I can feel it on both you and me now. I hope you don't intend for me to find out any further than that." She didn't think he'd throw her in but he continued to walk and there wasn't anything she could do about it. Her feet still dangled and she couldn't touch the ground even if she stretched her toes out. Sam was left with nothing to do but hold on.

"If you don't want to go for a swim you have to do two things. First, you have to kiss me and second, you have to tell me you missed me as much as I missed you. And if you didn't, lie to me anyway."

Intense eyes pleaded with her, he'd been starved of her affection and Sam knew exactly what he was feeling, she couldn't deny she felt the same. He came to a stop just on the waters edge and neither one said anything. He didn't put her down and they simply stared at each other for a long time as their understanding was spoken silently through their eyes. No words needed to be spoken. It was the first realization for both just how difficult life would be without the other. It was the first realization for Sam, that she didn't feel so alone.

Michael would comment years later that he was there the moment they fell in love.

CHAPTER 3

It didn't take her long to fit in, Grace and Robert made it easy for her to feel so comfortable, and Sam would soon come to see it was one of the reasons guests returned to the Inn year after year. You weren't really made to feel like a guest, you were family, and they treated you as such.

Carter joked one night at all the attention she was getting. "Am I to become second fiddle now?"

Grace smiled. "Of course not second fiddle. But I have to say, with this one by your side, you might not be noticed as easily."

"Thanks mom." He took the ribbing as the joke it was meant to be.

That evening, they went for a walk along the bluff and he pulled Sam into his arms as the sun made its way into the sea. "I hope they're not embarrassing you too much. They were thinking the worst and were happily surprised by you."

"The worst?" she laughed, "I'm afraid to ask why."

"All I told them was that you were female. I couldn't describe you in words so I didn't even try, told them they'd have to see for themselves."

"They must have been petrified wondering what you were going to bring home."

He looked into her striking blue eyes and could see her happiness there, could always read them as if they were physically connected to his own soul. "I'm glad you came."

"I'm glad you talked me into it. For insisting I give it a chance when I was reluctant."

"I told you, didn't I? I said you'd love it here."

Sam did fall in love with Cape Cod and everything about it. When they weren't working, summer afternoons and evenings were spent exploring the many wonders in the gentle surf. Rides across spectacular sand dunes and discovering the wild beauty of the National Seashore filled her days and nights. Often they traveled to Race Point at the Cape's furthest tip to see the sunset. Sandy beaches, lighthouses, quaint churches, sea captain's homes. Picturesque fishing villages captivated Sam's full attention. How wonderful Carter's life was to have grown up in such splendor of salty air.

It was a small, close-knit place weaved together by generations, the kind of place where everyone knew everyone else. Sam couldn't help but think of all she'd missed growing up alone and sheltered. In this little spot on the banks of New England, Carter's family and friends opened their hearts and homes to her, and Sam felt it a privilege to share their lives.

Carter's work involved not only doing things around the Inn, but he also used whatever time he could and began his own small business doing small remodeling jobs when he could find them. Word of mouth spread and residents were only too happy to give him whatever work they needed done. Sometimes it involved reconfiguring and remodeling an entire bathroom, and other times a simple window replacement, but he took great pride in whatever it was.

What Sam did around the Inn she didn't consider work. It was the most fun she'd ever had. She helped Grace with breakfasts and learned much about running the place and making sure everything was taken care of from clean towels to guest check-in. One of the favorite parts of her job was talking to people and getting to know them.

Sam had become quite adept by the end of the summer at making waffles and special sauces, but when she found some extra time on her hands, she began working on a newfound hobby of painting. Hadn't even known she was interested in it until she found herself in an art store and purchased some things. As she sat in front of a blank canvas, she dove headfirst into unknown territory, and after an enormous amount of paint was used, she finally finished a piece she thought presentable for anyone else to see. Not that she planned to show it to anyone, but it happened one day when Grace came into her room.

There was nothing in the painting but beach, water and sky. It was a plain and simple piece that had taken hours and days, and she didn't dare add more than a few white ripples of water along the edge. No sailboats, or trees, or anything else that would take the slightest bit of talent. But her colors were good, she gave herself that much credit, even though the scene lacked everything but the barest of necessities to look like a beach painting. Sam thought she could possibly master using the light in the correct way, adding anything more would probably throw her totally off.

Grace came in while she was in the shower and shouted through the closed door. "Sam? We're going out to dinner this evening. I've finally talked Robert into putting on a pair of decent pants and make himself presentable." The painting had been laying on top the bed, now Grace held it in her hands and smiled when she stepped out of the bathroom. "Sam, this is fantastic, I didn't know you painted."

"I didn't either." She began to brush through her hair. "And I wouldn't quite call it painting."

"This is lovely, something like this would go perfectly in the sunroom. Do you think if you have time, you could paint one for there? I'd pay you of course."

Sam looked at her face and wondered if she was just being kind but her expression was genuine and sincere, Grace couldn't be any other way. She actually liked it and wanted one. "You can have that one if you really want it."

"I'd love to have it, but are you sure? You don't look all too sure you're willing to part with it." Grace looked at Sam and saw an odd expression she couldn't quite read.

Sam laughed again. "I'm sure I want to part with it, if I have a stupid look on my face it's because I'm just a little struck that you'd want it."

"I'll pay you what you want for it, but you'd have to do something first."

"Paint it over? You want sailboats? I can't do sailboats, I probably couldn't even add another little ripple of wave."

"No, it's perfect as it is, but you have to sign it, there's no signature."

Sam obliged, happy to have a home for something she wasn't sure what she was going to do with after she'd finished it, and Grace had it professionally matted and framed from a store in Provincetown. She displayed it proud exactly where she said it would fit perfectly, the sunroom. Sam of course refused any money for it, was only too glad she'd taken it.

When Sam walked by the door of the sunroom one day it caught her attention easily. The last of the evening light came through the window and just the way the sun shone on it she would almost admit to herself that it did look pretty good. Then she decided it was probably the beautiful large white frame that made it so.

"There you are." Carter stepped behind her and wrapped her in his arms as his mouth tenderly kissed her neck. "You smell so good."

"That lavender soap your mother's been supplying me with all summer. I'm spoiled now and won't be able to do without, I went down to the farm today and bought a whole basket of it to take back to school with me."

"Your work looks great, doesn't it? Mom hung it today. I didn't know my little love was so talented, you never told me. Any other talents you're hiding?"

"I didn't know I was hiding this one, but I'm not quite sure it's talent, I think it's the frame that makes it look so good."

"Why do you do that? Why do you underestimate yourself, you're your own worst critic." He sounded peeved, it didn't matter what anyone told her about it, she didn't see the beauty of it.

Sam had never been encouraged to do things, never been told anything she did was worthwhile. It was all so new to her and she had to learn how to deal with it, learn how to accept compliments graciously.

"I'm sorry. Thank you. I'm glad you like it."

"And you? Don't you like it? Aren't paintings supposed to make you feel something? What does it make you feel?"

She looked at it long and hard before she answered honestly. "It makes me feel me. I know it must sound weird, but it's like this is who I am."

She wasn't Samantha Durham from the Durham Empire. Not the daughter of a wealthy prominent Virginia family, with no identity of her own. Sam found her identity. In the glorious wind that blew in from the ocean, on top a bluff overlooking vast amounts of water, as she walked barefoot through the sand or sat on a star filled night in an old creaky rocking chair that seemed to be made especially for her, Sam found her identity.

She found a person inside, a person separate from Joan and Montgomery Durham, and she'd come to realize they didn't define who she was. They'd merely been the vehicle to life but had never taught her how to live it. She'd discovered that here on the banks of New England. Discovered the freedom she needed to find her independence and her own spirit that now soared high above her parent's world.

Proof of that was evident in the signature of the painting. The signature was simple. Sam. Not Samantha, no last name... just Sam.

****

The end of the summer came much too soon for Sam's liking. She fretted about their return to school when it seemed she'd just settled in. For their last night she told everyone she was in charge of dinner and was making a traditional favorite, Lobster, and she'd gone to the fresh seafood market on the pier and with Ms. Paterling's help learned how to choose the best ones and given instructions on cooking them. But it was far from being as easy as the woman explained to her.

Sam didn't expect it to be so difficult. As she prepared the pot for the crustaceans impending doom she heard them click away nearby as if they sensed their demise. The clatter of their movement made her cringe and when she peered at them she wondered if she should blindfold them. All eight beady eyes stared at her as if she were executioner. Did they have minds? Could they feel pain? With the pot ready and waiting, it was after a few agonizing moments that her plans changed. Sam couldn't do it, she just couldn't go through with it.

With lobsters in tow she made her way down to the sea to let them loose, easily and carefully cut the first bands on two lobsters and threw them towards the water. However, just as she cut the bands on her third one and was about to throw him, she realized the first two had crawled back towards her. It scared her when she looked down to see one so close to her toes and she dropped the one in her hand close by, now she had three loose lobsters around her feet. Each seemed content to stay close to the last one still in the container, the one Sam couldn't get to for fear of a few toes being snatched. Whenever she got close, one seemed to walk in her direction and she'd jump and scream in fright.

She must have danced and squealed on the beach for ten minutes before Carter stepped out of the shower and heard the shrieks from his open bedroom window. Puzzled at first, it took him a few moments to realize what she was doing then he burst into laughter when he realized her predicament and went to her rescue. With a deft skill he retrieved all the lobsters and finished her task of setting them free.

When he turned to her, he was still laughing but she looked stricken.

"I couldn't do it." She said, tears almost on the brim of her eyes. "I couldn't cook them, and I promised dinner."

Carter pulled her into his arms, unable to stop laughing. "Then I suggest we go get dressed to go out, unless you think my parents are going to swim out to sea with a fork."

They all decided that Percy's Corner, a favorite local restaurant, was obviously much better prepared for steaming lobsters than Sam had been. Instead of a quiet evening for the four of them, they ran into several friends who joined them for dinner and like Grace and Robert, they found the tale amusing. Percy himself jokingly placed a tablecloth over the fresh lobster tank so she couldn't see them, and they all asked if she were going to set all the clams free at the next clam bake. It was close to midnight when they returned home after a fun evening.

"I promise that next summer I *will* make dinner, I just can't promise that it will be lobster. I'll leave that up to Percy who does it so well." Sam laughed as she stepped inside.

"Next summer?" Pop, as she'd come to call Carter's father, raised his eyebrows. "Do we have to wait until next summer?"

"Of course not." Grace chimed in. "She'll be back on long weekends and the holiday season is right around the corner. I know you have a family of your own dear, but don't forget you now belong to this one also. We expect to see something of you before next summer." Grace's words were a statement, said with a conviction that it wasn't open for discussion.

"I knew bringing you here was probably a bad idea." Carter teased. "They wouldn't care if I came back, as long as you did."

Grace swooshed her hand through the air and teased. "Oh Carter, that's not true. Who would I get to fix the porch railings when they break?"

Sam hung her sweater on the peg and went to the small desk and began filling the few guest boxes with papers that were printed out every evening of the breakfast menu for the next morning, what the weather would be like, and suggestions of things to do for the day. It had become habit no matter what time she came in.

"After tomorrow I'm going to have to remind Robert to do that, he hasn't done it in so long since you took over." Grace said.

"Don't remind me we're leaving tomorrow. I'm not ready." As she placed the paper in the box for the Baker's, she reached inside one of the drawers and placed a piece of candy in the box also. They had a son who ran down every morning to check the box and she'd been surprising him for a few days with the treat.

Grace put her arm lovingly around her husband. "Quite a few things he'll need to be reminded of. With you two here I think he's gotten lazy."

"Won't take me long to get back into it, I can't take for granted Sam will be back every summer to work. Once she becomes a big hotshot lawyer she won't be out here putting candy in guest boxes."

"Or painter." Carter added with a proud smile in her direction. "She's going to sign up for some art classes this year."

Grace beamed. "I'm so glad. You have such natural talent and I'm glad you're going to enhance it."

"I don't know what I'll get out of it, but it will sure beat corporate legalese language class." The last paper went in and she was officially done with her duties and Grace presented her with a gift.

"Just a little something for you to take with you, but it'll come in handy for your next visit."

She blushed as she took the pink wrapped box with a white curly bow. "You didn't have to do this."

"See?" Carter pointed out again. "You even get gifts. I don't get gifts."

Sam opened it and revealed a blue and yellow print bag. Grace teased her when she saw her personal items in a plastic grocery bag and had this one specially made from a shop in town from material that matched the quilt in her room. Knew Sam loved both the quilt and the print. And Sam knew the shop well, it was no ordinary bag, every stitch hand sewn with time consuming care.

She held it in her hands gingerly. At her parents home in Virginia she had a closet full of designer bags that meant nothing to her, this one had meaning to it and she was touched deeply. Grace put quite a bit of thought not only in the bag itself but using the material she loved, Sam looked at it as a way for her to carry a piece of this home with her.

"I thought it was a good size for your personal items or you could use it to carry some of your painting supplies. I hope you like it."

"It's perfect." She spoke the words softly, afraid her voice would catch as she felt the tears but held them back.

"Now I expect you to use it the next time you come home."

Grace's words were said casually, but the meaning of them hit her deeply. It did feel like home. Her parent's houses were large, pretentious and most times void of anything other than a showcase of the most beautiful material things money could buy. Including empty of her parents as they wandered the world while she wandered lonely empty halls and wondered when they'd return. It had never felt like this.

When his parents went to bed Carter made sure the windows on the lower level were locked then found Sam on the porch in the rocking chair, the bag in her lap.

When she noticed Carter looking at her she smiled. "They're so thoughtful."

"They care a great deal for you." He sat down next to her and took her hand in his. "Plus, I guess she figured if she gave you a resemblance of the quilt on your bed you wouldn't steal the whole thing. This will be easier to fit in your suitcase. Which reminds me, we'll have to leave fairly early tomorrow, are you packed?"

Sam groaned, leaned back and closed her eyes. "Don't remind me. Let me sit here and pretend we just got here and have the whole summer."

With her eyes still closed Carter rose from his seat, leaned over her, and placed the softest kiss on her lips then whispered. "I didn't really ask because we have to leave early, I asked because I wondered if you'd be busy tonight."

"Oh?" Sam didn't open her eyes as his lips moved to her neck and it was so slight it felt like a tender breeze, as if it were a cold breeze that made her shiver, yet at the same time she could feel the heat where his mouth was. "What did you have in mind?"

She was consumed by Carter's passion that night just as she'd been the first night they made love and every time in between. He had a way of making her feel so entirely and completely filled with contentment. There was such tenderness in the way he touched her, the way he loved her, he said without words that she was the most important thing in his life.

****

Grace was quietly watching Sam from the kitchen window when Carter entered.

"Mom, have you seen my keys? I was going to put the things in the car and..." He glanced into the basket on the counter and saw what he was looking for.

Grace laughed. "I don't know why you bother asking, you know when I find them I put them there. How many years now? And you still ask."

She didn't turn around and Carter came to stand beside her and the two watched Sam as she stopped, shielded her eyes from the early morning bright sun and looked out towards the horizon.

"I was wondering where she was, I thought maybe she'd gone with dad to check out the early fish market."

"She's been out there since dawn." Grace said softly.

"I'm going to have to drag her kicking and screaming out of here." He laughed.

Grace's voice that followed held all the compassion of a mother who loved her son dearly. "She has secrets Carter. I've fallen in love with that young lady as if I'd given birth to her, and I've come to know her just as well. It isn't something deceitful she's trying to hide, but there's something in her that's very unhappy."

"I know." He admitted with a soft knowing tone.

"At the same time I believe she loves you, I have this feeling she'll hurt you down the road. I don't know what it is, it's just something I feel in my gut." She turned to see his uneasy look and lay her hand over his. "But don't let my foolish words stop you from giving your full heart. I think it's what she needs."

She turned to leave and his words stopped her when she reached the door.

"Hey mom?" Carter didn't turn around when he spoke, his eyes still on Sam. He knew it was already too late, but he asked anyway. "What if I don't give my full heart, does that stop the hurt when it comes?"

"No son. If you don't give your whole heart to something, you'll miss the true joy of ever really having the experience at all."

"So either way it hurts." He turned to see the sad smile his mother gave him before she left the room.

"Good morning." Sam smiled sweetly as he crossed the grass towards her. Her heart lifted instantly the moment she saw him in the morning, as if she'd secretly been frightened it was a possibility she wouldn't.

"If I didn't know any better I'd think you were trying to hide from me so I'd drive away and leave you here."

"Any chance of that happening?" She put her arms around his neck and pressed herself to him.

"That's like saying I went down to Skippy McGee's fish shack and he chopped my right arm off and I didn't notice."

"He isn't evil." She laughed. She'd befriended a lonely old man who sat in a fish shack on a pier and Carter couldn't understand it. Okay, so she hadn't really made friends with him but she was working on it. "Okay, so he was extra ornery when I went to see him this morning but I think that was just because he was sad I was leaving." She could see the laughter in his eyes. "Okay, so maybe he is glad to see me go but he'll be surprised when I come back."

"So my plan worked?"

"Your plan?"

"My ulterior motive for bringing you here. So you would fall in love with it and could see yourself here for many years to come."

"I tried to resist just for spite." She teased. "But I fell in love with it regardless."

"And the many years to come part?" Carter pulled a ring from his pocket. A small diamond, more like a tiny diamond chip, on a gold band but he said one day he'd replace it with the biggest diamond she'd ever seen.

He explained that neither was ready for marriage, each of them would want to finish their education but to look at it as the pre-engagement ring he called it. A commitment to each other of a promised future together, a promised tomorrow.

"I love you Sam. You make me feel as if I'm just now starting to live. What do you think? Think you could spend the rest of your life with me?"

"I know it would be awfully difficult to spend the rest of my life without you." She placed her hand aside Carter's handsome face and with her thumb rubbed the small indent in his chin.

Carter put the small ring on her finger. "This is all I need right now, a promised tomorrow."

Carter kissed her softly. Her words fell just short of telling him she loved him and his mother's words, that she would hurt him one day, dominated his thoughts.

The wind blew around them, a wind she'd come to think of as the winds of change. The air felt different. It seemed to sink into her skin instead of breeze past it. It became a moment to savor because whenever it came she experienced something new. A new emotion, a new fear, it had come to signify an alteration in her life. Fitting it blew in at that moment as if to verify her feelings of it. It was sending her off into a different direction once again.

CHAPTER 4

When classes started that year, many things changed for them. Carter moved into an apartment with his best friend Michael. One of Sam's best friends, Shawna, went over to visit with her frequently and her and Michael hit it off tremendously. The four of them decided to get a larger house together so they found one, but in order to be able to afford it they had to rent out two of the other large rooms.

A student one year ahead of them, Blake Davis, moved into one room and a girl Nikki answered the advertisement for the other.

When Blake and Nikki got together as a couple and moved into one room, the vacancy then rented to a quiet girl named Sara who minded her own business but eventually fit in quite well and began to feel more comfortable as time went by.

They had a party one night and a guy named Richard, just as studious as Sara, ended up in her room all night as they discussed the particles of atoms or interpreted the works of Shakespeare. The others didn't know what they'd done all night, all they knew was that Richard never left.

The group of them all became quick and fast friends and Sam immersed herself completely in living with Carter on such an intimate level. She loved the feel of his safe arms around her every night and his smile in the very early morning. And no matter how busy and involved their separate lives were it comforted her to know he was always there at the beginning and end of every day. Their life in Cape Cod brought them so close together she could barely remember how her life was when he wasn't in it. Barely remembered her other life at all until her mother called and interrupted at times.

When the first major holiday of the school year came, Thanksgiving, all Sam could think of and look forward to was spending it at the Cape with Carter. But after an argument with her mother who thought it best she come to Virginia for the holiday a tinge of guilt began to build and she finally gave in.

"Great darling, that will be divine. We'll prepare the most fabulous meal. I'll invite... I'll invite everyone. A grand feast with all the trimmings."

Sam hadn't been there in months, with her parents in Europe for the summer and then off to somewhere else, there wasn't a reason to go. Felt she'd grown so much over the past year from being on her own and set her mind up to think things would be different now. Her perspective had changed as an independent young woman instead of the young child who hadn't a choice. She could have said no, but couldn't shake the feeling she was being selfish, unfair.

Now she had to break the news to Carter. As she walked back to the house she already wanted to change her mind again. Call her mother and refuse, but knew she should go. It was the day they were to leave for New England, their bags waited by the door and Sam passed them when she entered and found him reading the paper on the couch.

She sat down next to him, kissed him then rested her head on his shoulder. "Hey you."

"You were out early."

"I didn't wake you did I?"

"I'm awake the minute you leave my arms." He went back to the paper momentarily. "There's a Faberge' exhibit the week we get back from break."

"Since when are you into jeweled eggs?"

"I'm not, but its art and I thought you'd want to go."

As bored as he would be, Carter would put a huge smile on his face and enjoy it with her. Or at least pretend. He went back to reading and she studied his face, saw the slight change when she spoke.

"I've had a change of plans."

"What's that?" He said casually, not expecting what he heard next.

"I'm not going to be able to go home with you, I'm going to have to go to my parents for Thanksgiving."

"Hmm." He mumbled and pretended to read.

He wasn't sure what to say so he simply waited for an invitation that never came. Could only listen to her excuses as to why she changed her plans, their plans.

"If I go now I can probably get away with only going for a short time for winter break and we can have the entire time to ourselves." Even to her ears it sounded lame but she tried to rationalize it to sound better. It didn't. She had no viable excuse to cancel on him at the last minute.

"Sounds like you've thought it out well. Anything you've forgotten to think of?" His voice had an edge he couldn't hide, eyes focused on the blurred black and white print he'd stopped concentrating on.

"I hope you're not angry."

He closed the paper roughly and set it down beside him. "You change our plans at the very last possible minute, I'm waiting for an invitation that obviously isn't going to come, yes Sam, I am angry."

Sam tensed. "For one, I know how important the holidays are for your mother, she expects you this afternoon and she'd kill me for changing your plans. Or in the very least have my room rented to a customer the next time I went." Sam tried to rise but he stopped her.

"Don't, Sam, don't try to avoid this argument like you always do."

"Is that what this is? An argument?"

"It's going to become one. We've been seeing each other over a year now, living together for months, don't you think it's about time I met your parents?" He held tight to her arm.

"Not yet Carter, they're very protective, they wouldn't understand and I don't need the added tension and stress." She pulled away from him and rose, he too on his feet quickly.

"You're not a kid, you're an adult. Surely they want you to have a healthy relationship with the opposite sex."

"I don't want to talk about this."

"I do." He stated strongly.

"Then I guess you're right, this is an argument." She turned quickly and he turned her back to face him.

"I know you've told them about me. What is it, Sam? Why don't you want them to meet me?"

"It isn't you Carter."

"Then what the hell is it?" He shouted now. His normal calm reserve broke and he couldn't look the other way this time, couldn't ignore the subject as he'd done before.

"Maybe next time. Maybe..." She started to talk but knew she didn't mean what she said and stopped before she lied even more.

"Why don't you want me to meet them?" He asked straight up, something he'd never done but he was angry about it this time, thought he was an important part of her life but when it came to her family she made him feel like an outcast.

"Not now Carter, I don't need this now." Sam should have told him right there, he needed to know, but felt as soon as she told him the truth, Sam would cease to exist and she'd become Samantha. She wasn't ready for her two worlds to converge. Not yet. Not now when she'd only just begun to discover herself.

"Well I might need it now. Maybe I want to know I actually mean something."

"Of course you mean something, whether you meet my parents or not isn't going to change that."

Carter noticed that she wasn't going to elaborate on exactly what that 'something' was that he meant to her. She wouldn't say the words she loved him. And as he looked into her eyes he saw she wasn't going to change her mind about including him in her visit and no argument they had would do so.

"Have a good holiday. I'll see you when you decide you want to include me in your life again." He let go of her, grabbed his suitcase and slammed the door on his way out.

She stood in the silence, wanted to run after him but didn't. When she heard the doorknob turn, she expected to see Carter but was disappointed to see Shawna instead.

"What the hell was that? Carter just flew past me with barely two words to say, mumbled something about screwed up life, Happy Thanksgiving, and shot out of here so fast he left tire marks. Trouble in paradise?"

"Paradise it ain't. Just that Shawna, a screwed up life." Sam fought tears as she left.

After he calmed down, Carter cursed himself for getting so angry. He shouldn't have forced the issue, shouldn't have said anything. For whatever reasons, she didn't want him there and he had to respect it, even if he didn't understand it. It didn't make it any easier when he reached home and saw the disappointment on his parent's faces. Although he pretended he was fine with the change of plans, he saw the knowing look in his mother's eyes.

****

When she got to her parents home in Virginia they were delayed. "We're still in California, your father's meeting here has taken longer than planned but we'll be home before you know it."

Her mothers words could have been spoken to the ten-year-old child she was at one time... 'We'll be home before you know it.'... How many times had she heard the words? How many times had she counted on them being true? It was difficult to do, but she kept to her original feeling of changing her perspective that this time things would be different. Sam gave her mother the benefit of doubt and knew she'd be home, this time her mother knew she wasn't a young child who would forget they didn't show up when promised. It's what her mother always counted on when she was a child, she hadn't taken into consideration Sam had actually grown up.

She wandered the empty house for the two days she'd been there alone and thought of the wasted time she could have been with Carter. He'd been so angry and hurt it was all she could think of, but she didn't call him. Hoped he would call, but couldn't blame him when he didn't make the attempt either.

When Thanksgiving Day actually arrived she found herself still alone and no word as to when her parents would be there. Early morning changed to early afternoon and all she could think of was Cape Cod with the smell of cinnamon and muffins, only now imagined a kitchen full of people and the aroma of turkey and homemade pies. Could almost hear the laughter of friends who gathered, could see Carter stealing a piece of something or sticking his finger in a bowl to lick batter, and Grace playfully slap his hand as she handed him a spoon and told him to scoop the mashed potatoes from the pot.

Or maybe he played cards with old Mr. Parker and let him win as he usually did, then taking the ribbing in stride as it was rubbed in. Carter would always say... 'Next time, Mr. Parker. I'll be practicing up for next time.'

She knew those people. As she walked around her own house, she felt like she was waiting for strangers to come home. Had already planned how she would escape from her mother after she'd had too much to drink and her father would desert them and move to his office with the excuse of work. Sam never had a holiday like the one she pictured in her mind that was taking place far from where she was, and maybe her thoughts of what it would be like were just that. Thoughts, a picture, maybe something gleaned from sentimental movies and the imagination of a child. Maybe it wasn't even real at all.

Sam looked out the window by the front door, hadn't consciously stood in the foyer, she supposed it was childhood habit. When she turned to see Bea, the main housekeeper, she saw the sadness in the woman's eyes and without words the woman offered compassion she always found comfort in. Sam had fallen for it again, her mother dangled hope in front of her, only to snatch it away. She finally gave up her lonely vigil and luckily caught a timely flight out.

She didn't bother knocking when she arrived at the Inn, simply stepped through the door to a reception of warmth and people truly happy to see her. No one more surprised than Carter who beamed from across the room when their eyes met. The smile on his face went directly to her heart and in that one second of time, one of so many seconds that would comprise her life, she knew she'd never find everything she'd ever searched for anywhere else.

Sam spent that and many other holidays and weekends at the Cape with Carter, and when summer came again, and the summers that followed, their friends began going with them at times. During the tourist season many jobs could be found and they either worked at the Inn or found other jobs in town. Some stayed for only a few weeks at a time, others stayed all summer. They worked hard and played hard. Clambakes on the beach, boating, sailing, spending long summer days exploring different parts of New England with it's many opportunity of discovery.

Their intimate group formed as a lifelong connection. Over the years, each discovered themselves and each other amidst Cape winds, and Sam was one of them. With no knowledge of her family's wealth, they liked her for who she was, the person she had become.

They all went to Michael's parent's lake house once for a four-day break, another time Nikki, along with her brothers, was giving her parents an anniversary party and they all surprised her and attended. Of course, no one ever met Sam's parents, and no one asked questions after being told the simple fact that her family had a glass business in Virginia, and they didn't seem to need more.

Sam didn't feel she was lying, she just couldn't tell them. What did one say? My name is Samantha Durham and my family is filthy rich? She didn't want to give it over to them, continued to view it as maybe if they knew she was Samantha Durham and all that actually meant, she couldn't be Sam anymore.

Carter didn't argue about her going away alone, or mention or parents again. He instinctively knew not to mention it, respected her privacy and didn't press. Made up his own notions and ideas as to why he'd never met them. Perhaps they were dirt poor and it embarrassed her, maybe they just didn't get along, perhaps they'd been overly strict or possessive and she enjoyed the freedom without them. It didn't become important to Carter any longer. He knew in time she would share that part of her life, until then, he would take everything else. It was only difficult when she chose to go home for a few days at times and he'd have to get by without her, which wasn't easy. They'd become such an important part of each other's everyday lives it was truly as if he missed his right arm.

Carter talked to her mother once when she called the Inn and he answered the phone at the desk. Or rather, he didn't talk to her, he heard her voice.

"Waterside Inn, how can I help you today?" Carter answered automatically in the 'answer the phone cheery voice' his mother insisted upon.

"Is Samantha Durham available?" A woman's voice droned blandly.

"She is..." Carter thought she already sounded bored and they hadn't even had a conversation to be bored from. He quickly glanced around and saw through the window she was outside painting. "...not around right now, can I take a message? Can I ask who's calling?"

"Tell her to call her mother." It sounded like an order rather than a request.

"Your mother called." He said as he walked towards Sam from across the grass.

She responded casually even though she panicked on the inside. "What did she say?"

"Tell her to call her mother." He quoted her exact words. "Then she hung up on me."

"I'll call her back later." Sam said casually and put down her brush, no longer able to concentrate on her work after her mother's silent interference, plus she wanted to change the subject. "What do you think?"

"Looks like it will be my favorite."

Sam laughed. "You say that about all of them."

Unlike her earlier works, with a little help from a few art classes added into her school schedule, she learned to add much more than beach, water and sky. This particular one was an accomplishment that put all her studies to test. The Waterside Inn. Complete with the white rocking chairs on the wrap around porch, a basket of lavender beside the door, and Grace's prized tea set on the small table. All in it's surrounding beauty of grass and sea. Like the many others she painted, she would have it framed and present it to Grace and Pop who would lovingly display it proud as they did every one she'd given them.

"Are you finished with the one you wouldn't let me see?" Carter remembered she was working on two at one time, didn't want to leave either unfinished when summer was over.

Sam smiled to herself, reached down into her portfolio case and placed it upon the easel so he could view it. "I just finished it today."

It was simple, not as busy as the Inn. A painting of The Point that jutted out into the harbor with the large white gazebo, only she'd painted in what appeared to be a bride and groom. You couldn't see faces, but you could tell it was a man in a black suit and the bride's dress and veil seemed to flow freely in the wind, appeared to wrap the two of them together as one.

"I was talking to Nikki when her and Blake were here and we got to talking about weddings. I think one of these days I'd like to get married at The Point in the gazebo so I decided to paint it to see what it would look like." Sam smiled up at him, the words never gave a full commitment but the innuendo was there.

Carter placed his hands on her shoulders. "Looks like the perfect place. Who's the groom?"

"Oh, I don't know." She teased. "I have someone in mind but I'm waiting to see if he'll finish college or drop out and become a homeless guitar player."

As Carter looked at the painting he knew it would be them one day. It had to be. But still, in the back of his mind his mother's words returned as they often did at times. 'She'll hurt you one day Carter'. She would be wrong, wouldn't she? She had to be.

Sam admired the work and imagined it to be them indeed, what she didn't know at that moment in time was that it would be her last painting for many years to come.

****

It wasn't difficult for Sam to figure she'd gotten the phone number from directory assistance. But she'd never worried about that because her mother didn't like to talk to other people, so she didn't think she'd call a land line.

"I had to call that Inn. Why don't you ever keep your cell phone on? How am I to get hold of you?" Her mother started in on her immediately when Sam returned her call.

"I've told you mother, I can't keep it on. I'm working or in class, all you have to do is leave a message."

Joan went into a rant. "I've been thinking about you, why don't you give up this fool notion of working and come to Italy with us? We're going to cruise the Mediterranean, it's going to be wonderful. What are you doing there anyway? Sailing? Sunning? No, you're wasting precious time cleaning up after people, or cooking, or some such nonsense. If you want a job I can get you a job anywhere. Work with Durham now, side by side with your father."

"That isn't what I want, I'm perfectly happy where I am."

"I don't understand this little sojourn of yours you insist upon, what is it you want? I'll buy it for you."

Sam would have laughed if her mother hadn't been serious in her statement. It was sad. Sadder still Sam was the happiest she'd ever been in her life, and it wasn't enough. Would never be enough until she was what they wanted her to be. Sam could hear the clink of ice in a glass as her mother took a drink of gin, knew it had been quite some time she stopped watering it down with tonic.

"Just come with us for a little while, the McGuire's son will be there and you get along well with him."

"Well? The last time I saw him I was sixteen and he snuck up to my bedroom to smell my underwear! If that's not disgusting enough, he's a cocaine addict, does that not matter to you?"

"Everyone can go through a bad spell, but he's fine now, he went to one of those rehab centers. I know you've been spending all this time with Cartwright, your house man, but you can't be serious. It isn't as if you'll have a future with him." Joan said it with a laugh as if it were the funniest of jokes.

Sam was furious, held the phone tighter in her hand and stopped herself from screaming. "Don't do that mother, you don't even know him."

"I do know the kind of person that's right for you and the McGuire's son is quite a catch. If you don't snatch him up I'm afraid he may be gone soon." The lilt to the end of her last words was as if it were a threat Sam should be concerned about.

"Oh I wouldn't worry about that."

Then her mother changed her tactic but it wasn't as if Sam couldn't see through it. Joan huffed, her voice a passive sigh to elicit any compassion she could. "Forget about him, I just want you to come with us for a while, a few days. I haven't seen you in so long and it would be nice to spend time together."

"I came to Virginia for a week just last month, remember? You were there two days then went off to Florida."

"I don't know why, it was so dreadfully hot. Come to Italy, we'll have days, weeks, months if you want. I just want to see you Sam."

Sam wanted that to be the real reason, wanted to believe her words. She'd fallen into it as a child. Hung on every word when she told her from a long distance phone line how much she missed her and that she'd be home soon. Or how she promised not to drink anymore when she'd thrown a bottle at her then apologized profusely afterwards.

It was a child's heart that wanted to believe the reason she gave, a child's heart that reached out to a mother that wasn't there. Even now she saw it as that hope that dangled just out of reach but she'd suffered the ache of broken trust so many times she knew if she went to grab for it, it would be snatched away.

Sam didn't take the bait. "Go mother, and have a good time. I'll look forward to the postcard you'll send." She didn't need to add another to her collection of hundreds but she knew it would come. It always did.

"I am your mother, I could force you to come."

"No you can't." She sighed. Talking to her mother was an emotional roller coaster ride from one extreme to the next.

"I could insist, Samantha."

She shouldn't have fallen into it, should have listened to her patiently then hung up the phone but Sam didn't.

"You know mother, all my life you never wanted me to go anywhere with you, I was left at home, now you only want me to go so you can try to marry me off to some coke snorting asshole. Don't I mean anything to you?"

"Of course you mean something to me, I'm only looking out for you. I want you to be with someone in the lifestyle that suits you. And that's with someone like the McGuire's son, not some college bum who fixes houses that only wants to live off your money. He can't love you dear, it's your money he loves."

She'd heard it all her life. As if she couldn't possibly be good enough on her own for someone to love her, without her money she offered nothing worth having. So what were her parent's reasons? Why didn't they love her?

After she quietly hung up on her mother, she refused to cry, wasn't a child anymore. Sam stood on the bluff alone then heard Grace's call from the porch.

"Sam? Carter called a few minutes ago and wanted to know if you could stop by that house he's working on today after you go to town. The one on Ocean Lane."

Sam waved to let her know she'd heard but didn't go in right away, needed a few deep breaths to gain her composure back. Why did she let her mother make her feel like crap? How could she still get to her? Even as anger took hold, a tinge of guilt crept in alongside it.

Sam loved her parents, that unconditional love that came with birth but was she wrong to want more than what they gave? Was she supposed to feel guilty because she'd found something elsewhere? Something her parents never offered?

****

It took her longer than planned to get to where Carter was. She had to pick up a few things for Grace and made a quick stop to see Skippy McGee before driving down the long drive of the house on Ocean Lane. He'd been working on it since last summer for someone who wanted to use it as a vacation home and it was her favorite so far. She often gave her opinion on things with the other homes he worked on but this one she truly had a hand in the beautiful way it developed.

Carter loved his work. Remodeling and fixing houses to a new shine seemed to be what he was born to do. Architectural classes put him above most others in the business but he preferred manual labor skills just as much as drawing the plans. Liked to be involved in his finished project from the very beginning stages all the way to the end.

Painstaking care was taken to be true to the original style of the house when the client desired it, he even went so far as to make trim specific to a certain era if it wasn't available to purchase. Scoured everywhere he could for a type of brick and Sam once watched him make and assemble an entire floor of wood that was unlike anything she'd ever seen. Because of the way he worked, over just the last few years he'd picked up more and more projects for the summer and had already made a name for himself.

The driveway was long and lined with trees and once you could see the house in the clearing it looked both like everything you would expect to see and at the same time everything you wouldn't. It had been a complete remodel she'd seen evolve from crumbled ruins of a once beautiful Cape Cod style house that had gone neglected, to a pristine white picture of refinement with pretty yellow shutters and a front porch that looked inviting even though it was bare.

It was completely centered in vision with the ocean a wide vista behind it and Sam always had a lift of her heart just to see it. It reminded her of something she'd seen once in a story as a young child. Something in some far off dream world that looked so perfect, yet so unattainable to her.

Before she got out of the car she took a few moments just to look at it and calm her nerves a little from still thinking about her mother's phone call. Then she saw Carter open the front door and lean against the doorjamb with his arms crossed. Just seeing him calmed her.

"Where have you been?" He smiled as she walked towards the house. God he loved seeing her. Her dark hair hung loose around her face, a face without makeup it didn't need and her intense deep blue eyes that jumped with life. Only now, he could tell she was bothered by something and they'd been together long enough he could figure out easily she must have returned her mothers call. He didn't question it. "I see you didn't come empty handed."

"Of course not. Your mother sent you lunch and Skippy McGee isn't the only one in town I save my chocolate muffins for."

"Did you go see him first?" He said, as he walked down the steps and met her halfway with a kiss.

"I did. Are you jealous?"

"Of a mean old man in a fish shack? I think I'm safe. He hates you."

"He got up and walked out on me today." Sam said with an even tone and Carter laughed.

"Just left you?"

"I was chatting away and he just slowly got up and walked out."

He shook his head. "Are you ever going to give up?"

"I refuse. He's going to come around, I know it." She stepped closer and put her arms around his waist, needed to feel him next to her. There was a smudge of dirt on his face and she wiped it away. "I ought to charge you for consulting fees. Not to mention the food delivery."

"I'm but a poor man and have no money to pay you."

"Maybe you have something to barter?" She looked at him seductively, pressed herself against him more. "Maybe you could offer personal services perhaps."

He shrugged his shoulders. "If I have no choice. I may be a poor man, but I am one of honor and if you insist."

She kissed him with a passion, loved the feel of him so close to her, the way his arms wrapped around and held tight. Every second in his arms faded all her fears and anxiety, her uneasiness melted and the world was right. He loved her.

When he pulled away he only did so before he made love to her right there in the driveway. "I didn't know you meant right here and now."

"Why not?" She teased, but when she saw he would take her up on it she chickened out. "Okay, maybe not here."

Carter took her hand and led her to the door. "Not in the driveway anyway."

When he pushed the door open wider she gasped in surprise. It was one large great room and the entire back wall was floor to ceiling windows, the sea filled the room. Sun shone off the gleaming wood of the floor, a floor exactly like one she'd seen him do elsewhere, wide planks honed to a sleek shine, this one even more beautiful if that was possible.

"Carter, this is magnificent. I didn't know you'd done so much."

"You haven't been here in awhile, you're too busy visiting Skippy McGee instead." He had to admit it was impressive, the best work he'd done so far.

"I can't believe this is the same house." She whispered as she walked into the kitchen on the left, a two-way fireplace separated it from the big center room.

The wall of glass continued there as it did on the other side where the master bedroom was.

"This is incredible" She stopped in front of him with a look of awe. "I didn't know you'd gotten this far, the last time I was here you had plastic all over the window side, I had no idea."

"I didn't want you to see the windows so I hid them."

Carter was pleased with her reaction, had watched every moment with great interest, holding a secret inside he would pick just the right moment in the future to reveal. He didn't remodel the house for any client to use as a vacation home, he'd purchased it himself in a deal he couldn't pass up. And with all of Sam's innocent suggestions and opinions, he'd created something he knew would be exactly as she wanted. Maybe Christmas he would surprise her not only with an engagement ring, but the gift of a house they could begin their lives in one day.

As she pressed up to him, slid her arms around his waist, he could see the pleasure in her eyes and held back an urge to tell her then. But as she placed several small, soft kisses on his neck, it was all he could think about. Their life together. Their children running around. He'd planned for their rooms downstairs, then upstairs when they were older. Carter took her by the hand and pulled her back through the living room to the other side.

"The master bedroom is finished."

"It is?" She held tight to his hand and followed willingly, knew what his intentions were.

CHAPTER 5

The next time Sam's mother called, her demeanor was highly irate. Then it worried her when she called her cell phone several more times and left countless messages, this time in her drunk, whiny, child like manner. She was lonely, she had said, needed her daughter. Childhood guilt stirred within her but she tried as best she could to push it aside. Older now, she learned a long time ago she couldn't help her mother, Joan Durham needed much more than Sam could give her.

She did call her back once and the conversation, or rather, the semi-conversation with Sam talking and her mother crying left her even more agitated and yet concerned. Before she let her mothers words break through to her childhood fears, to make her run to a mother who sounded in desperate need, she called her father.

"Is mother okay?"

"Samantha, dear, do I at least get 'Hello father, nice to hear your voice'?"

She sighed and couldn't help but smile. "Hello father, nice to hear your voice."

"That's better, but I would have hoped you'd be calling to tell me you're coming to Italy with us."

"I really can't." She sighed, hoped it wouldn't be another argument, but her father never pressed as much as her mother always did.

"It would be nice to spend time with you, but I know you're busy. Italy will come later. I can't blame you for wanting to stay with your friends instead of coming with a bunch of old people."

"I'm having a good time here, at least you can appreciate that. Mother doesn't seem to understand why I'm even here."

"Enjoy the college days Samantha, after graduation I'll have you to the grindstone and believe me, it will be a grand day for me when I can put your name on your office door. I already have it picked out for you."

Sam didn't want to think about that phase of her life yet, she hadn't left this one, only would when she was forced to do so. She changed the subject back to the original reason for her call. "Mother has called a few times and her tone worries me, is she okay?"

"I was away for a few days but she'll be fine now. We've decided to go a little early so she can enjoy a Spa. That's seemed to pacify her for now. All you have to do is concentrate on getting your degree and getting back here, I need you in the office. Half the attorneys there are idiots and I know you'll be the one person who will be loyal to me, look out for the company's best interest."

"Yeah, Dad." She said quietly, he made her feel better about her mother but it was only replaced with thoughts of her future that was put before her. A future she pushed away to the back corners. "I'd better let you get back to work, I just wanted to make sure she was okay."

"Perfectly fine, let me worry about your mother. But you know, it would be nice to see you, why don't you arrange some time to come to New York before we leave? Seeing you always calms her."

It wasn't much to ask of her and she decided it would be nice to see them. With high hopes she made plans to visit.

****

Carter had been watching her from the porch as the last brilliant rays of sun disappeared and left her no choice but to pack up her paints and call it a day. Sam wore a pair of loose white gauze pants and a coral flowered top with a tie in the back the breeze played with, made it dance and flow as the wind picked it up and dropped it again at will. Just as it did with her hair that had come undone from a ponytail. She'd been so engrossed she hadn't noticed.

Her back still to him, he continued to watch intently after she packed her paints and clasped her hands together. Reached them high above her head and stretched her body in an arch. Instantly he wanted to be standing in front her, stroke his hands up her inner arms and kiss the soft part of her neck just between her ear and the crevice of her collarbone. Could feel the softness that was now so familiar, could almost hear the sigh she would emit. Carter never could have imagined such intense love existed.

Sam walked across the grass towards him as he still sat on the porch but she hadn't noticed him yet, it was obvious her mind, thoughts, and eyes were elsewhere. But when she looked up a slow smile crossed her face and the beauty of her struck him, as it always did. Not only her physical beauty, but also the smile that said she loved him. Even if she hadn't said it out loud.

When she reached him she set her things down, sat next to him and fell into the crook of his arm as he put it around her. He felt so good. So solid, he was the only thing in her life that felt so anymore.

"I didn't know you were home yet, how long have you been here?" Sam sighed and couldn't get close enough to the clean fresh smell that was Carter just after a shower.

"Long enough to fall in love with you all over again."

"Any fish today? Were the waters kind? What's the deal with that anyway? You got to go fishing and I babysat the Wagner's kids."

"You were probably better off, it was a little rough, there's a storm coming in."

His words had different meaning for Sam. The time came closer when she would have to explain the life that had been planned for her, that time passed quickly and he would have to know about Samantha Durham, Corporate Attorney to Durham Corporation. Although she should have told him a long time ago, and urged her mind to tell him then, it didn't happen. When it did, that was the storm she worried about.

"Are you going to tell me what's wrong?" Carter spoke softly, as if his understanding tone would encourage her to answer him.

"There's nothing wrong."

"I can see it in your eyes, and its different this time Sam, I'm worried." Carter didn't normally press her, but this time there was something desperate that frightened him. He felt as if she wanted to say something but changed her mind. There were still so many secrets in Sam's life she'd yet to reveal, he began to think it was possible she never would.

Sam snuggled closer to him. "There's nothing wrong, nothing that sitting right here for the rest of the day won't fix. I was all over today, had the Wagner kids and that wasn't an easy task, they wore me out."

"And you love it as much as they do, I think they come every year because the kid's want to spend time with you. I'm afraid if you're not here one year, they're going to want their money back." He tried once more as he whispered close to her ear. "What's wrong, Sam?"

"Summer's fading away from us, I always get down at this time. I'm worried how Skippy McGee will survive most of the winter without my chocolate cheesecake muffins."

Carter had to laugh. "You and Skippy McGee. A mean old man who sits in a fish hut on the pier all day and doesn't like you. He's probably the only one in town, is that why you go see him every Friday and take muffins? You can't stand there's one hold out? Last week you cursed him till Sunday because he told you that if anyone in town would listen to him, he'd gather them all up to run you out. I thought you weren't going back?"

"I think he's coming around." She laid her head against his chest and chuckled at the absurdity of it.

"The mood you've been in, you'll probably be good for each other when you make your weekly visit tomorrow."

"Have I been that bad?" She tried her best not to let it show but obviously she hadn't done well.

"Not too bad. It doesn't make you unbearable, but I'm in love and can't be impartial. To me there's nothing that would make you unbearable, unless you brought Skippy McGee home with you."

"He'd never come, he thinks I live in hell."

The sound of Carter's spontaneous laughter exploded, it seemed to echo for miles and signal out to anything and anyone that life was good. There was laughter in the air. Sam had fallen in love with the sound.

He shook his head trying to understand. "I keep trying, but I can't understand the fascination with Skippy McGee. When I was a little boy I skirted around that fish hut as far as I could, had nightmares of him throwing me into the water just to watch me drown. Or slapping me up on his table and gutting me just like a fish, then chopping me up for bait. And here you are, after almost four years now going to see him at least once a week just to sit and listen to him grumble."

"He's lonely. And he lost his love."

"He's lonely because he's a mean old lunatic who's alone and wants to stay that way. And you believe that old story about losing his love?" He asked.

"It's what most people in town say, is there another reason you never told me about?"

"I don't think he lost her, I think she's probably floating around underneath the pier or maybe he keeps her in that big white cooler."

"He isn't dangerous or evil. And of course he hasn't said so, because he doesn't talk to me much to say anything other than 'go away', but I think he does like my chocolate muffins."

Quite a few things were said about why Skippy McGee was a miserable old coot, but most of them involved a tourist who came to town one season in his much younger day. He'd fallen madly in love and no one more surprised than he when he asked her to marry him and stay in Cape Cod forever, and she agreed. They married. But it was only a few months later she'd left him a note while he was out fishing one day. Cape Cod wasn't exciting enough for her. She needed more. Moved to Florida where there was warm sun and lively action all year long.

After that he looked to any tourist as if they were the one's who'd wronged him. Said Cape Cod had to be in your blood in order to belong, anyone not born and raised there was an outsider. Laws should be made to keep them out. Barriers put up. Whatever it took. He aimed his hate and distaste towards Sam. From the first moment she'd met him, Sam had become his target.

His words to her ran the gamut. 'Get off my pier... go away... go to hell... if I throw you in and you drown, no one will know...' Her favorite was always... 'City girl ain't got no business here, ain't your place. Go on home.'

So endearing, but Sam went back week after week in the summer and at times when she came in the winter months. Often, she found herself just sitting in the grass by the water and looking at his old fish hut. There were days she had to swallow her fear and build up the courage to face him.

When she did, she sat quietly while he ignored her. Or she'd chatter away, while he either ignored her or fussed at her to leave. Sometimes it was a few times a week, or a quick stop when she was in town for a short time. But she always made it a standing appointment to at least go see him every Friday, whether he liked it or not, and took muffins.

Carter pulled her close and kissed her, stirrings of passion strong as he teased. "I like your muffins."

"Is that all you like about me?"

"What kind of question is that? It's only one of a million things."

"Like?" Sam asked with a serious tone, her eyes seeking answers from his.

Carter saw a need, a need to hear his words and he formed them carefully. "I like the way you're so excited when school's almost over, then the way you become sentimental when the summer's almost over. I like the way you shiver when I kiss the palm of your hand." Carter took her hand and kissed it where he spoke of. "Or when your eyes light up when you're extremely happy about something. Like when mother hangs a new painting. You insist she doesn't have to feel obligated to hang it, yet when you see it your eyes light up when no one is looking..."

"I love the way you call my father Pop, and the way you sometimes call my mother Mama Grace. And I even like the fact you feel guilty about it, as if you feel you're being disrespectful to your own mother somehow."

Samantha listened intently to this man who made her feel so loved, who knew her inner self like no one else on this earth.

He stroked her cheek softly as he continued. "I like the way you look in the morning, there's a glow of a fresh new day in your eyes. And I love the way you have a look of satisfaction at the end of the day when the moonlight shines in them. I love the way you've made Cape Cod your home, as if you've always been here..."

"The way you greet repeat guests every year as if you've known them all your life. The way you have that tells them you've been waiting just for them." He touched his lips to hers tenderly. "I could go on for the rest of the night, but I'll say one last thing. As much as I don't understand it, I even like the way you worry about Skippy McGee."

****

As Sam prepared to go to New York to see her parents, the people on the Cape prepared for a storm and it left her uneasy. She'd never been through a hurricane but those on the Cape organized game plans that came from experience. Boats were secured as best they could be in and out of the water, furniture from first floors moved to higher floors, other possessions were confined to safe places. Grace and Pop along with other Inn, motel and hotel owners relocated guests elsewhere for safety. Windows and doors were boarded, valuables packed and safeguarded elsewhere and anything else that could be done to avoid as much damage as possible.

"I wish I could stay and help." Sam pressed against Carter and looked up into his handsome face. "I feel bad leaving when there's so much to be done and I'll be able to do nothing but worry. Is it going to be really bad?" Sam looked out to calm waters of Nantucket Sound that gave no indication of anything amiss.

"Around here we never underestimate the power of a storm, we just prepare for the worst and hope for the best. With it coming in, that's the only reason I'm glad you're headed out. At least I know you'll be safe."

"I can't believe it's supposed to come today, it looks like any other beautiful day. Will you call me later?" Whenever she was away from Carter she always had her phone on as opposed to always off when she was around him.

"I'll call." He kissed her lightly but Sam pressed into him hard, needed much more. Carter wrapped his arms around her and held tight, wanted to give her whatever reassurance she sought.

"I'd better leave before I change my mind." Although she said the words she didn't pull away. "I hate to leave, you understand, don't you Carter?"

Sam did what she felt she needed to do, that he understood. "Yeah Sam. I understand."

So she left the Cape, and as she looked into her rearview mirror saw Carter standing there with his hands inside his worn jeans and a sad expression on his face. She gripped her hand on the wheel and forced herself to drive on even though she didn't want to. Afraid if she took her hands off, the car would turn itself around on its own and go back to where she wanted to be, where she should be.

Maybe if she went back and told him, explained everything, even take him with her to meet her parents. But as many thoughts that told her to go back and tell him, just as many prevented her and she screamed to herself the entire way... I'm not ready to give up Sam... I'm not ready to give up Sam... I'm not ready to give up Sam... It was the logic she used for just over an hour as she drove to Boston Airport where a private jet awaited.

The pilot smiled broadly, he'd been with her father for years and knew her well. "Nice to see you Ms. Durham, it's been quite some time."

"Hello Mr. Rob, how have you been? How's the family?"

She kissed him on the cheek and they gave each other a quick hug. For Sam it was like seeing an old friend from her other life, the life she stepped back into periodically when needed. Back and forth... back and forth... something had to end, something had to happen and she would eventually have to bring the two together. It was driving her crazy. Torn between two worlds, loving one and feeling obligated to the other, and yet her unconditional love made her love the obligated world just as much. Sam held onto her high hopes that things would be different, kept repeating it in her mind until she believed it to be so.

An hour later she was whisked off the plane and into a waiting limousine. It surprised her little that her parents weren't there in person, she reminded herself which life she was in. The world was different here.

"There's my baby." Joan threw her arms wide and some of what remained of her drink splashed out.

Sam hugged her. For all her mother's faults, she always did appear truly glad to see her, when she ever took the time to do so. But then again, it was hard for her not to think it wasn't just the alcohol that made her glad to see her.

Growing up she'd always felt the roles were reversed most times, from an early age of eight years old she could remember feeling the mother and Joan the child. Her mother would break down at times, become irate and scream at her, then the next cry like a frail baby and Sam would hold her, console her as best she could. It was a twisted emotional reversal. There were feelings of concern and empathy she felt now as she held her mother. Worried about her.

Joan pulled back and looked at Sam intently. "Look how tan you are, but my dear, look how big you've gotten. You must be a size eight at least." Joan looked to her and tried not to look perturbed but the smile showed the obvious disapproval.

"It's so nice to see you also. And I'm not an eight, more like a size ten, maybe even larger." The moment of feeling at least a little happy to see her mother subsided.

"I've bought you some new clothes but we'll have to buy more, I think they're all a size four."

"I've never worn a four in my life mother, and I don't need any new clothes." She turned to her father and gave him a kiss on the cheek. "Hello father."

"Of course you need clothes, look at how you're dressed."

She took a second to look at herself in 'Sam's' clothes, a simple pair of jeans, a white t-shirt, and a pair of tennis shoes. Joan Montgomery had probably never worn a pair of tennis shoes in her life.

"I'm comfortable." She argued, automatically put in defensive mode.

"You look... sloppy." Joan's face scrunched up like a child's then she shrugged. "Come to your room and try on the things I've bought you, you might be able to squeeze into them. If not you can pack a few things you have in your closet here and we'll buy new when we get to Italy."

Sam stood where she was, her feet refused to move, her mind refused to take in her mothers words. They'd discussed it, fought about it, and she didn't want to hash it out again. Maybe if she just ignored her.

"Come along, Samantha." Her mother had begun to walk away, now Joan stopped and waited.

"I just walked in the door and I don't want to try on clothes I don't need. Can I just put my things down and relax? How about breakfast? I'm starving." She looked to her father for help.

"We discussed this Joan and you understood." He talked to her as if she were a child.

Joan didn't seem to hear. "But there's not much time Samantha."

"She's not going with us Joan." Montgomery said more firmly.

"Oh, you said that, but I'm sure she's changed her mind, haven't you dear?" Her mother looked to her with a broad smile as if it were so.

"No mother, I haven't. I came to visit for a few days before you go." Samantha found herself like her father, talking to her as if she were a child who needed to understand something complicated. "How about I make you happy. I'll wear something new you bought and we'll go out for breakfast. The Four Seasons, you love it there."

Joan huffed with impatience. "Samantha, we're leaving in an hour, there's no time for breakfast."

Sam froze and stared at her mother. Not only had she gone to great lengths to get there, but she'd left Carter and his family when there was a hurricane on its way to Cape Cod. And for what? One hour of quality time before they jetted off to the Italian Riviera.

Sam looked to her father for sober answers, maybe she was too drunk to remember when they were leaving and was mistaken. He shrugged his shoulders.

"A quick change of plans. They could only get into the spa tomorrow, the only available date. It's difficult to get reservations there, so we leave today." Montgomery's face looked apologetic. "I'm sorry, I should have told you about the change in plans but I was afraid you wouldn't come and she really wanted to see you before she left."

Sam smiled crookedly, nodded her head and spoke with a slow dry tone. "Of course. And of course she wanted to see me, had to tell me how big I was and how sloppy I looked."

"I hope you understand Samantha." Her father watched her, she'd always understood, but he didn't see the acceptance in her eyes now.

"But it's okay." Joan was ecstatic and Sam also thought delusional. "You're coming with us. I've bought all the clothes you need. They'll be entirely too small but we'll buy your wardrobe when we get there. I'm making you go, by force if I have to."

"You can't, that's kidnapping." She stated dryly, not amused.

"Not if it's my own daughter, it's intervention, I'm saving you, like they do with those drug kids except I'm saving you from yourself."

Sam didn't say another word and began to walk towards the door.

"Montgomery, get her before she gets away." Joan shouted the words as if she truly planned on taking her by force if she had to.

He touched her arm slightly and assured her there would be no kidnapping. "We're not going to force you Samantha, as much as I'd love for you to come to Italy with us I don't share your mother's ideas."

"Oh, I'm not worried about being kidnapped, I'm worried about remaining in this room for one more minute. I have quite a few years of frustration that's about ready to explode."

Joan screeched from across the room, all pleasantries gone, and the smile no longer on her face. "Samantha Durham, all I want is for you to meet the right people, you're not getting any younger. It's about time you settled down and the McGuire's son won't be available long."

She glared at her father now. "Do you share her same sentiments? You want me married off to the highest bidder?"

Montgomery spoke in a calmer tone. "Your mother just wants you to start meeting the right people Sam. I understand you've been having fun in school and whomever you've been seeing is fine, for that phase of your life, but what is he? A plumber? A handyman? You'll be a corporate executive. The heiress to something much bigger."

"You've never even met Carter and yet you make assumptions he isn't right for me. He's studying to be an architect and remodels houses right now and does a damn fine job. And guess what? He and his family have made me the happiest I've ever been in my entire life. Does that not mean anything to you?" They didn't know what she loved in life and weren't interested, they never had been, because it wasn't their version of happiness.

Joan started crying. "See Montgomery? I told you, she doesn't even want to be with me anymore."

"Now that I'm an adult, all of a sudden you want to spend time with me? Why now? Why not when I was a child? What was wrong with me then?" Sam glared at her and didn't know why she waited for an answer because it was hard for her mother to understand anything, much less have to really think about something important.

"You're holding it against me that we traveled. Is that why you don't want to spend time with me?" Joan cried.

"You're never physically around, or emotionally for that matter." Sam just wanted to leave, wanted to get out of there because she could feel the heat rise like bile in her throat.

"I think those people are brainwashing her Montgomery." Joan sniffed and finished the last of her drink in one swallow.

"That has to be the reason I spend time with them." Sam's words dripped in loathing sarcasm.

"Is it a cult? What are they doing to you? Are you being drugged? Well, you're coming with us. I'm your mother and..."

"You don't know the meaning of the word 'mother', it's more than giving birth to someone. What have you ever done for me besides that?" The words sprang out as her frustration began to build to a dangerous level.

"How ungracious of you! I've bought you everything you ever wanted."

"But you didn't give a shit about what I needed. Bought... bought... love is not for sale, you can't buy it! That's all I ever wanted and you could never give it to me because you were either too busy or too drunk."

Her father held one hand in the air as a signal to stop her. "Now Samantha, I'll not have you say things about your mother that way."

"You're not blind to it, you're in denial and choose to look the other way, well I can't anymore. Neither one of you have ever been there for me, at least she has an excuse of being drunk."

"My entire life has been building this company for you, and yes, your mother comes along on many of my trips because you know how difficult it is for her to be alone. Is it so wrong to spend my entire life building something for you? The proudest day for me is when you walk into the office and take over."

"I told you those people were doing something to her." Joan was crying again, this time sobbing as she poured another drink.

"Doing something to me?" Sam's voice rose loudly, the absurdity of all of her mother's ramblings took hold in her gut. "Grace and Pop care whether I'm truly happy, you care whether I have enough money to go buy my happiness somewhere. A Prada purse doesn't make me happy. A new car doesn't make me happy. Superficial ornaments, all decoration. It's all a farce. It doesn't make you parents who want to provide for your child, it makes you parents who don't want to give up anything emotional because you might have to feel something..."

"It's a trade off. Give me the frills and you don't have to give anything of yourself. Provide me a bank account and a Prada purse and that should take care of everything. Lord knows you don't have time for anything else. A Louis Vuitton handbag isn't love, it's a fucking handbag."

Joan gasped in horror. Montgomery's voice tried to remain calm but he could see the situation moving out of control. "Look at the way you're talking, isn't that proof you're being influenced by common people?"

"Its proof the both of you aggravate me so much I resort to cursing."

"That's it, you're coming back to the real world." Joan walked towards her with determination and would have physically grabbed her had Montgomery not stopped her.

Sam continued to rage. "The real world? The real world is people who get up everyday and hope the weather will be kind to them so they can fish. It's how they make a living and it's going to supply food for their table. The real world is a mother who shops at the second hand store for a nice pair of pants so she can buy her baby a brand new outfit for his Baptism. It's a man who sells his car and gets a bike because his wife is sick and there are medical bills to pay. That's the real world."

"Bums. They're bums Samantha. It's nothing but a bunch of people who have accepted their lot in life and have no drive for anything else."

"What else is there? What's out there you're looking for mother? You travel all over the world trying to find it and you haven't yet. You look for it in the bottom of every bottle you empty and it isn't there, is it? It's just an empty damn bottle! Well I've found something..."

"Carter doesn't care how much money I have or what my net worth is. And Grace and Pop don't give me a thousand dollar purse for my birthday and a postcard from somewhere saying how sorry they are they can't be there. They give me much more than you ever could. They've given me a piece of themselves, a piece of their lives, and that's worth more than you could ever understand."

Everything Sam ever felt spilled out with the emotion of pent up frustration she held back for so long and she couldn't stop it from happening. As if the last pin had been pulled to detonate a bomb and everything poured out, shrapnel flew about the room damaging everything in its wake.

"You two have spent your entire lives making sure I've had the best clothes, the best of this, the best of that, did you not notice that I didn't care what the label said or how much it cost? I didn't even want those things, all I wanted was for maybe my parents to be there on my birthday. Or take me somewhere because you wanted, not because you want to marry me off to someone you feel is worthy. Someone who's nothing but a drug addict but you don't care about that, all you care about is the fact he comes from what you consider the right people with the right kind of money. You can't trade me off like cattle, you parade me around when it's beneficial to you, then let me be when I'm of no use."

Joan sobbed uncontrollably now. "She's crazed Montgomery, I tell you she's crazed, they've done something to her."

"The only thing they've ever done is loved me, was that too much to ask of you?"

Sam looked into her mother's eyes and saw guilt there. Joan knew the way she'd treated her only child was wrong and yet had never done anything to change it. When she looked to her father, his eyes revealed a sad shame, he knew her hurtful words were true, but yet like Joan, never did anything about it.

What a perfectly lovely life the three of them appeared to have on the outside with all the trappings of wealth, and yet how miserable and tormented each of them were inside the beautiful walls hung with Matisse and Renior.

When Sam spoke again, her voice was soft now, a resignation in her words. "I'm going home. There are people waiting there who want to give me more than an hour of their time. They'll share their lives with me because they love me and care about me. Unlike you two who have a twisted and distorted version of the meaning."

CHAPTER 6

The storm approached the Cape with furious rage. Sam now considered her decision to return one that put her in perilous danger as the winds raged, and the rain pelted the car in sheets making the wiper blades unable to keep up. Downed trees along the road became her obstacles. Items of debris flew through the air and Sam gripped the wheel as tightly as she could because it was too late to turn back now.

Carter screamed at her to stay away when she told him she was coming back. "You won't make it Sam, by the time you get here you'll be in the middle of the storm."

"I have to, there's no where... there's no where else to go." Sam needed to get to him desperately. She was shaking over the encounter with her parents, they didn't care about her at all, they couldn't possibly love her. It's all she'd ever wanted. Carter would make her world right again, it was the only thing that could.

"Get a hotel, go back to school and wait there."

"Carter I need you... I..." But the cell phone connection went dead.

Now experiencing what he warned her to stay away from, she wished she'd listened. Determined to get there as quickly as she could to tell him everything about her he'd never known, Sam left New York with a purpose and now feared for her life as she passed a shed blown from it's footings that now lie against a bank. The same gale force winds that caused it now rocked her car. The drive was made more difficult when something hit her headlight and broke it, leaving her with only one. All she prayed was to get to Carter and tell him everything.

But Sam's purpose would not come to fruition. She made it to the safety of Waterside Inn and Carter's arms and they rode out the rest of the storm, but afterwards there was so much damage that clean up took everything they had. The Waterside Inn itself received minimal damage compared to others. Sam was shocked when they drove through one section and an entire house blocked the road. Boats were torn from moorings and smashed against the embankment of trees. She would have told him but now her problems and worries seemed so minimal compared to friends who'd lost their entire homes in one quick moment.

Electricity was a precious commodity afforded only to those with generators. Ice and water were being distributed, food, clothing, any items of need. Some from outside sources others from neighbors who'd been more fortunate, including taking in people who had no home left and no place else to go. Anonymously, Sam spent thousands from her trust fund and arranged for things discreetly.

Once repairs were made to the Inn their concentration was to neighbors who hadn't been so fortunate and although Sam wanted to weep every time she met someone who'd lost everything, she put on a strong persona and dug through rubble for anything that could be salvaged. Their most prized possessions were family pictures, a special piece of jewelry from a loved one, notes or cards, personal items and memorabilia so valuable to their family lives. She dug through mud, water, hermit crabs, dead and live fish and everything else Mother Nature had dropped on their doorstep to find it for them.

There were times her reserve broke and she cried with them over things they'd lost. Sam openly wept beside a mother who crumbled over remnants of a baby's photo album, or a grown man who had lost the only precious keepsake of his long dead grandfather. Priceless memento's that could never be replaced with any amount of money, items that tied their lives together, things she herself had never had. There was as much pain in not having it, as there was in losing it. As Sam helped them all try to put their lives back together, Carter used his well-honed skills to begin rebuilding in the construction process.

One of Sam's first worries was Skippy McGee, but she didn't know where he lived, all she'd known was the fish shack on the pier. He was so eccentric that he probably tried to ride the storm out there. When she got close enough to see, she was surprised to find it still standing, there was roof damage and wall pieces' missing that he was now trying to repair, but it was still there.

Sam didn't say a word as she walked onto the pier, picked up some tools he had laying there, and began nailing boards. It wasn't the type of work she was skilled at, but it was a haphazard shack anyway and he didn't look as if he was being particular. He nailed down odd pieces over open space anywhere he saw one. They worked in silence, each of them engrossed in what they were doing and Skippy finally spoke when it was apparent she wasn't leaving.

"Ain't you got nothing else to keep you busy?"

Sam continued to work without hesitation. "I do."

"Then what you here for? I didn't ask for your help, don't need it."

"If you did, you wouldn't ask. Maybe that's why I'm here."

"This don't mean you belong here." He set his hammer down and went inside. Old arthritic knees could no longer hold him up to the physical task.

As he sat inside and rested she continued to work until she no longer saw one open hole. Even climbed up on the roof and almost fell into the water, but nailed down the two largest boards she could find that would keep the rain and weather from penetrating.

Sam was sweaty and dirty as she opened the door and leaned against it, wiped her forehead with the sleeve of her shirt. "Think you need anything else?"

"I didn't need that. I'd a done it myself. Hell, I thought it'd be a winter project to keep me busy but I guess it won't now. All you city folk in a hurry for everything, and you ain't nothing but a city girl. Think you can come here and fix anything, you ain't got no business here, git on out of town." He huffed as if he'd planned it for the winter and now it was her fault he wouldn't have it to do. "Go on back to where you belong, it ain't here."

"When will I belong, Skippy?" She asked the question with innocence. Her voice soft and childlike, she truly wanted to know his answer. When he didn't answer, she repeated it a little louder, it told him she wasn't going away, he had to answer her. "When will I belong?"

Slowly, he raised his eyes to hers. Hard gray eyes bore into her. They were intimidating, cold, but they didn't waver and neither did she as she waited for him to speak. He stared for what seemed an eternity and she forced herself not to turn away, not to be frightened of his intense gaze that seemed to look into the depths of her soul.

"I'd see it, and I don't." He finally answered and looked away again.

Sam did what she could in Cape Cod. Physically put in as much muscle as she had along with helping people financially through ways that would keep her anonymous. While Carter stayed behind to lend his carpentry skills she returned to classes late when things were fairly under control and she felt she could be of no major use to anyone.

With so much that happened, all the work that consumed them, she of course pushed away once again her confessions. But this time she didn't have to worry over when and how she would tell him. It would be forced upon her as Sam was thrown from one storm into another when the family lawyer called with news that would change the path her life would take.

****

She'd been in the library when Richard found her hunched over a book, engrossed in her task of playing catch up with her lessons. He ran in, disheveled and out of breath, stood before her with a face drained of all color.

"Sam." He gasped.

She looked up, immediately prepared herself for bad news of some kind. "Where's Sara? What's happened?"

"It isn't Sara. You got a phone call at the house, he couldn't reach you on your cell phone. A Preston Burke. It's your parent's, Sam. It's urgent."

Along the beautiful coast of the Italian Riviera, Joan and Montgomery Durham lost their lives when the car they were driving veered off the road and crashed violently. Both were killed instantly. Although they hadn't suffered, it was little help to ease the numb anguish that engulfed her. The news hit Sam with hard force, the shock of it paralyzed her and immense grief consumed her along with remorse over so many things that would always be left unsaid between them, but even more, so many things that had been said.

Preston arranged for her immediate return to Virginia. Suggested she get there as quick as possible before the story broke because the business world would be rocked by the news. Reporters would swarm the campus in search of her so the private jet awaited her anytime she was prepared to leave.

It was Nikki who packed her bag while Sam sat at the window, lost in her own thoughts. She hadn't been paying attention to what Nikki was talking about but the words finally broke through and Sam began to listen to what she was saying.

"We're all coming with you, including Blake who's on his way now. The others are throwing some things together and Shawna is trying to figure out how we're getting there. Hopefully she can borrow a friends huge SUV the six of us can fit in, if not, we'll take two cars and drive down because it would cost us a fortune to fly. But Sara is trying to find you and Carter a flight now."

"Carter, oh my God, I haven't even..."

Nikki touched her face gently and quickly reassured her. "Richard called him first thing, he's halfway here."

The need to see him grew in intensity and Sam couldn't think of a time in her life when she needed someone more. Just knowing he was halfway to her gave her a slight comfort but also a feeling of urgency for him to hurry to her side.

"Sam, is there someone else I need to call? Any relatives, other family, just tell me what to take care of." Nikki asked but Sara entered the room before Sam could answer there was nothing she had to do.

Sara came in with a piece of paper that had scribbled notes that covered it. "There's a flight in fifteen minutes that of course won't work, but I can get a non stop that leaves at eight this evening."

Another feeling of guilt, this time towards her friends, coursed through her. They all went to work doing things they thought necessary and lost in her sorrow she hadn't been paying attention. Sam wanted to tell them not to come. Knew they all had classes, jobs, and other things that would have to be rearranged. Blake, who graduated last year was leaving his new dream job he'd only just begun and driving from a few hours away to join them.

She knew she should open her mouth and refuse any to go out of their way but she needed them, Sam needed them all. There was no one else in her life that would see her through this and in her moments of weakness she didn't know how she could do it alone. So much would have to be explained, and she wouldn't know where to begin, but somehow, she knew with them all by her side, she would get through it.

"We won't need a flight, and no one needs to drive. There's a private jet waiting whenever we're ready to leave."

Sam had spoken softly, without anymore explanation, and Nikki and Sara looked to each other then back to Sam but didn't say a word. Only spoke in whispers to each other when they left her room, each concerned she may be delirious with emotional pain. But they understood when Richard silently walked into the house with the newspaper in his hand that explained more to them, revealed it on the front page headlines. Joan and Montgomery Durham killed in a car crash in Italy. Survived by one daughter, Samantha Durham.

No one asked for explanation. No one said a word other than words of comfort and support as they all flew to Virginia and escorted quickly and secretly to the Durham Estate that was larger than most hotels they'd ever been in. And on that day, just as busy. Many people rushed about the house, a flurry of activity as upper executives took meetings in several rooms and people came and went around them. A tragedy such as this, with someone like Montgomery Durham, did not involve mere funeral arrangements, many intricacies had to be taken care of.

She looked around at the flurry of activity and something deep inside took hold in her gut. Sam had been around these people long enough to know they were vultures, they would take her apart. Pick at her piece by piece until there was nothing left. They'd already taken over the house and just as quickly would want to manipulate her.

No matter what was to come she could either be looked at as a docile creature to be handled carefully then taken advantage of, or she could take control immediately before they all swallowed her up. Defenses born from within flowed through her veins and from somewhere deep emerged another side of her.

One of the long-standing house staff members came up quickly, and without the formality her mother always required, the dear woman took her in her arms in a tight familiar hug.

"I've been waiting for you. How's my girl?"

"I'll be fine." Sam looked to the others. "I've brought some friends with me and they'll be staying."

"I'll take care of them right away." Bea touched her face sweetly. "I have a kitchen full of food and…"

"They might be hungry." Sam remembered her offerings well, Bea thought anything could be solved with good food.

No doubt, someone secretly radioed him or did what they needed to inform her father's long-standing attorney that she'd arrived, he was at her side in moments.

"I hope you don't mind, Ms. Durham, we decided it best for everyone to meet here. The media has been camped out at the offices since the news leaked."

"So, no official statements have been made yet?"

"It's hit the papers of course, but nothing official. We're getting ready..."

Sam interrupted right away. "Good, I'm sure I'll have to rewrite it before it's released and I know you've already made arrangements for everything so we'll have to get together so we can make changes."

"Changes?" He questioned with puzzlement.

"I'm sure changes will have to be made, I'll have a say in what's released. I'll meet you in an hour."

The young woman before him was far from what he expected to arrive. Not having been around her much over the years, Preston expected someone more like her mother. Expected a shriveling, needy girl to show up and be glad people were being paid to take care of everything for her. Instead he was faced with someone far different.

"Had I known you wanted to contribute I would have waited, but the statement is scheduled to be released in fifteen minutes."

"And I know with one phone call from you, it can be stopped." Sam stood her ground on the one shaky square of marble in the vast foyer full of hundreds of others. But it was only hers that shook, and it was also only on the inside, on the outside she stood solid.

"Of course, but it has to be done as quickly as possible."

"I said I'd meet you in an hour." Sam persisted without hesitation.

"I'd say thirty minutes at the most, shareholders are getting nervous. I've set the library up as my temporary office, we can meet there."

"I've never liked the library, I'll meet you in my fathers office in an hour." Sam stared at him strongly and waited for objection.

Each knew it was more than words, it was a subtle press for dominance that he wasn't sure he wanted to give up. Especially not to someone who didn't know anything about what was going on, even if she was Montgomery's only child. Had it been a son he may have looked at it differently, but given no other choice, Preston was the first to concede.

"I didn't mean to be insensitive, of course, settle in and we'll meet later."

When they stepped into her room that was probably as big as the entire first floor of the Waterside Inn and lavishly decorated with rich silk and chenille, a bathroom with gold fixtures and imported Italian marble, Sam knew how intimidating it probably was for Carter. She lay her purse down on a chair and noticed the few luggage pieces were already there, they'd been delivered by way of the back stairs.

She watched his back as Carter walked over to the window and looked out beyond to the vast amount of hilly land dotted with horses. Nothing had yet been said about all that had been revealed to him in the last few hours, his only concern was for her needs. It tore him up he could do anything for her but take away the distress she now faced. He stared at something in the distance or nothing in the distance, Sam wasn't sure what exactly he gazed upon, but he hadn't looked at her.

"Who was that?" He finally spoke without turning around.

"You mean my fathers attorney?"

"No, I mean the fragile woman I walked in with and the woman I'm standing in this room with now. The one who pulled the power play?" Carter saw it for what it was.

"I made a quick decision when I saw a house full of suits. I could either be fragile as you said, like my mother was, or I could take control like my father would. These people are Durham Corporation, and they may have looked out for my father, but now they're looking out for their best interests. The wealth may not be important to me, but my dignity is. I can't stand by and let anyone take advantage, and that's where all their minds are right now."

Carter ran his hands through his hair but remained there with his back turned. Sam walked over and touched him lightly, rubbed her hand down his side and felt him tense up.

"What are you thinking?" She asked.

"I'm thinking, things I shouldn't be thinking right now. You just lost your parents and we can discuss everything else later."

"No, tell me now. What are you thinking?" His mood frightened her.

Carter turned around, took her in his arms, and pulled her close to reassure her. "No, Sam, not now."

CHAPTER 7

Sam was relieved when Carter agreed to attend the meeting with her when she asked. Not only did she need him for support, but it was too late for drawn out explanations, she might as well throw him into her other world now. He was already halfway there.

"I think it best we meet alone, some of our discussions will be sensitive information." Preston began to object when he saw Carter present.

"And I think it best he be here." Sam stated.

It was settled. Carter had been standing by the window looking through some books on a shelf and remained there while Sam sat in her father's chair, Preston and the others across from her.

She felt her gut instinct had been right. Two other men accompanied Preston and it gave her the suspicion she was a lamb about to be dragged to slaughter. Her defenses went up as they were there to talk her into what was best for her and the company. Sam wasn't listening to anyone else's opinion of what was best for her at that point, she didn't know herself, but she knew she couldn't follow along with what their version of it was.

"There are many things to be done. First decisions have to be made about the funeral, a public statement, and stockholders meetings. Most of it you don't have to worry about of course, I'll take care of everything." Preston sounded sympathetic as he assured her there wasn't anything she would have to do but get through it.

"I'm sure that's been done already. You didn't wait for me to get home to make plans Preston, you've already made plans and you will basically suggest things and make me feel like it was my decision. Let's get this over with as quickly as possible. Just tell me what you have and I'll tell you whether it's what I want or not."

They discussed many things and most she disagreed with and changed, the main thing was a more private funeral than the circus it would become. Sam didn't see it as an event, she saw it as the death of her parents and they would be buried quietly with dignity and respect. Her mother was probably having a fit. Would have wanted the whole world to attend, hire the National Boys Choir at the very least. But her mother was no longer here.

The important pivotal point came when she disapproved of the official statement. Unbeknownst to them she'd contacted her father's assistant who supplied her everything she needed to be informed. Including an accident report, initial autopsy, everything that told her exactly in what manner her parent's lives ended.

"The official statement we're to make contains all the pertinent information but I think one of the most important things is being left out." Sam passed each of them a copy of the new one she'd devised and watched their faces.

"We can't do this. The death has a major impact as it stands alone, there's no reason to put something out there to exacerbate the problems we're going to face." Preston was the first to object and the others quickly followed.

"It's bad publicity. No disrespect Ms. Durham, but I feel it best you let us handle these kinds of things the way we know how."

"And how is that? Push it aside as if it didn't exist? Anyone who'd met my mother suspected it if they didn't know for sure. She was an alcoholic. Her being drunk behind the wheel of a car caused this accident, maybe it's important for people to know that and it could possibly help someone. Even the wealthy can't buy everything, not even immortality. They're not immune to tragedy, and tragedy that could have been avoided is the worst of all isn't it?"

"We're financially in trouble as it is, you can't put another hole in a sinking ship. I strongly disagree on this, and can't be a part of it." One of the men spoke as if his word would be the last one.

"You don't have to be, you can leave now."

"If that's a threat to my position with this company, it wouldn't make a difference. If this is released, we probably won't have a company and my job will be gone anyway. This statement..."

Her voice never wavered, her stare intense as she finished his sentence with her own words. "This statement will be released. Again, if you don't wish to be a part of it, you can leave now. I'll wait for you to close the door."

Preston leaned towards her, his voice slow and condescending as he tried to be patient. "I know there are quite a few things you don't understand and I'll explain them at great length if you want to know, but the main thing is we're in the middle of reaching an agreement on a merger. A merger this company needs to survive. The bad publicity makes the stock go down, that makes the company worth less, which in turn makes our position vulnerable in negotiation."

Sam too leaned his direction, bringing them even closer. "And I'm an adult that doesn't have to be talked to like a child. An adult I remind you, that owns this company now."

He slowly leaned back in his chair. "Spalding Edwards has to be called."

"Who the hell is Spalding Edwards?" Sam almost shouted.

"He owns the company we're merging with. In the least, I think he should be consulted."

"You can tell Spalding Edwards anything you want to tell him, but unless I see a signed contract that says he has any say with what goes on within this company, it's none of his business. None of you sitting here will make this decision and neither will Spalding Edwards. The statement will give the exact cause of the accident."

"This is a big mistake." One of them muttered.

"If so, it will be my mistake. My mother didn't do much when she was alive, but maybe in her death she can help someone else. It's a disease many people suffer from."

"Okay, so we'll come up with a version of the truth."

"It will be the truth. A lie will only cause more problems later on."

Sam's statement didn't go unnoticed to Carter who watched her intensity from across the room.

None of the men knew what else to say to try and change her mind, but all of them knew, right or wrong, there wasn't a thing they could do about it. Other than hire someone to declare her incompetent and they'd have to do it quickly.

Preston's secretary knocked on the door then opened it without waiting. "I'm sorry to disturb you, Spalding Edwards is on the phone and he's adamant about speaking with you Mr. Burke."

Sam sat back in her chair. "I can see you'll have a stroke if you don't talk to him, by all means, take the call Preston. Tell him what you feel he needs to know."

They waited as Preston spoke in low tones and only his end of the conversation could be heard. He revealed what they'd been discussing, made it known none of them felt it a good idea and tried to talk her out of it. Sam sat back and listened to him talk, then took the phone when it was handed to her.

"I knew your father well Ms. Durham, he was a good man, and you have my sympathy."

"Thank you."

"I hate to get into business like this so soon, but Preston told me what you're considering."

"No Mr. Edwards, it isn't something I'm considering, it's a decision that's already been made. If it affects you and any business dealings we may have then I guess that's a judgment call you'll have to make." Sam stated her words with finality and there were no other options she would consider.

"My first instinct is to thank the God's. I can lower my price by millions when the stock falls tomorrow."

"You have that option."

There was dead silence between them. A silence that extended to the room when all that could be heard was the ticking of a clock somewhere. Sam didn't break her reserve and Spalding was the first to speak.

"My deal will still be on the table tomorrow as stands. The original agreement on price your father and I made will be honored, even though the offer will be millions more than your company will be worth after your press release."

"After the funeral when I can get down to business, I'll possibly consider it."

Spalding couldn't help but appreciate her gumption. It crossed his mind she'd already had a better offer, or perhaps she was bluffing, only wanted to make it appear so with her aloofness. So sure of herself, some would see it as an arrogant gamble. Maybe she already decided she wanted more and this was a prelude for further negotiations, he couldn't be sure. The only thing he was sure of, Montgomery Durham was in her genes, there was no doubt of that.

"Very well. Again, I share your grief Ms. Durham, and I'm truly sorry. If there's anything I can do you'll let me know?"

"There'll be nothing."

"I have to say..." He stopped her for one more comment before they hung up. "You'd make your father proud."

Sam replaced the phone and didn't indicate to anyone the words spoken between them and showed no indication she was going to. Only concluded the meeting.

"Unless there's anything else I should know, I think this meeting is over." It was a statement and not a question.

All the men left without the notions they'd come in with. No one considered Sam to take an active role of any such kind, it hadn't crossed their minds, but there wasn't a thing they could do about it. Even as they listened to her one sided conversation with Spalding Edwards, from their end, it sounded as if she'd just ruined the deal that would save Durham Corporation from demise. Financial instability was already a concern and the merger with Edwards was to be their savior. Sam hadn't shared the discussion, as far as they knew it was now ruined, or would be tomorrow.

When the door closed Sam sat and stared at it for a long time. Her father's words rang in her head over and over again as the reality of her surroundings overwhelmed her... 'The proudest day for me is when you walk into my office and take over.'... followed by her words of anger afterwards as she lashed out. Mean, angry words she was now ashamed of. How proud had her father been after that? Her parents died thinking she meant every hateful thing she said, even if she did at the time, they didn't deserve to die thinking that's the only thing she'd ever thought of them.

Sam hadn't realized she'd leaned back and closed her eyes, didn't know for how long but it seemed forever as the words pounded her from all sides. And she'd forgotten Carter was even in the room, until he kissed away the unnoticed tear from her cheek.

****

Beatrice informed her that her friends were all settled in comfortable rooms and they now gathered in the pool house. Sam and Carter walked quietly, neither spoke as they made their way to the dwelling that sat literally on the waters edge, so close one could dive out into the pool easily. It was complete with living quarters just as opulent as the main house and was as large, if not larger, than Carter's entire home. Sam was embarrassed by the enormity of the obvious signs of wealth that surrounded them. She'd never given it much thought before, now as she walked with Carter, she was fully aware of how pretentious it all was, from the walk across the stone patio and path to the entire grounds that surrounded them.

"How did you guys manage to find a quiet place in this house?" Sam said as she walked in the door and they all looked to her and Carter.

Each of them saw something different between the two but of course no one said anything, no one quite sure what it was, but they didn't look the same. It would only be so obvious to those who knew them well that something was going on, something wasn't right.

"Beatrice has been running people out of here so we could have it all to ourselves." Richard answered as he discreetly looked to Sara with slight concern in his eyes.

"We've been talking about how she'd make a great football coach." Shawna laughed. "Michael calls her Attila the Hun."

"She could have our team at the top of the ranks in no time." Michael commented and looked to Carter but saw no laughter in his eyes.

Nikki put her arm around Sam and led her to the couch to sit down. There was no need to wait for explanations to why Sam would hide her life from them, therefore they all decided as a group the best way to deal with it was straight up. "We've all decided we aren't going to hold it against you that you're filthy rich. Sara was the last hold out though, only because she paid for the last lunch when you forgot your purse."

"Guys, I..."

"Don't." Blake sat on the other side of her and took her hand in his with the brotherly kindness she was used to. "We don't know why we didn't know about all this, and we don't care. You can explain it to us later if you want, or you don't have to explain anything at all, that's your choice. Right now, you have more important things to deal with. We only wanted to bring it up right away because we didn't want you to have it on your mind."

They didn't bring the subject up again, started chatting about many other things, Blake's new job, Sara having to add two more classes to her already busy schedule, Michael's sister having another child, making it her fifth. He joked that she needed someone like Beatrice to keep her crew all in line. Half of it Sam heard and the other half was lost in an empty space somewhere as she looked about and pretended to pay attention. Smiled or chuckled when it was appropriate and a few times caught herself doing it when it wasn't appropriate, but no one seemed to notice. If they did, they didn't say anything.

Her two worlds finally converged together. It wasn't what she imagined, certainly not in the way it came about, but they all accepted it so easily without question. All but Carter, who contributed to various conversations but barely looked at her, hardly spoke directly to her. So much he held back right now but she knew in time it would be dealt with. Sam only wished she had the confidence to think the best. As she caught his eye, she saw the distance between them, and it only seemed to grow with passing time.

There were no viewings or pre-funeral pomp and circumstance, soon after their deaths the funeral was as she wished, quiet and respectful. A list of the most important fifty people was made and adhered to. Sam refused to budge on the number much to everyone's chagrin, especially Preston Burke who insisted on certain business associates for relationship purposes, Sam insisted it wasn't a business function and wouldn't give an inch. Not even Spalding Edwards was granted admittance, even when he showed up and expected to be let in.

With Carter by her side and her friends surrounding her, Sam made it through the long day. It was after midnight when she showered and reached the bed where Carter lay on his back with his eyes closed. She snuggled in next to him and he held her tight against his chest with his arm.

"This is where I want to spend the rest of my life. Right here in your arms." She sighed and closed her eyes, let him soothe her just by his touch.

Her words shot through him. Just days ago nothing would have come to mind but to assure her it was where she would always be. Now, he wondered exactly what she meant. Did she mean this bed specifically? She wanted to spend the rest of her life here at the Durham Estate and wanted him here with her?

There had been many thoughts he had since his discovery, most of them he'd kept silent and would continue to keep silent for another time. Shock, anger, and betrayal were prominent, but through all that came his love for her. The main thing to deal with was that she'd just lost her parents, and he would deal with his own issues at a more appropriate time.

"I talked to mom today, she's beside herself they couldn't be here for you."

"I told her I understood and I didn't expect her to be. With Pop's broken foot and a house full of guests, she would have had to shut down all over again. And they've just gotten back up and running after the hurricane."

"It's been an enormous day, why don't you get some sleep, Sam?" He kissed the top of her head and rubbed his hand up and down her back in a soothing motion.

"Are we going to be okay?"

"We'll be fine, get some sleep." He said the words but there was fear that grew underneath the surface.

Their friends said little about the change between the two. Nikki assured her that she wasn't concerned it would have a lasting effect. "It's quite a bit for him to process, just give him time to absorb it all."

"I guess, I'm just not sure Nikki, it feels different. It feels like there's something going on around me that I don't know about, but I can't put my finger on it."

"You've just suffered a drastic blow, Sam. Your emotions are in turmoil as it is, don't worry about Carter, he should be the last of your worries."

He should be, Sam thought to herself, but he was first in her worries. She should feel confident in their relationship, confident in his love for her, but she felt so unstable and unsure. About him, about her life, it was as if she'd walked through a door to another side and she wanted to go back.

"What do you really think about all this?" Sam questioned. She believed what they all told her, that it didn't change things, but she seemed to need reassurances.

"I'm still in shock, Sam, but I understand."

"You do?" Sam looked into her friend's eyes and saw it there. Nothing had changed between them. "I hated lying to everyone, but..."

"Don't explain it to me. You had your reasons and I don't care what they are. And you didn't lie to us, none of us ever asked you about your financial position in life. None of us ever asked if you grew up in a privileged lifestyle. It wasn't important to any of us then, and it isn't now."

She knew Nikki spoke the truth, spoke for all of them, Sam saw in each of their eyes the acceptance she needed for them to know she was still Sam. Still the girl they knew and they didn't look at her or treat her any differently.

A week after the burial everyone was flown back on the private jet as Carter and Sam remained behind. There were things that needed to be taken care of, both with the estate and between each other. Growing tension could no longer be avoided and every time Sam brought the subject up, he dismissed it, but she could wait no longer, something had to be done.

"I know you've been waiting for what could be considered a respectful time, and I don't know if there's any rule that says when that is, so I might be breaking it. But I need to know what's going on with you."

"I don't want to deal with this right now. We'll have time to do that later."

One of the main reasons he didn't want to deal with it then was because he knew her state of mind was fragile, she'd just lost her mother and father. On the outside she appeared solid as stone and spent the week meeting with executives and the decisions she was making were so much different than decisions of before. Those involved mere choices of whether to use blue or green paint, or if she should add cinnamon to the pecan sauce that morning. He did his best to try and rub the tension and stress from her every night but the things she was dealing with were huge, he didn't feel she'd be in the best state of mind right now. Things could easily get out of control. With availability of hindsight, Carter would have stuck to his guns and waited. Later, he would ask himself many times if it had made a difference in the direction their lives would take.

Sam continued head on, needed to get it out in the open. "How much later? When later? Tomorrow? Next week? No, we're going to deal with this now. It's money, that's all. Why do I feel like it changes things, and why does it have to?"

"It isn't the money."

"I'm sure the money plays a part."

"I can't deny that."

"Talk to me Carter." She refused to let him ignore her this time when she saw his reluctance. "If the main thing isn't the money, then what is it?"

"It's the fact that for almost four years I feel like you lied to me."

"My entire life I've grown up knowing people look at me different when they find out I have money. When I went to college I wanted it all to end. No one knew who I was or where I came from. I didn't intentionally lie, it was just easier not to reveal certain things."

Carter had given that thought and knew it would be one of her reasons, but it still didn't explain it all. "I can understand that, but don't you think after four years of knowing me, you could have trusted me enough to say something? If after four years I hadn't proved my love, how much longer would it have taken?"

"I was going to tell you after I saw them in New York, the weekend they left for Italy, but then the hurricane hit and there wasn't time.

There were so many times I wanted to tell you, so many times I had the opportunity and didn't. I should have."

"But you never did, now I see you as someone I don't even know. I'm starting to think you never intended to tell me." The thought plagued him and now it was finally out.

"How can you say that? Of course I would have eventually told you."

"Maybe I didn't fit into this, Sam." It was a sad realization for Carter.

"What do you mean?"

"Maybe all this time I was only fooling myself thinking we had a future together. I was the college boy to have fun with and you were just waiting until school was over to leave and come back to this. That's why I never knew, I was never supposed to."

"Carter, that isn't true." Sam was hurt by the words, that he would think that of her.

"I could understand the first year of being together, maybe even the second, but after almost four years? Would you have ever told me?"

"I should have, I know that. And it was always my intention, but there never seemed to be a right time."

"I suppose another four years still wouldn't have given you ample time. All the holidays you left me, all the weekends, why couldn't I be a part of it? You never wanted me to meet your parents because you never intended for me to."

"It had nothing to do with that." How was she to explain in a quick moment that it had to do with her being Sam and not Samantha? How could she explain the feeling of being another person separate from her parents and their empire and make him understand? Make it convincing and not the excuse it would sound like.

"Prove me wrong. Tell me you love me, Sam, you've never said the words in all this time, say them now."

She looked into his eyes, saw in them so many things and wanted to say the words he longed for, but couldn't. She'd spent her entire life loving her parents, only to feel they'd never loved her back. Child emotions that had been given so unconditionally were shut out at an early age, and deep in her mind Sam often associated that feeling with Carter. If she loved him, would he shut her out? Even though he always told her, how was she to believe him when she wasn't even sure the meaning of the word?

Like her business skills, maybe it had been bred into her and she was incapable of it. The words were on the tip of her tongue but fear stopped her. So many emotions overwhelmed her. She'd loved her parents and lost them, would she lose Carter too? Sam didn't need to ask herself that question because she already knew the answer.

"You can't say it." He conceded softly.

"But that doesn't mean my intentions were wrong. You know me, Carter, more than anyone ever has."

"I don't know anything anymore. I left Massachusetts with one person and arrived here with another, like watching a metamorphosis before my eyes."

"So I've stepped into the role my father always wanted me to be in, is that so very wrong?" Sam even surprised herself when she spoke the words.

"It's certainly answered quite a few questions. Is this what you want? To live here and run Durham Corporation?"

"I don't know." She'd never considered it before but she couldn't let go of her father's words, and the guilt of her rage against both of them. "I know I can't leave right now. My father was in the process of a merger, it's going to take weeks for that to be complete."

"Had you told me that and not told me to stay, I would have left with the others. What am I supposed to do, hang around and wait for your other personality to come back? Besides the fact I have a year left of school, I'm not going to be Mr. Durham, or the in house repair man. Am I to fix the windows when they break? Design a new stable? Put on an addition?" Carter looked around and huffed cynically. "Yeah, you could use another five hundred square feet in this expanse of twenty thousand."

"How ironic is this? Most people I worry they *like* me because I have money, now I worry you *hate* me because of it."

Carter sighed as he walked slowly to her and pulled her into his arms, pulled her close and held tight for a moment before he spoke. "Never hate Sam, I could never hate you no matter what. I wouldn't care if you had a billion dollars."

Both had to chuckle lightly at the statement.

"Samantha." Beatrice came into the room and accidentally interrupted them. "Oh I'm sorry, I didn't realize you were in here Carter."

"It's okay Bea." He smiled to the kind woman he'd come to know so well throughout the week. One who shared so much with him, enlightened him in so many ways when she revealed a lifetime of stories about Samantha Durham, the woman he'd just now discovered. Through a staff member, he'd learned the other side of a woman he'd loved for years.

"Can you give us a few more minutes Bea?" Sam questioned.

"Just wanted to let you know Spalding Edwards is here." Bea announced, and then left the two alone again.

She'd been waiting on him, now just wanted him to go away, but it was Carter she feared leaving. As she looked into his eyes she read so many things there, fear, uncertainty, sadness, and she now regretted her choice to push forward with her demand for answers. If she hadn't pushed, if she'd waited, she could have put the confrontation off for much longer, but she couldn't change that decision now, they were deep into it and there was no turning back.

"I know this is an adjustment, but..." Sam began to speak and her words faded away with the unfinished sentence.

He touched her face but didn't kiss her. It already hurt too much as he longed to hear the words. All she had to do was tell him she loved him and he would have endured being 'Mr. Durham' until they could move past this, but the words never came. He pushed her gently away from him.

"You go on, Edwards is waiting."

"Will you be here when I get back?" Her tone indicated she already knew the answer.

"No, I have to go home."

With everything he had, all he wished was for her to give it all up and come with him. But it was only one sided as she wished for the opposite, that he would stay.

"Something can be worked out, don't leave Carter." Her voice pleaded with him.

Carter stood a few feet from her but could have been miles away as he looked into striking blue eyes that had lost something in one short week. Even they didn't look the same, and the crack of his heart seemed to resound in his chest.

"You've already left, Sam." Carter whispered sadly before leaving her life.

****

He didn't go back to school right away, he went home to Cape Cod and to Ocean Lane. Carter stood before the magnificent house he'd built for her, for them, and for the life he once envisioned. Through the storm it was exposed and open to the rage of winds and rain that had taken down much bigger structures. Unprotected, vulnerable to the fury of Mother Nature's rampage as she demolished everything in her path, but the home he'd so lovingly built had come through the hurricane completely intact. How, he wasn't sure. Not even a missing shingle, absolutely nothing out of place. It stood majestic and strong and he almost wished it had been completely destroyed.

CHAPTER 8

The separation from each other was an adjustment for everyone. Both of them an important part of a group of friends they shared and neither willing to give that up, they came to understand it would not be easy to avoid each other, they wouldn't be able to just walk away and live two separate lives. There were many occasions they would have to be together as marriages began, or other events came along, and in the beginning it was difficult.

Anger was the first stage they went through. Each harbored feelings the other should have put more effort into working it out somehow, coming to an arrangement that would have suited them both, and blamed the other when they'd made no attempt. They'd had time to stew and let the hurt boil, so when they met up again six months after their parting it resulted in a clash of resentment.

They had the occasion to all get together for Nikki and Blake's long awaited engagement party. Everyone was there, and of course their close knit group of friends had their notions that once they were together again, things would be fine, things would somehow work themselves out. But both Sam and Carter put on a face of disinterest towards the other, managed to ignore the fact that either was present until Carter found her alone.

"I've been wondering about something, do we have to file a no-marriage divorce paper or something? Or does it automatically take effect after a certain period of time. I'm assuming we're officially over since I haven't heard from you."

It was hard for Sam not to notice the coldness in his voice, it was a tone she'd never heard from him before, and it now sent a shiver through her. It also caused her to react the same way as she spat back. "You're the one who left, it was up to you to call."

"And you couldn't find a phone that worked in that mansion? Surely one of fifty might have had a dial tone if you'd checked."

"If all you have to say is something sarcastic, just don't talk to me Carter."

A hard cold wall was put up between them, one that was evident still when they met up again for the actual wedding. It was Sara who put a stop to it when she saw them arguing outside of the restaurant after the rehearsal dinner. She'd stepped outside and shouted at them which made them hush immediately, Sara was the quiet one, neither had ever witnessed her raise her voice in an angry manner so it halted them instantly. She easily made them feel guilty for what they'd been doing to the others without even realizing it.

"You two have to stop. Do you think you're the only ones affected by this split of yours? Do you know what it's doing to all of us? More important, do you know how this is affecting Nikki and Blake?" Her voice held a high-pitched frustration. "She asked me after the engagement party if they should postpone it. Said maybe they should give you two more time to work your problems out and then they could get married when things settled down. If they were willing to do that for you, do you think you could be willing to help in giving them a day that should be one of the happiest in their lives? If you two keep fighting like this all they're going to remember is how miserable we all were because we know you belong together and there's not a damn thing we can do about it."

Then her voice changed to her more gentle tone. The one they were used to. "I don't know what you two are going through, but I pray every night you'll get through it and we can all get back to normal. In the meantime, do you think we could concentrate on helping two of our best friends have the most glorious day ever?"

They were quiet when she left. Each felt the guilt of what they'd been doing to not only themselves but also everyone around them, adding tension and stress to a day that should be nothing but pleasant. From then on, they were at least civil and indifferent to one another. Each still torn by the emotions they couldn't let go of so easily and by the time the next affair came along it became easier.

Over time and years, somehow, they'd moved back to a familiar place they knew well. Best friends. They still fought on occasion, but most times about normal things friends disagreed over. Called each other at times or she'd send an email to remind him about someone's birthday, or to pass on news that someone was sick. Let him know when Michael lost his job once and could probably use some support.

Carter would call her at the oddest times, and sometimes talk about the oddest things. He was a bachelor on his own, the other ladies in their close knit group of friends were busy with husbands and children and he'd playfully make it known she was a last resort when he needed an opinion or an answer to something.

When Rebecca was born, the first child of Nikki and Blake, Carter showed up a beaming Godfather with gifts designed for a much older child, included among them a pink bike with all the latest bells and whistles, which she wouldn't possibly be able to use for years. After that, Sam got into the habit of calling him with gift suggestions when the other kids came along and reminders of their birthdays. And he called once at three in the morning for cooking advice.

"I need your help," he said.

"I'm not bailing you out." She stated half jokingly. "Not at this hour, call back at a decent time."

"Remember those waffles you used to make with the pecans? What was the sauce? How do I make that?"

Sam moaned and rolled over, pulled the pillow over her head as if that would make him go away and she could go back to sleep. "Carter why are you making waffles at three in the morning? Do I want to know this?"

"Mom is sick and Dad's off on a fishing trip."

Her attention and awareness was immediate. "Is she okay? How sick?"

"Just a bad cold, but you know her, she's miserable and she'll get up to work anyway. If I make it now she'll get up, it will be done, and she can go back to bed knowing everyone is taken care of."

"Did you call Janice Downs? She used to help out sometimes."

"She's sick too. The entire Cape is one big virus bug, I'm almost hoping the guests will get up sick and not want to eat anyway. Of course, they could be sick after they eat breakfast then we'd just have a whole new set of problems on our hands." He continued to look through the cabinets for something that resembled a put together breakfast meal. "I'm forcing her to stay in bed, told her I'd take care of everything and that would work fine if she didn't have any guests at the Inn, but there's three families who will be up in a few hours for breakfast and all I can offer is..." He pulled a box from the shelf. "Chocolate pudding. Or a cake, I can probably manage to throw some water and eggs in a bowl. Cake isn't a bad thing for breakfast is it? Do you remember where she keeps the cake mix?"

Sam laughed. "Carter, your mother won't have a single mix of anything to make a meal. She doesn't use things from a box."

She walked him through the recipe step by step, not only the sauce but of course the waffles as well, he originally thought they'd be the frozen kind to pop into a toaster but his mother Grace had nothing pre-made or pre-packaged in her kitchen. The Waterside Inn at Cape Cod served nothing but the best breakfast made from the freshest ingredients. It brought the most loyal guests back year after year.

Having helped her for four years of her life, Sam knew that fact well, she also knew how to walk him through the process step by step. She'd stood there in the same kitchen and knew by heart where every ingredient could be found, every pot, pan and utensil or appliance needed. Pictured it as she told Carter exactly where to look, and over a long distance telephone line, like a well-oiled machine, they worked together. One by memory and words, the other doing the hands-on work until a full breakfast of waffles with pecan sauce, fresh fruit, shredded potato casserole and slices of honey ham was complete with fifteen minutes to spare before guests rose and expected to dine at six a.m.

"Give Grace and Pop my best?" Sam knew what the answer would be, but asked anyway.

"Can't do that," he stated with finality, there would be no question, "I'm not a messenger."

"Not even this once? I made your breakfast."

"Not even this once," was all he said before he hung up the phone, and then called back two seconds later before she'd even replaced the portable receiver. "Thanks, Sam."

Carter would do many things for her if she asked, but he continued to refuse to pass along messages to his parents for her, and Sam couldn't do it for herself. They were never far from her thoughts, but slowly she had to let them slip away over the years, wasn't able to hold onto the connection that used to be a lifeline for her.

The two moved to a comfortable place with one another, two people with separate lives. Although they seldom saw each other, they talked on the phone, sometimes frequently, sometimes months would pass, but the anger and resentment had long subsided. Subconsciously she felt the menial excuses she used to call him, was her only connection and she couldn't come to break it. So as strange as it seemed at times, she held on to hearing his voice on occasion and got through any face to face encounters with minimal damage. Built up a reserve over time that helped her stay detached in order to keep the emotional distance unbroken.

The years carried on, and others in the group went on with their planned futures as weddings and children came. Nikki and Blake now had a girl and a boy aged ten and eight respectively. Sara and Richard followed whose son Richie was almost five and the last time they all had a chance to get together was to celebrate Amy's first birthday, Shawna and Michael's only child. They converged on their lake house and Sam lavished the little girl who called her 'Aunt Tam' with almost an entirely new wardrobe, unable to decide which outfits she wanted, she purchased them all, an entire suitcase full. She had also gifted her with her first stock certificate just as she'd done with the other children on their first birthdays and birthdays that followed.

Trenton reluctantly went with her that weekend and managed to get through, unlike Carter's second wife he brought along and even though they all tried to make her feel comfortable it became painfully obvious she didn't fit in when they argued constantly and left early. The difference with Trenton was that he simply remained indifferent to her best friends. In a way, Sam suspected he knew he wasn't going to fit in and didn't want to, but for her he participated at times. Not often, just enough to look like he at least made an effort.

"I'll go if you really want me to," he'd say.

"There's no reason to go if you actually don't want to, which I know you don't."

"It isn't that I don't," he'd lie, "I have a few things that need to be worked on, I could get them done and not have to be pressed about it next week."

Other times he made an effort were a few dinners when someone was in New York, and in the five years they'd dated exclusively, once or twice he'd accompany her for a weekend away with them, other times she went alone. Most times she had one reason or another why she couldn't attend at all and even though she and Carter were in a different place, she couldn't deny her decision was influenced by whether or not he would be there. It all depended on how vulnerable she felt at the time. They still acted like the best friends they were, still considered each other among the dearest people in their lives. And although she'd learned to bury deep feelings of the past, sometimes her defenses felt weakened and she declined, needed the drive of her work to keep her moving in a forward direction.

So over time, she and Carter gradually moved beyond their initial pain. Years and distance worked to their advantage to get them back to a familiar place they knew well. Best friends. Still an essential, significant part of each others lives, only in a different capacity.

****

After Trenton's proposal to her, Sam felt like a spectator, certainly not a participant as she watched not only the very public proposal and all the fanfare that came with it, but also everything that followed that evening and the weeks after. Wedding plans began to quickly evolve around her as Harriet Edwards, Trenton's mother, immediately moved into high gear. Hired a wedding planner and took total control and Sam didn't mind a bit, welcomed her skills and expertise in preparing for events.

"I think if I write a list and you write a list we could make it easy to make sure we have everything covered." Harriet said when she called her at the office one day.

Samantha had been in the middle of a conference call she'd put on hold and was now highly irritated but tried to sound patient. "Harriet, we'll have to discuss this some other time. I can't be disturbed in the middle of the day like this, you'll have to call me at home."

"It's Saturday. Normal people are home on a Saturday, but you're never home. You're always at the office so I didn't have a choice. All I need is a list."

"Then you make one, I wouldn't know the first thing to put on it." She looked to the blinking button on her other line, there were six people waiting on her. "I really have to go Harriet."

"But don't you..."

"No I don't. I don't want to think about all those things you've told me I have to think about. I trust your judgment, just let me know what you decide." Samantha didn't have time for frivolous interruptions.

She went along with everything. It was easier that way. Not only because time was a valued commodity to her, but there was no desire to put so much effort into an affair that would become the social event of the year. To her, it was simply the next natural step to a relationship.

As she finished the conference call, Samantha was finishing up her preparation of notes for contract changes for the meeting she had in less than an hour, when she was interrupted again. This time her cell phone and she saw it was Carter.

Samantha was impatient, her appointment across town. "I don't have much time Carter."

"And friendly greetings to you too." His voice reminded her to get out of work mode.

"Sorry, a frustrating day."

"It's a weekend, isn't it Saturday?"

"Crises management." She put her pencil down, rubbed her eyes, and decided to take a few calm moments.

"Same here, you sent an email reminder of Rebecca's birthday, but you didn't tell me what to get. I know, I'm pathetic, but you normally send a link that's directed to the perfect thing. When I saw it wasn't there I panicked."

She thought about his question to Nikki and Blake's daughter. One of the roles she'd taken in his life was to keep him on track. As a bachelor, once again after being married twice, he needed help when it came to things women typically took care of. She decided that after his gift of a bicycle with all the bells and whistles to a newborn.

The boys he seldom had a problem, but he was so lost when it came to the girls. "Sorry, I'll send another."

"Thanks."

"Hey, Carter..." She looked to the enormous diamond ring on her finger and thought of telling him, but the words didn't come. Let someone else tell him. That's how she found out about his marriages. "Never mind."

"I know you want to chat but I can't. Some of us have a life on Saturdays."

"Thanks for the reminder." She said it sarcastically and continued. "While we're on the subject of reminders, you did remember Shawna's birthday, didn't you?"

Carter was silent.

"Carter?"

"You didn't call me, or send an email." He blamed it on her as his only viable excuse.

"You can't remember it on your own for one year? It was two weeks ago, did you at least call her?"

He was silent again.

Sam spent five minutes lecturing him about how she couldn't be liable for his irresponsibility to not at least have a calendar. An appointment book, which she knew he had, and could put his own reminders into, he couldn't rely on her all the time. If it was important for him to keep his friends close, then it should be important enough to remember it on his own.

Carter waited patiently for her finish scolding him before he spoke again. "Does that mean you're not sending the email about Rebecca's gift? Should I go ahead and get a hockey table?"

****

After a long grueling day, Samantha was anxious to get out of the bitter cold that hit the city. Grateful for the warmth as she stepped inside the building when the doorman held the door open for her.

"Evening, Ms. Durham. You have a package at the desk."

"Thanks, Mr. Winters," she thought her mouth must be numb when she smiled because it didn't seem to bend right.

Not wanting to carry a large box upstairs and dispose of it later, she could get whatever was inside out and leave the outer package there. So she opened it at the desk as the assistant chatted to her.

"It's been a bitter winter, huh? I'm not a winter person, I'm spring. I can't take the cold as well anymore. Guess these old bones..."

Sam screamed loudly. The assistant jumped up and only frightened her more and she screamed again, turned much too fast and knocked the box on the floor. It burst open the rest of the way and four live lobsters escaped. Sam cursed Carter, it hadn't been the first time, but it scared her every time.

His note read... Thanks for coming through. Rebecca loved her gift. Also, if you could send me a link to buy one of those calendar things, I promise I'll become more responsible and fill it in. That's after you send me what to fill it in with. After this, I'll be responsible. Then I'll only have to be reminded of gifts. But after that...

"Ms. Durham?"

She looked up to see the doorman had scooped up the lobsters and put them back in their box.

"What do you want us to do with these lobsters?"

Sam peeked inside. "I guess we can't throw them in the Hudson River can we?"

Samantha didn't mention the incident in the lobby when she opened the door to Trenton's penthouse. He wouldn't find it as amusing as most. Her old life and the one she lived now clashed in their differences just as her ruby and diamond earrings and the worn faded bag. Seldom did they meet and Samantha was the neutral territory in the middle.

She set her keys in the tray atop the Victorian walnut credenza in the foyer. An ornately decorated piece Samantha always considered overly ornate with its floral marquestry design, embellished with gilt metal decoration. She considered it obnoxious, he considered it a highlight of his antique collection of furniture, a prized piece.

She assumed correctly when meeting Trenton and the first time seeing his penthouse, he was more interested in what it cost than what it looked like. The credenza evident, the price tag of a little over twelve thousand dollars was all the proof he needed to feel it would impress.

"I thought we were going out to dinner?" He came around the corner and saw her sorting through the mail. He took it out of her hands, put it down, and pulled her close and repeated when it seemed she didn't even know he'd spoken. "I thought we were going out to dinner?"

"The meeting ran late." Samantha didn't put her arms around him because she was still cold, so she bent her elbows against his chest. "I hope you have a fire going, I'm freezing."

"I will. Why don't you go change, I'll go make the call to cancel dinner."

Sam thought of the lobster dinner the doormen were having that evening. "How about steak tonight?"

"As long as you let me cook it, you burnt the last ones." He kissed her and was about to pull away but remembered something. "Mother has set up a meeting with several caterers for day after tomorrow."

"That's fine, as long as she knows I won't be there."

"Of course you'll be there. It's your wedding."

"It isn't my wedding, it's supposed to be our wedding and she's made it hers." She rubbed her temple, felt a stress headache coming on as it often did after her long day of work. And just when she thought she could relax.

"She's only helping."

"But I don't even care that it's hers, I trust her decisions, she can decide on the food choices."

"She could, but it makes more sense for you to."

"If it's so important, you go. What do I care what people eat? It's food. Whatever I decide will be the wrong thing anyway. If I want steak, she'd want seafood. If I want baked potatoes, she'd want mashed. I'm saving us from arguing, she can go and decide what we'll eat, it really makes no difference to me."

"I've already told her you'd be there," he continued.

"Since you've already taken that liberty, you can take another liberty and speak for me and tell her I won't be there. Did it ever occur to you to check with me? Did anyone ever bother to see if I had plans? You and your mother don't run my life. She can plan the wedding, run the entire affair, I hand it over to her, but I don't appreciate you or her making my plans. I can't go, I have a meeting scheduled."

Trenton tensed slightly, knew he wouldn't be able to avoid the fight he saw coming. He'd only done it because his mother needed an answer and he couldn't get hold of her, so he made it possible for her to go.

"I'm sending Peter in your place, it's already arranged."

Samantha had just been about to lean into him and welcome the shoulder massage she knew he'd give her until he spoke his words. Her eyes shot daggers through his.

"Are you crazy? What do you mean you're sending Peter in my place? It's my job, my responsibility, and I'll be the one to take care of it. Not Peter. And I don't work for you, you have a lot of damn nerve thinking you can arrange anything for me. Who the hell do you think you are?" It angered her more that he would do such a thing more than it angered her that he and his mother thought they could make her plans.

"Samantha, I just did you a favor. You have the wedding plans to keep you busy and after we're married it's not like Peter won't eventually be taking over for you. He might as well start now getting into the swing of things."

She couldn't move, frozen in place as she glared into eyes she thought she once knew so well. Since their engagement she'd begun to see a side of Trenton she wasn't sure she liked. Certainly didn't like the hints he'd dropped of how their lives would be after they married, as it wasn't in her plans to change anything.

It took her several days for her to gain control of her anger and calm down. She stayed at her own place across town in a much less ostentatious part of Manhattan. Experienced one of her mini breakdowns as she liked to call them, had them on occasion when the world seemed to close in on her. When things pounded her from all sides she had to get away from everything and take time for herself. When her concrete hardness seemed to melt and soften around the edges it left her vulnerable and she needed to be alone to build it up again. She'd get control of herself, focus on and vision the road ahead, and then go on as usual.

Trenton had been frantic in her absence, but she wouldn't return his calls and he let her simmer. Now leaned against the door of her office when he was told she'd come in that day. Held an enormous bouquet of irises, there must have been one of every color, and a crooked guilty smile on his handsome face.

Samantha looked up from her desk. "Flower deliveries are to be left in the lobby."

"I was granted special permission." He closed the door then rounded her desk and leaned against it.

"Remind me to have someone fired."

He looked to her face and saw the forgiveness, it had driven him crazy to be without her. "I can't promise you a smooth road ahead, but I have no doubt you'll put me in my place every time I need to be reminded what my place is in your life."

"If we're getting married, I think some adjustments are in order." She spoke seriously now, as handsome as he was there were things that needed to be said. "It's important for you to understand that you have no control over my end of this business. I do my job and I do it well. You do your job and you do it well. You are under no circumstances to ever interfere with my portion of it ever again."

Trenton placed his offering of flowers in front of her and bent down and kissed her. "I'm sorry, I was out of line. I've had to listen to my father for days, and believe me, he'd much rather be without me than you. And I learned my lesson, Peter screwed the deal up big time and everything's a mess."

"It's already been taken care of. I got a call from the owner of Cedis Enterprises begging me to meet with him, we scheduled for tomorrow."

"Come here." He took her hand and pulled her up to him, she stood in front of him while he remained sitting on the desk. Trenton kissed her sweetly, held both of her hands in his. "I love you. It's been hell trying to wonder when you were coming back, can we agree not to do that again?"

"I don't foresee we'll have a problem again, haven't we already agreed that you have no control over my plans? If you like, I could write up a contract and..."

He stopped her with another kiss.

Trenton was a strong powerful person that was used to getting his way in everything business, and that used to hold true in his personal life until he'd met Samantha. Such a strong personality herself he still had to be reminded on occasion she refused to be anything other.

****

Time restraints prevented her from calling her best friends on the phone about the engagement, so when she met with Nikki, Sara and Shawna for a girl's weekend she planned on breaking the news but didn't have to. The first thing they noticed about her was of course the ring. It shone like a beacon on her hand.

"Look at that rock!'... 'Why didn't you tell us?'... 'Was it a Christmas present?'... 'New Years present?'... "I've never seen a diamond so huge.'... 'This is the news of the year and you never said a word.'... All of them were shocked, even though they knew it would one day happen, each held her own reservations Sam would actually say yes.

They barraged her with questions she answered automatically. Trenton didn't want to wait for next year so a late summer, possibly early fall wedding was planned. If she lacked enthusiasm, they never said anything. Like everything else personal, Samantha treated it with nonchalance.

"Is this what you really want?" Nikki was the first to question.

"What kind of question is that? Isn't it the next logical step? We've been together five years now, living together for months, I can't picture myself at fifty years old living with Trenton and still having my own apartment on the other side of town."

All of them noticed she hadn't answered the question directly, all of them but Sam who'd become adept at skirting certain issues and didn't think anything of it.

"Doesn't that tell you something?" Sara asked.

"It tells me it's about time we get married."

"I mean doesn't it tell you something because you've been living with Trenton yet still have your own apartment?" Sara raised her eyebrows and didn't wait for an answer. "Logically, you're thinking like a business woman. You're moving ahead because it's expected, but in the back of your mind, maybe it's not what you really want."

"I've kept my place for security reasons. How was I to know he'd propose? And I wasn't sure living together would work out, it would have been foolish to get rid of it." Samantha felt on the defensive, her friends knew her like no one else.

The three women became quiet. Sam would take the plunge of marriage to a man who would do his best to pull her away from them all, they knew it, yet there was not much they could do about it.

"Then it's settled, we're all going to Bermuda in May." Shawna announced as a statement of fact.

"Bermuda? What does that have to do with anything?" Sam questioned.

Nikki was the one to answer. "We were saving it to talk to you about it. There's a small reunion planned with some old college classmates, a cruise to Bermuda."

"I don't know Nikki, I've been so busy with everything that's going on right now, we're..."

Nikki interrupted, stopped her immediately. "I don't want to hear all that business crap. You're one of the owners of the company, you can do anything you damn well please. Besides, if you don't go with us now, once you get married we'll never see you again."

"That's not true, my getting married has nothing to do with us." She looked somewhat offended but didn't take the comment seriously. As she looked to the others, all three women had the same look in their eyes as if it were so.

"You know Trenton doesn't like us." Sara added. All three were prepared to stack up against her.

Samantha sighed. "It isn't that he doesn't like any of you, he doesn't know you that well."

"And he doesn't want to. You don't have to defend him, we don't mind. It's just the type of person he is. His personality is a little different from ours, that's all."

"We? You've all discussed this as a group?" Samantha asked, looked to each one to see confirmation.

"At great length I'm not ashamed to admit." If Nikki was anything, it was honest. She had no qualms in telling the truth.

"So you've been talking behind my back."

"No, not behind your back, I just told you so it doesn't count as behind your back."

"You have a point." Sam admitted with a laugh.

"Say you'll come. Our last hurrah before your wedding. We'll never get the chance again for all of us to do this together and you know it." Both Shawna's face and voice pleaded.

Samantha took the words to heart and they scared her a little. She had to admit there was probably some truth in them, even if she didn't admit it openly. She looked to each of their faces and sighed. "I guess May gives me enough time to prepare everything before I can get away."

"Ahhhh! I'm ecstatic! I knew you couldn't refuse, especially if I dangled Bermuda in front of you. Tons of people are already scheduled to come."

They talked about the people who would be there, all of them kept in so much better touch with friends from college than Sam ever had. Only keeping in contact with her own important circle of friends but they kept her informed and updated over the years.

"All the guys are up for it? Including Carter? If he knows I'm going, he may change his mind."

She had yet to tell him of her engagement, but it was for no reason other than they had a silent agreement, they didn't talk of personal issues. Their common ground was their friends and they stayed in neutral territory. She didn't even know where he lived. Of course he'd moved from his parents long ago but anything she'd ever sent him was to that address. He never said and she never asked.

Nikki laughed. "Blake told me you two had a battle. Said Carter called him up screaming something about becoming responsible, said you blasted him for forgetting Shawna's birthday."

"He can forget it every year. I got the most enormous bouquet of flowers delivered. I'd never seen anything like it, and it made Michael jealous until he read who they were from of course." Shawna looked a little hesitant to continue. "I think he might need intervention soon. Talking about marriage again, just a few rumblings but we all know how impulsive he can be with taking wives."

Of course Sam looked unfazed, she always did. But if he did get married again, she'd do as she'd always done. Smile, congratulate him, send him a gift, and pretend it didn't bother her. She would even go out of her way to make any wife he had feel comfortable around them. Only in the secret of her mind did she always find fault with whoever was at Carter's side.

"Have you met this one?" Nikki asked.

"None of us have." Sara answered.

Nikki chuckled. "I wish he'd find a hobby or something. He could be married by now for all we know."

"If he is," Shawna added, "I guess we'll meet her on the cruise because he said he was definitely going."

Sara held her glass in the air for a toast. "To all of us together again in one spot for more than a very short day or two, I don't think that's happened since our younger days at the Cape."

Sam couldn't help but be thrown back into a day long past. Thought about their days on the Cape and knew a week with all of them together would be so much different than they once were.

"You can't change your mind now." Nikki had seen the shift in Sam's eyes. "No second thoughts. You agreed and we'll make you stick to it."

"I won't change my mind, I just wondered why Sara had to remind us it was the 'younger' days, are we old enough to use that term?" She laughed easily and pulled herself back quickly.

They all picked up their glasses, held them in the air, and toasted in unison. "Bermuda here we come."

PART TWO

Letting Go

CHAPTER 9

They all weathered the changes over the years and remained intact, through it all, the eight of them emerged as a whole. Made it through Carter's two wives and girlfriends in between, and Sam's few other male companions she'd dated briefly. And now that she was officially engaged, they knew Trenton wasn't going away.

As Sam prepared for the trip, she had an odd feeling of premonition. Something lurked on the outskirts of her thoughts and she couldn't place her finger on it. Felt both excitement and trepidation at the same time.

There was question in her mind as she had to wonder how long it would last, had to wonder what would be the breaking point that would change them all completely. Put an end to a rare union of people who seemed to depend on the others for survival, fed off each other's souls.

****

Trenton wasn't happy about it, and though she told him he didn't have to go, he promised he'd enjoy himself as they made their way to the cruise terminal where their ship awaited. When they stepped out of the limousine Trenton hired to carry them from the airport, squeals of laughter lit up her heart but made him cringe.

"I thought you'd never get here!" Nikki screamed as she ran to greet them.

"Some last minute work to get out of the way."

"We were beginning to think you'd changed your mind." Sara greeted her with a huge hug, followed by her husband Richard and all the others who waited for her.

There was much laughter and chatter as the old friends quickly stepped into familiar ways. It had been a few months since she'd seen some of them and told them how great they looked, or as in Michael's case, he looked like crap and she told him that too.

"What happened to your hair? Shawna get mad and shave it off in the middle of the night? If that's the case I'm sure you deserved it. If you did it on your own you ought to be shot, you look like a convict."

"He decided he wanted to try a new look." Shawna's eyes rolled in agreement with Sam.

"You probably scared Amy to death!"

Michael rubbed the top of his head, just as their young daughter did. "She actually loves it, rubs it like Aladdin's lamp."

"But I make the wish." Shawna added. "I wish for his hair back."

Everyone greeted Trenton. The women gave him a slight hug, unwanted and uncomfortable on his part, and the men shook his hand.

Her friends tried as best they could to be pleasant every time they saw him, but it was obvious he didn't share their enthusiasm.

"Nice to see you again." He nodded politely and lied, already bored with the group he had nothing in common with.

Carter would be late so they made their way inside to board but they were separated when Trenton and Samantha checked in as Suite Guests. Though she would have preferred to be closer to her friends, Trenton insisted they book a suite, said he wouldn't be satisfied with anything less.

"We'll all meet up on the top deck for our first frozen drink after we settle in." Nikki shouted as Trenton and Samantha boarded ahead of them.

They were escorted to their cabin that would be very comfortable for their week's stay. A living room, separate bedroom, refrigerator, VCR and stereo with CD library. A well equipped marble bathroom with tub and shower, and the floor to ceiling bay windows afforded them a wonderful view to the sea.

"This will do." Trenton put his rolling bag in the closet, took off his suit jacket and loosened his tie immediately.

"You don't sound very enthusiastic. It's lovely, it will more than do." Her voice was a little on edge because of his greeting towards her friends. "You certainly weren't very happy to see my friend's, you could have been a little nicer. It wouldn't have killed you."

"That's to be determined by the end of this week."

As she looked out the window across the port as they prepared to sail, he came from behind and put his arms around her. "I'm sorry. That early meeting this morning put me in a bad mood and I'm taking it out on you."

When he embraced her tenderly, she allowed the edge to fade, refused to start the week off letting his bad mood get to her. "It's been a stressful day. A stressful few months actually with all of the wedding plans, let's just enjoy this week okay? We need it."

"That I can totally agree upon," he said.

"That's nice to hear since we've agreed on little the past few weeks."

"Wedding plans do have to be made. Mother wants everything to certain specifications, it will be a very high profile affair."

She could feel her heat rise again and pushed it away to the back of her mind. "No more wedding talk, let's go meet the others for a drink to start this vacation."

"You go on, I have a little work to finish."

"Work?" Sam raised her eyes. "It's vacation."

It didn't surprise Sam he opened a briefcase full of work. Whether it was true work, or just an excuse not to have to hang out with her friends she wasn't sure, either way, it didn't matter.

Samantha found everyone already on the open deck with drinks dressed up with umbrellas and fruit. More had joined them and it seemed every lounge chair held someone from her college years past. Some she recognized, others it took a few moments and it was fun to see how they'd changed.

"Sam Durham, I heard you were living in New York. I was sure I'd have read by now you having a gallery showing." The woman had been in a few of her art classes.

"I'm afraid I outgrew my interest in the hobby and took another direction."

"I can't believe that, you were the most talented of anyone." She was truly shocked by the news, was sure Sam would have pursued it.

"A girl's gotta' make a living, and I couldn't see myself living as the starving artist. I went into corporate law instead. What about you?"

Some of her classmates hadn't known her full story. Believed her to be the girl she'd presented then, your typical average college student. She now told them the truth, only kept information at a minimum. A simple statement of being in corporate law and didn't elaborate on more.

Although they all mingled with others, the special group of them always ended up congregating together. Like a radar spot that automatically drew them all to one place. It wasn't as if they excluded others, they were all so comfortable together, each and every one shared a past and a present. They talked, laughed and caught up on each others lives. The only one still not there was Carter.

Nikki looked across the top deck and often glanced down by the pool deck. "I don't know where Carter could be. Who talked to him last?"

"I called him this morning and there was no problem. I hope nothing came up." Sara looked to Richard. "Your cell phone is on, isn't it?"

"He'll be here." Michael assured them.

Just as Sam thought he wouldn't, she looked up and saw him make his way, talking and laughing, through the crowd. When he made his way to them, another round of greetings came. Hugs, kisses and handshakes for one of their own. Sara greeted him first with a pretend, angry, motherly tone.

"You haven't checked in with me, I told you I need to hear your voice at least two times a month. It's a good thing you have that irresistible smile, or you'd be in worse trouble." Sara gave him a big hug.

"I'll make it up to you this week." He easily kissed her cheek, held onto her when she hugged him. Carter didn't take for granted the people who cared deeply about him. Just being around them helped him through the toughest times of his life.

All the others followed and when he reached Sam he placed his arm around her shoulder, affectionately kissed the top of her head. "Hey."

She smiled up at him. "Hey stranger."

It was a comfortable friendly greeting. No different than it'd been with the other women standing there. It was always their way, as if they'd never shared a bed together.

"Stranger is right." Nikki said. "How long has it been? I think the only one of us you've seen is Michael lately, Blake and I feel a little left out."

"And thank God he saw Michael. If not he'd be married again by now." Shawna remembered the night her husband had talked him out of it.

Sam was under the impression he had married, no one told her otherwise. "No wedding? When was anyone going to tell me, I was about to send my third gift."

Carter put his arm around her again. "That's what I was waiting on, I wanted you to send the gift first."

It was later, after everyone gradually wandered off, when Carter acknowledged her engagement.

"I heard congratulations are in order." He picked up her left hand and thought it felt heavy with the weight of the huge diamond. "But you know me, I've never followed the order of things very well."

"Am I at least going to get a gift? I've sent you two."

"I can only imagine where you're registered." God she looked good. His life would be so much easier if she didn't look so good.

Sara told her Grace had been ill. She was relieved when Carter told her she was fine now. Kidney stones gave her some trouble but she was as healthy as ever.

"Next time you see them, give Grace and Pop my best?" Sam knew what the answer would be, but asked anyway.

"You know I won't do that Sam."

"Not even this once? I've sent you wedding gifts."

"Not even this once."

Carter would do many things for her if she asked, but he'd told her a long time ago if she wanted to talk to his parents she could call anytime. Visit anytime. He refused then and continued to refuse to pass along messages. It was probably the only thing in the entire world he wouldn't do for her.

And Sam couldn't do it for herself. For reasons unknown, and many she speculated on, she let them slip away over the years. Now felt it too late to go back and salvage any sort of connection they would have now.

Trenton never joined her on deck and she found him still working when she went to the room. With some time before they were to meet others, they took the opportunity to wander the ship and explore its many corners. An entire city afloat that offered everything anyone could need.

There were many places people sat and relaxed in quiet, or livelier places people gathered as everyone was excited to be on vacation. They stopped inside the jewelry store and gift shop and then Sam purchased a few bottles of Bermuda Gold for herself and to take back home as souvenirs for her assistant and others.

After checking out the immense lounge where shows and entertainment could be found most evenings, they sat in a quaint place and listened to a singer belt out a few old Irish tunes. She was beginning to relax already. Knowing the entire week was ahead of them, she was letting go of thoughts of work and all there was that would be waiting for her when she returned.

Sam found the ship quaint. Intimate areas and friendly people welcomed them at every turn and she became immediately familiar with the layout. Realized quickly the smiling staff would become friends throughout the week as she passed several of them who always said a few words of greeting. Always had a smile and at the ready to help.

That evening at dinner they were joined by Shawna, Michael, Sara and Richard. Nikki and Blake were eating later and Sam didn't know about Carter nor did she ask. Conservation flowed and even Trenton contributed at some points. Sam knew he was making a huge effort, even when she could see his irritation they didn't have a particular wine he wanted but was presented with another choice he was completely happy with.

Marcelis, the wine steward, promised he would enjoy it and Trenton was pleased. After that he took his word without question and learned much from a connoisseur he didn't expect to find.

After dinner, he retired to find someplace to smoke his cigar and she joined the others to see a comedian in the lounge, then drinks afterwards on the open deck where a calypso band played. Everyone was in vacation mode as passengers learned island dances and froufrou umbrella drinks flowed in abundance.

The night air was sea fresh as she watched her friends dance below. They'd tried to coerce her into joining them but she declined, instead ran for the safety of above when they weren't looking. As the gentle wind caressed her face her mysterious premonition returned. The winds of change blew in, the wind that she could feel seep into her skin instead of brush past it. Changes were about to unfold, and she didn't quite know yet if it was something to welcome or something to fear. It was as if the wind itself had been responsible for placing Carter right beside her, she jolted when she heard him speak.

"There was a time you would be the one dragging them onto the dance floor, now you escape?" Carter easily settled himself next to her, his arms resting on the banister just as hers.

"We have to grow up sometime."

"Grow up? Why?"

"Because that's the way life works."

"Then that explains it. I don't have a clue how life works." And for him, it was much too demanding to try to figure it out.

"Unless you have a secret, I don't think you're getting any younger."

"Getting older and growing up are two different things. We all get older, but that doesn't mean we have to lose ourselves in the process, does it?"

"I hear the insinuation in your voice."

"I didn't try to hide it." Carter laughed and changed the subject. "What happened to Buster Brown? Not used to the nightlife?"

"His name is Trenton Spalding Edwards." She felt she immediately had to defend her soon to be husband. "And he's probably trying to finish some work he had to bring."

"I certainly didn't think he was cutting loose somewhere."

"He's a nice man Carter, you'd like him if you got to know him."

"Please don't make me," he said. "I'm sure he's pleasant enough, but I'm surprised at your choice. He doesn't suit you."

"You're the expert on who suits me?"

"Consider it friendly advice."

"I don't think I'll take advice from a man who's been married twice. Almost three times. Seems you're not the one to advise anyone of what's right for them when it comes to relationships." Sam waved to Nikki when she looked up from below.

"Hey, that one hurt. Those divorces weren't my fault, and it was only twice. I went to Vegas remember?"

"Left number three at the alter, how kind."

"We both agreed it wasn't the best thing to do." Carter turned the other direction and leaned his back on the railing, a better position to look at her directly. "Do you think we could agree on something?"

Sam looked at him then. "That would depend on what you had in mind."

"I thought maybe we could both agree that it doesn't have to be awkward between us."

"It's never awkward between us."

"We've never really been together for a full week. A day or two here and there, but that barely gives us time to say hello. This is a little different, I thought if we cleared the air early, we could avoid it."

"We have a past Carter, but that's all. It doesn't have anything to do with us now."

He didn't take his eyes off her as the moonlight seemed to shimmer and bounce off her hair. Carter knew she tried to avoid his gaze by purposefully looking straight down to the people dancing below. "Maybe you're right."

"Maybe?" She questioned.

"Technically, doesn't the past have everything to do with what we are?"

"You know what I intended for the words to mean. What we had in the past doesn't have anything to do with us now. We're different, we're not…"

He waited but she didn't finish and he pressed. "We're not… what?"

"Why are you making this difficult?"

"Making this conversation difficult? It's just a friendly conversation. Or is it that you're uncomfortable with this conversation. What were you going to say? That we're not together? We're not in love? What exactly did you want to say but didn't?"

"We're not what we used to be. We're friends, there's no need to ever feel awkward."

Maybe being friends wasn't enough for him any longer. When he first looked into her eyes, as always, he could only see a tiny glimpse, a tiny piece of the girl he once knew. With just the first glance it was there, then disappeared quickly. And as always, Carter yearned to see it again, to see the full Sam he once knew.

Yesterday, he would have told anyone he was over her and he would have pretended to believe it himself, but she pulled him with an invisible magnet, just as she always did. Even in the distance she tried to keep, he felt the connection between them just as strong as he had years ago, it was hardly gone, no matter how much she pretended it was.

Yet this time was different. This time she was engaged to be married to another man. Had made a commitment that would pull her even further away from him. The thought of being on the verge of losing her forever sent strange thoughts into his head he couldn't get rid of.

He wondered if Buster Brown knew her as well as he did, if they shared what they once had. Had to tell himself it couldn't possibly be so, he didn't think there was anyone on earth that could have shared what they did.

Carter looked away from her and sighed playfully. "It's just as well we're merely friends now. I'd never be able to keep up with your lifestyle. I never would have guessed you to fit so nicely into a high maintenance role."

"Kiss my ass Carter."

"Which would look a bit better if you wore something that made it possible to see your ass instead of those clothes that look like you're getting ready to go to a board meeting."

"Not only are you kidding yourself to think you're an expert on relationships, you're also a fashion critic now too? My how you've expanded your talents." But it did make Sam think about her plain black pants and jacket she wore. With the white shirt she could have passed for one of the staff instead of a guest, all she needed was a nametag.

Carter smiled crookedly. "As a man, I think that alone validates some authority I have to decide what looks nice on a woman."

"Are you saying I look like shit?"

"I'm saying you don't look like you." He paused before he went on. "What happened to the Sam I used to know? How has she been?"

"I may have grown up and wear different clothes and carry myself in a different way, but I'm still the same person."

"Are you?" Carter raised his eyebrows and challenged her.

"Just because I've grown up means I've changed?"

"Just because Buster Brown is at your side doesn't mean you had to."

"I'm still my own person Carter, he doesn't have anything to do with what I've become." Sam pushed herself away from the banister and began to walk away. "Speaking of Trenton, I should go find him."

"If you find Sam, tell her I miss her." Carter called after her. She didn't turn around but he knew she heard.

CHAPTER 10

Trenton's refined taste included a passion for his fiancé. When Sam entered the room the previous evening after a night with her friends, she seduced him from his work but he was willingly lured away. Displayed a side of her he didn't think he'd ever seen, if he had, he surely would have remembered. He thought of it when he opened his eyes and heard her in the shower.

He always woke just after the first light of dawn, Sam even earlier. He'd never been able to figure out what time she actually rose in the morning, sometimes wondered if she slept at all.

"I was going to go on deck and get some coffee, want me to wait for you?" She asked as she began to dress.

"You go ahead, I'll shower and meet you later."

She knew he would get into work, if they were in New York, they both would. On weekends they rarely relaxed, simply worked at home in their separate offices. She kissed him before she left with a knowing smile.

"Don't work too hard."

As the sun rose on the horizon Sam sat for a long time by herself before Sara and Richard joined her. Then Shawna and Nikki as they explained their respective husbands were being lazy and wanted to sleep in.

"It's not everyday I get to wake up and enjoy a sight like this, I won't waste any time in bed." Nikki sat down with her cup of coffee and sighed. "Isn't this glorious? Sitting with friends at sea. When was the last time we all enjoyed a morning like this together?"

"I think all five of us were at my house last, but we sat in my backyard with our coffee, certainly doesn't compare to this."

Sara laughed. "Not in the least. If I were at home right now I'd be making my list for the day. By this time I would have had all the beds made and laundry in, it's heaven just to be able to walk out of the room knowing my bed will be made when I get back."

"And mints on your pillow when you return tonight." Carter said as he joined them. "But Richard probably does that for you at home doesn't he?"

Richard defended himself with a joke. "I put rose petals on the bed instead."

"Right." Sara chimed in. "If you did you'd probably use the entire flowers, stems and all, and forget to take off the thorns."

Sam felt Carter's hand touch her shoulder and squeeze as he walked by her and sat down next to Shawna. Why did he still have to make her feel so special? A slight touch on purpose just to let her know he was thinking about her. It was just a touch Sam, a casual touch he'd give anyone, don't read anything ridiculous into it. She wished he'd gotten a beer belly, gone bald, and lost his teeth. It would be easier to be so close to him.

"Where are Michael and Blake?" Carter asked.

Nikki rolled her eyes. "Sleeping in."

"Michael may be awake and trying to find one of those green nets to drive golf balls into." Shawna sighed. "The man is possessed by the sport. I'm looking forward to seeing Bermuda and all he can talk about is the golf courses."

At that moment one of their old classmates, Brian Phelps, joined them. He had several children from many girlfriends. Arrogant. Conceited. He was everything each of them thought he would turn out to be.

"Golf? Sounds like a conversation I should be part of. I've been looking for some golfers in this bunch. Do you play Carter?" He sat down and pulled up a chair, made himself comfortable.

"Not me. We're talking about Michael, he's the one you need to talk to."

Brian turned his attention to Sam. "Your husband plays, doesn't he Sam?"

"I don't have a husband." She corrected him with a tone of annoyance.

"Sorry. Your fiancé', your significant other, your intended, whatever term you prefer, I'll oblige."

"If you're referring to Trenton, yes, he plays."

"I'll have to talk to him, maybe we can get together for a round or two."

It didn't go unnoticed that he seemed more interested in talking to Trenton than he did with Michael about golf. She knew the type of person Brian Phelps was, knew it was because of Trenton's financial position he would be interested. Brian was networking. He was a Wall Street wonder boy who made money for people, he'd love to get hold of their accounts.

"Yeah, talk to him." Carter said sarcastically with a tinge of anger. "He probably knows more about golf than Michael, I think Michael's only experience has been putt putt."

The group dispersed in different directions not long after. Shawna and Sam went for breakfast together as the others went elsewhere.

"This first day and I know already I'll have to be forced to leave. They make your beds, turn down your beds, want to carry your trays. I've never had so many people wanting to do things for me. You're probably used to all this but I'm going to suck it up all week long." Shawna set her tray down on a table by a window.

"Trenton is used to it. When I lived on my own, believe me, the bed never got made, but he has someone come in every day. I've never even met her, I'm gone before she gets there and home long after she leaves."

"I don't know how or why you do it, meaning your work schedule. I have to be honest, if I were rolling in your money I'd have it all. Maids. Butlers. Someone to feed me grapes while I took a bubble bath."

"I'd forgotten there was such a thing. When was the last time anyone ever took a bubble bath?"

"Wait till you have kids. Amy loves her bubbles."

"I'm leaving it up to all of you to have kids. I just get to spoil and play with them, you all have the hard work. A perfect arrangement." Sam sipped her coffee.

"But you have to have kids, you love kids." Shawna could tell by her face she didn't consider it at all.

"As I said, I have all your kids. That's all I need." As hard as she tried, she couldn't see kids with Trenton. Sam wasn't even sure she would know how to be a mother, she hadn't had the best example.

"Kids or no kids, if I were you, I'd sit around and eat bonbons. Chocolate one's."

Sam could picture her doing just that, without a guilty feeling in her body for the indulgence. As Sam glanced around the room, she noticed Carter on the other side sitting with several of their classmates. He hadn't noticed they were there.

"That Mindy is a piece of work, isn't she?" Shawna commented when she noticed also.

"I don't think I remember her." She didn't look familiar, but then again, she couldn't see her face well. It was practically buried in Carter's chest as she openly flirted. Kept leaning against him with a giggle that grated her nerves. There were several other people at the table, but the woman's attentions weren't on them.

"Mindy Turner. Just got her third or fourth divorce."

"Well, guess Carter's in good company. Must be some sort of divorce club. Maybe he's trying to catch up, he's only got two under his belt. And what is it with Vegas? Hasn't anyone explained the traditional wedding process with him?"

"No one knew until after he'd done it. But don't blame it on us, you talk to him also." Shawna reached across and took some extra sugar off Sam's tray.

"Gifts, important dates to remember, strange things in the middle of the night. Never his marriages, never his women."

"I've always wondered how you two could get along so well. Guess it would be hard to talk about those things." Then she questioned. "Strange things in the middle of the night?"

"One instance, Grace had a cold and he didn't want her to get up and make breakfast. So he called me at three in the morning and I walked him through it step by step. Another time he called at four in the morning and wanted me to go on the internet to find out a fact to settle a bet. I gave him the answer that would make him lose, it cost him a hundred bucks. That was my revenge for waking me."

Shawna was quiet and hesitant when she spoke again. "Do you ever think back? You know, that 'might have been' thing? Ever wonder what it would be like now if things had turned out different?"

Sam looked down through the window beside her and watched the sea pass by them, contemplated her answer, and then she laughed. "Yeah, I think I might have been wife number one, his first ex. The other two would have come after me."

"Maybe with three, he could get into the divorce club like Mindy." Shawna joked, knew Sam felt much more than she stated but also knew she wouldn't elaborate.

They both looked over as the group was leaving, Mindy close on Carter's heels. He still hadn't noticed they were there and Sam didn't look for too long, began talking of something else.

Pale bodies lined the edges of the pool. Lounge chairs were filled both with a sea of winter white and the occasional tanning bed occupant. When Shawna and Sam joined them after wandering the ship and checking out the various activities, it was apparent Nikki And Shawna had been there quite some time. Their clue, a collection of bright colored empty souvenir cups.

Sara raised her glass towards the waiter. "We need more please Enrique, and add two more for our friends. I am shameless Sam, sitting in the sun with a frozen drink in my hand, what could be better?"

"Indeed." Nikki agreed with her sentiments. "We were going to get lunch but decided the fruit hanging off the side of the glass counts as a meal."

They whiled the day away together and as usual the four of them spent the afternoon with no loss for words. Each moment that passed, slowly took with it more and more of Sam's stress and tension from her New York life. She didn't think of work, contracts, meetings, wedding plans, it was only among these people she could let her cares float away and truly relax.

****

That evening Sam dressed in red print capri pants and a white sleeveless blouse, it would have looked pristine and proper had she not left a few of the top buttons undone. Dark full hair fell around her face and shoulders. It wasn't often it was free of its confines of something to hold it back and it framed her face of bare minimal makeup.

Trenton tore his eyes away from his paperwork long enough to glance at her. "You look... different."

"Different? Not nice? Not good? Just different?"

"It's different for you." He didn't elaborate.

He had dinner with her that evening then ran off to the casino for a few hands of poker, while Sam went off with the others. If anyone thought it odd they chose to spend so much time apart they didn't say anything, except Carter and she took his teasing in stride.

"Buster Brown's out bar hopping elsewhere isn't he? He's such a party animal, it must be quite a job trying to control him."

"I know you like him, you just can't admit it can you? And his name is Trenton."

Carter noticed the way she looked that evening as compared to the stuffiness of the previous. Hair casually tossed free, the slight hint of her breasts, he smiled inwardly.

"What happened to you last night? You turned in a little early didn't you? We were all in the dance club until the wee hours."

She was sorry she'd missed it. "Other plans."

"A little romantic time with Buster?"

"What kind of question is that? A little strange, don't you think?"

"I don't know if your romantic time was strange, I wasn't there." He watched her as she tried not to smile.

"You know what I meant. That topic of conversation"

He shrugged his shoulders. "I was just wondering if you were thinking about me or him."

Sam's mouth fell open and then shocked laughter came out. "If that's not the most arrogant thing I've ever heard you say."

"Maybe arrogance, maybe truth." His boyish smile caught her.

There was casual ease between them. Always was. It was the added playful flirting that surprised her but she went along against her better judgment, didn't listen to the tiny voice in her head that tried to shout a warning.

"Please, don't kid yourself."

"You don't have to admit it. I think I know."

"Don't you have amusement to keep you busy? Must you hound me at every turn?"

"Just enjoying your company while I can. Who knows, this may be the last time we'll ever see each other again." Carter took the opportunity to instill the thought in her mind that what they had wouldn't survive her marriage. He wanted her to fully realize that.

"I wouldn't be able to get rid of you that easy."

A while later she was dragged onto the stage. Nikki, Sara and Shawna wanted to sing when karaoke started and a microphone was forced into her hand under protest, and to Sam's horror she found herself in a spotlight with the others. An upbeat Gloria Estafan song began and cheers from the crowd and the music got louder and they sang and danced like the once young college kids they were. Sam was taken away by the moment, but as soon as it was over, escaped back into oblivion.

"Hey." Sam smiled when she saw Trenton there and had walked straight to him.

"Quite a performance."

"It was fun." She needed water desperately, her mouth felt so dry from the singing and dancing and she was still trying to catch her breath. "I need a drink, are you staying for awhile? Do you want one?"

"Don't you think you've had enough to drink? It's not like you to go up on a stage and embarrass yourself."

"Not myself, but I obviously embarrassed you." Sam spun around and walked away from him, joined the others at a table with a large smile and fell into their conversation without missing a beat.

Carter watched the interaction take place and smiled inwardly. This would be even easier than he thought, he wouldn't have to do anything because Buster Brown would take care of it for him.

Later that evening she stood on the top deck alone, needed the fresh air. Carter came up from behind and had no reservations as he put his arms on either side of her, placed his hands on the railing alongside hers, and put his head close.

"Buster Brown not appreciate your singing talents?"

"I can't really blame him, can you? And to use the word talent is highly exaggerated." Sam made no effort to move, rested easily with her back against his chest. It surprised her she felt so at ease, but like that day by the pool, it was around her friends she could truly relax.

Carter's voice was a soft whisper, his mouth close to her ear. "What about your painting talents? Do you still paint Sam?"

"I keep trying to tell you, we all have to grow up Carter."

"And I keep trying to tell you, we don't have to lose ourselves in the process."

Sam went to move but his arms remained, trapped her in as she leaned against the banister and faced him now. "What are you trying to do Carter?"

"As a friend, I don't know if I can let you go through with it."

"I don't recall asking permission. I've been doing as I choose for a long time."

Carter leaned in slowly and pressed his lips to hers, felt the softness that in an instant seemed to replenish him like water to a lost man in a desert. Her lips parted slightly, then just as she began to respond, she just as quickly pulled away.

"That didn't mean anything Carter, it doesn't change things." Sam didn't move, looked as if it hadn't affected her in the least.

"Doesn't it? Don't you question at all your motives for marrying?"

"That's never been a question."

"Is it because you love him?" His words were a tentative whisper, he was afraid of the answer she may give but he needed to know.

Sam looked at him for a long time, debated lying and telling him she did love Trenton, but she couldn't. "I thought you wanted to get along this week, didn't want it to be awkward between us."

"You don't feel awkward, you just want to avoid the issue. Why are you getting married?"

"Why are we having this conversation?"

"Maybe because no one else will have it with you."

"There's no one else to question me, they all know I'm old enough now to make my own decisions." She huffed with exasperation, didn't want this kind of confrontation she'd previously feared.

"They're all afraid to flat out say what they feel, but I have nothing to lose. If you won't tell me why you're getting married, tell me why we didn't."

"Because you left. Ran off with some girl who had blonde hair and big boobs, married her I might add." Sam tried to lighten the air.

"On a rebound after waiting for you, and that's not what happened anyway." He remembered it well, changed his life forever. "You stayed in Virginia and I never heard from you again."

"I thought you'd come back." In a weak moment of emotion, she couldn't stop the soft words that came.

"Don't turn this on me Sam. You were the one that chose a different life." Carter let his hand slip down her arm until he took her hands in his. "All you had to do was say you loved me, and we could have gotten through anything."

But I did love you, she wanted to confess, but it was too late for that now.

CHAPTER 11

Founded in 1612, the town of St. George loomed ahead to break the blue monotony of the horizon. Azure water changed colors as reefs became visible and more clearly defined beneath crystal clear water as the ship sailed into the small channel. Dressed in traditional old garb of days gone by, a town crier stood along the rocks and waved a delightful welcome.

Blue, pink, yellow and green pastel houses lined the shore and flowed down from the top of the hill in staggered color. Strangers waved to passengers who lined the decks as the ship pulled slowly into its dock. Sam stood among them, waved back to locals excited to see their arrival.

With her attention focused far out to the island and the surroundings, Sam hadn't noticed when Trenton joined her, but when she turned around he was there.

"I'm sorry again about last night, I seem to be saying that quite a bit these days. You seem to be bringing out the worst in me lately and I don't know why."

"That's a hell of a way to apologize, maybe I just bring out who you really are." She was tired of fighting but not so willing to give it up as he'd hoped.

He put his arm around her and kissed her with affection. "How about we spend the entire day together?"

Sam couldn't help but wonder if it were an option or a given for her friends to spend time with their spouses. Was sure it was natural for them to assume they'd see Bermuda with their significant others together, and yet her soon to be husband made her what she could only see as a peace offering. It didn't matter. It was the way he was, the way they were together, and she accepted it.

"I'm spending the day with Nikki and Sara and whoever else decides to join us, you're welcome to come."

"I'm in your hands. Shopping? The beach?"

Sam watched his face and as usual it was difficult for him to hide that it obviously wasn't something he would look forward to and she chuckled. "You really don't have to go."

"I will."

"Apology accepted, I won't hold you to any more obligations," she said.

It would work out better if she were alone because he hated the beach and that's what she wanted to do. So he decided on golf with two men he'd met the evening before and she met Nikki and Sara as planned along with their husbands Blake and Richard.

"Just us?" Sam asked, unsure of what everyone else's plans were, she hadn't talked to them.

"Shawna has a spa appointment, Michael was going to try and get golf in and Carter went off earlier on a moped. We were going to get moped's but..."

"Don't let me stop you, you four get moped's and I'll head to the beach, that's all I want." Sam certainly wasn't going to rent a moped by herself and drive it, and they only sat two. "I'll do some shopping and walking around first, maybe come back and catch up with Shawna and we can meet you guys later?"

Tobacco Bay being the closest beach and it was where Sam would head to later, and they could meet up there whenever they decided. Or if they even wanted to, it certainly didn't bother her to spend the time alone.

History was just outside the ship with a replica of the Deliverance. The shipwrecked founder of Bermuda, Sir George Somers, built it to continue his journey to his original destination of a Virginia colony, and there was also a statue that paid honor and immortalized him.

King's Square was the beginning point for tourists. The Town Hall waved its flags proud and replicas of a pillory, stocks and a ducking stool made for pictures to send back home. When they were in use, punishable crimes included gossip among other petty offenses.

Sam took her time as she wandered through a few stores. A glorious day formed as she headed east to Duke of York street where she found St. Peter's Church, believed to be the oldest Anglican Church in the Western Hemisphere. Built of cedar with a palmetto-leaf thatched roof in 1612, the structure had to be rebuilt when a hurricane in 1712 almost completely destroyed it. It had been restored many times, adding a tower in 1814. One of the cherished treasures was a mahogany alter, the oldest piece of Bermudian furniture on the island.

Sam stepped inside a comforting darkness. There were no lights on, but as her eyes adjusted from being in the glaring sun, it was light and airy as the sun filtered through the open windows. Open cedar timber beams stood strong above her and the floor and pews a deep wood. There were a few people milling about and she noticed a familiar form leaning against a window and looking out.

"Have a lot of sins to confess?" Sam whispered as she stepped next to Carter.

"I wouldn't know where to begin." He teased then looked around appreciatively, told his reason for being there. "Had to see this, excellent examples of the architectural styles of the 17th to 20th centuries. Amazing what they could do with what little they had, not like they could plug in a saw."

Sam left him to continue exploring and went outside to the churchyard to see tombstones that told stories. Epidemics, shipwrecks and war. Unmarked tombstones that represented the segregated slave section and she also viewed the grave of one of Bermuda's governor's, Sir Richard Sharples, who was assassinated in 1973.

She didn't look for Carter when she left, for all she knew, he'd already gone. But when she walked down the steep steps toward the street, he leaned against his moped and waited for her. Her pace slowed as she came to a stop in front of him.

"I was headed up the hill to the Unfinished Church, want to go?" He asked casually.

"I'll walk."

"I know Samantha wouldn't think it proper but I know Sam wants to." He handed her the extra helmet.

"You think you know everything about Sam, don't you?"

"Want me to tell you how many intimate details I remember?"

"I don't need to be reminded you actually do know almost everything there is to know about me." She put the helmet on and reluctantly flung her leg over the bike.

They drove up the hill to the head of Duke of Kent Street to the Unfinished Church now maintained by The Bermuda National Trust. It was a magnificent gothic structure that began in the 1870's but suffered a series of problems that prevented its completion. Parish infighting, financial difficulties and a damaging storm left massive walls of stone but a ceiling open to the sky. Pillars and arched window openings that were never filled with glass as originally planned and a floor of earth left a ruin of impressive beauty. From one of the window openings she looked below to the town and could see their ship rise above the buildings from its position at the dock.

Neither one spoke as they walked around and enjoyed the beauty of it, there was no one else there and Sam eyed Carter several times as he was completely absorbed by the architecture. She knew it bothered him it was never complete. Knew it's what he was picturing in his mind, what it would look like had they finished it.

When he glanced in her direction she smiled. "Going to build one in Cape Cod so you can finish it?"

"It's a thought."

"And you'd build it by hand, wouldn't you?"

"I'd certainly give it a go." As they walked out together Carter put his sunglasses on, assumed she would be going with him. "Where to now?"

"I'm going to go back to the ship and find Shawna and go to the beach. You can go wherever you were intending to go."

"Shawna and Michael took off on a bike a little while ago."

"Oh. Well then I'm walking to Tobacco Bay."

"The others are at Horseshoe Bay over in Hamilton. I'm going now, you're welcome to come along. No sense going to a beach by yourself." He started the bike and waited patiently for her to decide.

Hamilton was across the island, which she could have gotten a bus or ferry but didn't. Instead, Sam wrapped her arms around his waist and held on. He wasn't reckless, but he wasn't timid either. Passed cars and buses, jumped here and there in and out of traffic, and had no fear as he skillfully maneuvered strange territory. Sam enjoyed it more than she wanted. They rounded a corner and when she saw they would be going downhill, with a childlike scream of delight, she held her legs out to the sides and her arms in the air as she laughed.

Just the wind that blew through her hair made her feel free. Warm sun on her bare legs and arms as the beauty of Bermuda presented itself around every turn and Sam was almost disappointed when they reached their destination.

"Where is everyone?" She asked when she saw no one around with a familiar face.

"Maybe it was Tobacco Bay. I could have been confused." He didn't even pretend to look around for them.

She slapped him on his arm. "You didn't! You lied to me on purpose!"

"How else was I going to get you on the bike?"

"Carter, how could you?"

"Don't pretend you're mad either." He took his helmet off and laid it on the seat. "You had a great ride."

"Such a sneak. Why did I trust you?"

"So we spend the day here, quieter anyway. By the time we get back to Tobacco Bay, they'll be gone."

"I could take the bus back." She threatened and didn't move from her stance.

"But you won't." He un-strapped the few things from the bike, handed her the small bag she carried, and took his towel as he walked towards the beach.

As insane as it was, he'd concocted a plan when he hadn't been able to sleep since the moment he saw her with Trenton, as an officially engaged woman. Hoped silently for years she would see things differently and find her way back to him. Now urgency coursed through him and he knew he had to do something.

He could get her to fall in love with him again. Actually, to remember she loved him because he didn't believe she'd ever stopped, maybe forgotten, but never stopped. He had a week to convince her she didn't want to get married to the wrong person. It was the last chance he'd ever have, there wouldn't come another time or opportunity like the one presented him.

Carter lie back on a towel and let her be. Although a reluctant hostage, Sam totally relaxed once her toes hit the pink sand and turquoise water, it was the first time she'd been at the very edge of the sea in years. She watched as small ripples of waves rolled over her feet. With each roll of water back out to sea it seemed to take with it not only grains of sand, but stress along with it. Solitude. It renewed her tired spirit.

Then nothing but the sound of ocean birds and rushing water when she decided to lie back and close her eyes on a towel. It reminded her so much of many lazy days on the Cape they shared. The memory of a simpler time in her life filtered into her mind and she hadn't even realized the moment she fell asleep, but when she woke, the light of the sun was dim as it was setting into the sea.

"I was about to go buy blankets for the night, I thought you'd never wake up."

Sam shielded her eyes, a sleepy daze still there and looked up at Carter who stood above her with supplies of food and drink.

"What time is it?"

"You don't have any appointments, you're on vacation, remember? I thought you'd be hungry, at the very least thirsty." He sat down on his towel and placed the food between them.

Sam sat up and took his wrist to look at his watch, couldn't believe the time. They'd gotten there before noon and she'd fallen asleep soon after. "It's 7:30, my God Carter, I've been asleep for more than six hours."

"I told you, I was about to go buy blankets for the night. I was afraid to wake you so I just kept watching your stomach to make sure you were breathing. And I rented an umbrella from a couple on the beach that weren't using theirs so you wouldn't burn." He held the box in his hand before he opened it. "Hungry?"

She hadn't slept for six hours straight in years, it was all she could think about until he mentioned food and she realized she was starved. "I don't know, by that look in your eye I'm wondering if I want to see what's in the box. Is there another choice? Box number one or box number two?"

"No choices. It's very prevalent in Bermuda, one of the mainstays of their diet when it's in season. However, their season actually ends in March so this is imported, probably from Maine." He opened the box to reveal lobster. "I think he looks familiar. I think you let him go at the Cape, didn't you?"

"Will you never let me forget that?" She snatched the box away from him and immediately began to crack through its shell.

He laughed heartily. "I can't tell you how many times I've laughed about that over the years. I can be sitting anywhere, doing anything, and it will pop into my mind out of the blue. As clearly as I see you now, I picture you hopping all over the beach like you were performing some sort of odd ritual."

"You even send live lobsters to my doorstep just to remind me."

"I've sent you other things." He handed her a bottle of ginger beer after he opened it, then opened one for himself and took a drink.

"The canoe was a great one."

She'd called Carter and suggested a robot toy that Richie really wanted for Christmas one year and he assured her he would get it and send it. It was a hot toy that year and it was important because Sara hadn't found him one and she was so relieved when Carter was going to get it. Sam told him she would be 'up shit's creek without a paddle' if she'd reassured Sara and he didn't come through.

Her doorman called her downstairs one day for a package Fed Ex delivered, an enormous box he helped her open and when she did revealed a full size canoe. The note read... Sam, just in case you end up shit's creek without paddles, a canoe will come in handy.

"Guess a canoe didn't come in handy in New York. No appreciation, I was just looking out for you. And no trust, you didn't think I'd get that robot and send it. I actually didn't send it, I went Christmas day myself, took it personally and it made me look like a king in his eyes." Carter cracked a piece of his lobster and teased her more. "What did you get him that year? A blue sweater or something?"

They feasted on delicious lobster and Ginger beer as the sky lit up and changed colors, beautiful shades of yellow and orange colors commingled together to make one glorious sunset. Sam closed her box with nothing but shells left and leaned back on her arms with a sigh.

"I can't believe I slept all day and that meal was the best I've had in a long time."

"See, I know what's good for you. You belong with me." He tipped the bottle up and finished his beer.

Casual words that fell into the playful flirting space and Sam looked into his smiling eyes. Couldn't be mad as he looked so innocent, appeared harmless. "I belong back at the ship, Trenton knows we're friends, but I certainly don't need to be here with you watching a sunset."

"You don't 'need' to be, but you want to be."

"A day running around the island is one thing. I don't think my fiancé' would appreciate a sunset and lobster feast on the beach." Sam began to pick up the trash they'd created. It felt so easy to be there with him, in her relaxed state she could sit there for hours.

"You're right. If he appreciated such beauty, I guess he'd be here with you instead of me." It wasn't only the sunset he described.

"I know what you're doing. I know you're just trying to make him look bad."

"I think he does that on his own."

"Don't Carter. Just give him a chance. I know you haven't seen the best of him, but he's been under some stress at the office and I'm not making excuses for him when I say he hasn't really been himself." Sam had experienced it since the engagement.

"To make it up to you, I'll let you get me drunk and take advantage of me." He said with a sly smile. "Hell, you don't even have to get me drunk, you can just take advantage of me."

"Will you ever change?" She had to laugh.

"God, I hope not."

In the back of her mind, she secretly hoped for the same. She'd gotten the trash up but they still remained facing the sea and the magnificence of an ending to the day. Carter broke the silence when the sun had all but disappeared.

"Another day gone. Life is short Sam, are you sure you know what you're doing with yours?" His voice was not teasing but serious.

"I'm sure." She was surer a week ago.

"You happy? I don't mean with Buster Brown, I mean with life in general, are you truly happy?"

Sam didn't answer him because anything she said would sound contrived and planned. Carter ignored the silence to his question, instead, he stood up and reached out for her hands and pulled her to her feet. When he pulled a little too hard she fell against him but didn't pull away. Their lips only an inch apart, they stood that way a few moments until Carter finally spoke.

"Don't wait for me to kiss you Sam. I felt guilty after I kissed you last night. I'm going to win you back, but I'll do it fairly. My conscious won't let me initiate cheating with another mans fiancé so you're going to have to make the first move."

She wanted to kiss him desperately. It was the atmosphere, she told herself, nothing more. Don't do it Sam, don't take that first step or you'd fall.

"Why do you have to have morals now?" She huffed and turned away.

Carter laughed at her anger, the effect he had on her. Knew it wasn't going to be easy but the obvious signs gave him hope, and that was more than he'd had in a long time.

CHAPTER 12

"I was beginning to worry about you." Trenton was dressed and ready for dinner when she returned. When he kissed her, he noticed a relaxed air about her that seemed odd, he hadn't seen it before. "How was your day? You look like you had a good time."

"It was great. A little sightseeing, St. Peter's Church, the Unfinished Church, and then the beach, I was all the way over in Hamilton and didn't realize what time it was." Quickly riffling through the closet she chose an outfit and talked to him on her way to the shower. "How was your day?"

"A great course, but those two I played with weren't exactly up to par, guess I should screen my golf choices a little better." Trenton pulled his cuff down and put his sport coat on.

"I wonder if Michael got a chance to play today, I know he wanted to. We should have coordinated it better and you two should have played."

Most of the others had eaten except for Sara and Richard so the four of them enjoyed a nice dinner together, then instead of running off elsewhere Trenton joined her afterwards. Sam was grateful, and seemed to cling to his arm, wanted him close to her. Felt a little unsure of herself and there was safety in his nearness.

Every Tuesday evening during the cruise season, St. George hosted a little street festival in the square. Music filled the air, vendors set up tables, tourists and locals alike wandered the square on the calm, warm evening. Quite a few alumni classmates attended and Richard and Sara remained with them until they all wandered off in separate directions.

Sara wandered into a souvenir shop, Sam next door into a small art gallery and the two men elsewhere. Wonderful pictures were displayed and she spent quite some time enjoying them, flipping through bins of matted watercolors. But she left without a purchase and noticed Trenton had run into some business acquaintances while he'd waited for her in the square.

"There you are." He put his arm around her proudly. "This is my fiancé', Samantha Durham."

She almost held her hand out and could only be glad she didn't when one of them opened his mouth. He leered at her with a disgusting look.

"I've heard many things about her. A hard nut that had to be cracked if you wanted to get to the sweet meat inside. What a package she makes, sweet meat indeed." He began to laugh at his own words, thought nothing of his disrespect.

Sam wanted to bash his teeth in. Not only because he talked as if she were invisible, but because to him it had been the funniest thing. His large belly shook disgustingly as he snorted and laughed, reminded her of a pig that discovered the gem of an apple in the mud. She felt the instant red-hot fury of her blood that rapidly surged faster through her veins, boiled to the surface of her skin. A quick retort left in the air of her open mouth because Trenton intervened abruptly as if the words hadn't been said.

"I hear you acquired yet another..."

His voice trailed off behind Sam who promptly turned away, had closed her mouth before the rage flowed out like lava, and kept walking straight ahead of her. Just walk Sam, don't turn around and don't go back, just walk straight. Take deep breaths and walk straight ahead. Her straight blind path led into a store where she bought a bottle of water. Not because she wanted it, only because she couldn't just stand there and fume like a mad rabid dog, and didn't want to leave without buying something. Maybe it could cool the rage that boiled inside.

"Hey sweet meat." Carter whispered in her ear, said it to tease, to joke about it, had overheard the conversation and knew she was on the verge of explosion.

"Go away, Carter." Sam tried to grab money out of her purse quickly.

"An endearing term, sweet meat, in lieu of muffin or cupcake, guess they're out of date and old fashioned now. And to think, I never thought I could learn something from Buster Brown. I might have to start using it."

"He didn't say it." She didn't have the patience to find the exact amount or wait for change so she slammed a ten-dollar bill on the counter, grabbed her water, and stormed back outside.

"Might as well have, I didn't hear him defend you." The jab was another attempt to help open her eyes.

The more Sam thought about it, the madder she became. Her blood now raged as if behind dam walls that cracked, threatened to break, and could destroy an entire village if released. Liberation was what it needed and across the way she saw her target still standing with Trenton. She was headed in their direction until Carter grabbed her hand quickly and pulled her in the opposite direction down a dark street instead.

"As much as I'd love to see blood shed over that, I think it might be better for you to calm down."

"Calm down? Did you hear that pompous, overbearing shit of a man?"

"Which one?" He made it no secret he included Trenton in her description, he just as guilty for accepting the words. He grabbed her hand again when she turned and pulled her along without letting go this time. "Okay, no more digs at Buster."

Every step took her further away from it physically, further away from it emotionally. Eventually she calmed enough to slow down and stopped to sit on an old concrete ledge, closed her eyes and groaned in frustration to release the last of her intense storm. Carter hadn't said another word and didn't as he sat down next to her.

"You should have let me go back." She finally said after a few moments.

"Some people you can't do anything about, it's the way they are and no amount of pointing out their flaws as a human being would change them. Waste of breath."

"Sounds like a bunch of crap, it would have made me feel better."

He laughed and looked at her face. Her head still back and her eyes closed but she appeared a little more settled. "Plus, I saw no reason for you to be arrested for fighting in the square." He took her bottle of water she hadn't opened, twisted the top, then took a sip and set it on the ledge. "Besides, I needed to get out of there myself because I could see myself being arrested for fighting in the square. We'd be detained in the stocks and then treated to the dunking stool for public humiliation and punishment."

He saw the smile cross her face and then she opened her eyes to look out to the calm water basked in moonlight. Sailboats bobbed and awaited their fisherman for morning.

"He was quite a character, reminded me of a bad guy in a kid's cartoon." Carter flung one leg over the broken concrete wall and straddled it to face her.

"People like that come with the territory. I've had to deal with that sort of thing for years. I've worked four times as much as any man to prove myself only to have someone like that come along and refer to me as 'sweet meat', and only because I'm a woman. The least respected thing in the boardroom. It's not the first or last time someone will try and make me feel less than what I am. I've discovered that men, for some reason, can accept any other man of equal power, but are deathly afraid if it's a woman."

Carter never put much thought into what she'd gone through, never thought about the business side of the Samantha he'd never known. Now he pictured her clawing her way through suits to make herself count for something. "The years couldn't have been easy on you."

"I held my own. It was tougher in the beginning, everyone dismissed me as basically nothing, but I've gained respect from most. I probably went a little overboard at times, there's quite a few that fear me, but that's a good thing too. At least they take me seriously."

He pictured Sam jumping around on a beach in the dark with shrieks of terror while trying to stay away from a lobster. That was the Sam he knew. The one before him faced off in powerful meetings with men who ate people like her for breakfast, he never fully pictured her that way. He'd only caught a glimpse of that side when she faced off with the lawyers when her parents died.

"I don't defend the people you've had to deal with, but I can see how they would immediately underestimate you and try to take advantage. Hiding behind demure, innocent, beautiful blue eyes, is hell on wheels."

Sam was slow to speak, her voice low. "I learned from the best. When my mother was in one of her angry drunks, a 'whiskey drunk' I called it, and went on a rampage throughout the house screaming at anyone in her path, I used to hide underneath my father's desk. It's the only room she never went in. I'd sit there all day long and sometimes my father worked from there so I'd listen to him on the phone, or when he took meetings." It was explanation for the transformation that had taken place when he died, and the person she'd become now. "All I wanted to do was stay away from my mother, I never realized how much I actually picked up, didn't even think I was hardly paying attention."

"You paid attention well." Carter smiled, didn't say his words with anger, but understanding. "I only saw it once when you faced off with your fathers attorneys but I bet Preston Burke never underestimated you again."

"He never had the chance, I fired him the day after you left, along with at least six other corporate heads. One a day for a week, like taking a vitamin." Sam found she was unafraid to reveal things, even the way she'd felt. "It empowered me, made me feel like I at least had control over something."

At the time, she'd felt so helpless. Had no control over Carter leaving or the way her life had suddenly turned. In business, she'd taken the reins and held on tight. The only thing that could be heard was the water lapping against the shore below them and a few voices in the far off distance. She had turned to face him while she talked, now each of them straddled the old wide wall that was anything but smooth, with its broken chips and worn surface. Carter took both her hands in his.

"Are you happy, Sam?"

She lowered her head, eyes downcast, and then turned to look across the water again streaked with moonlight. Carter wasn't sure if there were tears in her eyes or if it was just the way the light from the moon reflected from them in the darkness.

"We all live with the objective of being happy," she answered.

"So that's all I get." Indirectness didn't surprise him.

"What about you?"

He stared at her for a long time. Deep blue eyes that pulled him into her soul only because he knew the way there from memory, but as much as he hated to admit it, so many years had passed and they now held a certain unfamiliarity.

"Yeah, I guess we all live with the objective of being happy."

They sat quietly for a long time, then left and found the others sitting on the outdoor deck at White Horse Tavern, a quaint establishment that looked out to the docked ship. Her lights reflected off the water giving the ship an even brighter glow against the black sky.

Quite a few classmates were there and Carter slid onto the picnic table bench next to Richard, Sam slid on the opposite side next to Sara.

"Hey you two." Sara smiled.

Sam could see the look in all their eyes and regretted walking in with Carter. They thought things they shouldn't.

"Carter, I..." Richard was about to warn him but it was too late.

Mindy squealed loudly when she saw Carter and wrapped herself around him. It was obvious she'd had too much to drink. "Carter, I've been... I've been looking... for you."

Mindy insisted on squeezing in when there was obviously no room and was basically hanging onto Carter so she wouldn't fall off.

"I don't know how long she's been here. She was here when we got here." Sara informed her with a whisper in Sam's ear.

She could see how unpleasant it was for Carter and Sam had to look away, afraid she'd burst into laughter at the look of horror on his shocked face. A woman was literally throwing herself in his lap and he didn't know what to do, he looked so uncomfortable and embarrassed it was charming.

Mindy wouldn't let him be. Her chatter never stopped once and being polite, and not knowing what else to do, he listened. Caught Sam's eye once and she could read his screams for help.

"Sam?" Mindy squinted her eyes as if she couldn't see her clearly.

"Yes, Mindy, it's me."

"Sam, I just... a long time... long time ago you and Carter... I don' want to intfer... inference... with anyone. I don't think you two... are anymore... are you? You and Carter... anymore? You done... with him Sam?"

Her and Carter exchanged glances. Sam wasn't sure if it was her imagination or if the entire place went quiet, she was sure her own table of friends did.

"Yeah, Mindy, I'm done with him. He amounted to nothing you know, just a homeless guitar player."

****

The next morning when she woke, Carter was the first thing on her mind and it bothered her. Bothered her more than knowing he'd been the last thing on her mind the evening before.

She decided to take Trenton up on his previous day's offer of spending the day with her. There were no plans with the others until later that afternoon, so the two took a cab across the island to Hamilton. There were many things to distract her as they walked around, shopped, then found a nice restaurant for lunch, but although there were many things, it didn't work. Sam's mind was preoccupied. If she were in New York, it would be easy. She had her work. It's what drove her.

"I've repeated it twice already." Trenton said across the table from her.

"What?" Sam finally looked up at him.

"I asked you twice if you wanted me to order wine with lunch."

"Oh. Sure."

Trenton looked at her oddly, she'd been looking at the menu but was so totally lost somewhere. "Did you just shut down? Are you so relaxed without work, this is what it does to you?"

"All of a sudden I felt tired. Just started reading the menu and it put me in a daze. Sure, order appetizers."

"With the wine?"

Then she remembered it was what he asked and they both laughed at her puzzlement.

"I'll be better after you feed me." Her reassuring smile was believable.

She looked across the table to him as he concentrated on the extensive wine list. He looked more relaxed to her. His handsome face a little softer somehow, even tinted a little by the sun. He placed the wine order and they ordered food, they both took the waiters recommendation of a seafood dish.

"How did you know about this place?" It was Trenton's suggestion to come there.

"The men I was talking to last night." He looked at her with trepidation to mention it. "They have a place here, made some suggestions."

"Pig man?" She stated her nickname for him, it still irked her. "That's what he reminded me of."

"Max isn't the most tactful of men. The other one, Stewart, owns Grosover Communications, he's here for a big golf tournament going on. And Max Maines owns a good portion of California."

"So that makes his ignorance acceptable?"

"No, but I can't choose the people I do business with, and we might have some dealings with Max coming up. Hoping to anyway. We want to get rid of those real estate holdings, remember? He's shown some interest."

"Oh." Sam picked up her wine glass and smiled and Trenton looked at her with curiosity but didn't question it.

She would love to have it come to fruition, would look forward to him sitting across her desk. It would make him wish they'd come to blows in the square instead. It would be difficult for her to inflict physical pain, but there were many she negotiated with who left her office emotionally battered and wounded. If he wanted their holdings bad enough, he would be in the palm of her hand.

"I'm actually going over to Max's place this evening. I couldn't find you last night, but I didn't think you'd mind if I accepted his invitation."

"As long as I'm not expected to go with you."

"Believe me, the thought didn't cross my mind. I'm smart enough to know that if we stand a chance to have him as a good prospect, it might be a good idea for me to work on all the preliminary negotiations."

"Leave it to you to find business here," she said.

Trenton didn't tell her it wasn't by accident. It was by accident he'd run into him, but he'd previously planned on calling him while he was there. Her college friends who resorted into their youth when they were together, wasn't his attraction to the trip.

"Business and golf, it isn't all work. I'd like to play tomorrow but I haven't planned anything yet. Anything I can't miss on your schedule tomorrow?"

"We're not in the office, I don't have a schedule, remember?"

He chuckled. "Hard to believe, but you're actually managing very well without one. Something I thought I'd never be witness to."

"You ought to ask Michael to play with you. He's a golf fanatic." Sam didn't think she was going to push her friends on Trenton and it wasn't her plan. But she didn't see any reason they had to be so distant.

****

They returned to the ship late that afternoon and Trenton didn't join her when she met the others for a boat ride to Hamilton for the street festival there that night, they enjoyed the sunset along the way.

"So, did it work?" Carter asked as he sat down beside her in the seat Nikki had just vacated.

"Did what work?"

"Spending the day somewhere else. Did it take your mind off me?"

How did he have that ability? Sam asked herself. Some sort of mind game. She wasn't that obvious, was she? Just confident pot shots in the dark, that just happened to be right every time.

"Very much so. It was refreshing not having you hound me." Sam smiled with confidence. Of course she didn't tell him he didn't have to be physically present to hound her.

Nikki was only getting up for a moment but she hadn't returned and Sam suspected it was because Carter was there. Through the years she'd listened to insinuations and casually dropped hints from her friends about her life with Carter. Everyone still hoped it had all been a nightmare. It never bothered her, but she wondered if they would continue even after her wedding day.

"So did you have a nice day with Buster Brown, even if you were thinking about me?"

"It was very nice. Thanks for asking. I know you like him, you just don't want to admit it." The words said jokingly sounded absurd, even to her ears.

"No matter what I think of him, it still doesn't change that he's the wrong person for you."

"You wouldn't admit that you liked him anyway."

Odd thing was, there was a part of him that wanted to like Trenton. If he lost in this battle to win her back, he would at least be assured she was with a decent human being. In a strange way that would make him feel better if he was the one to walk away alone, but he hadn't found that quality from Trenton yet. Regardless how much he knew Trenton must love her, it wasn't enough. He wanted more for Sam. Even if that meant her life wasn't with him.

When Carter spoke again, his words were serious. "Isn't it more work for you to pretend to love someone?"

It was as if he could expose her, knew the right buttons to push to make her question herself. Make her admit, even if only in her own mind, the connection they had was hardly broken. It made her angry, with him, and herself.

"Maybe you should stop pretending you know me as well as you think."

"I know you're mad right now because I'm right." He said to prove his point. "I know I'm the last person you're thinking of at night, and the first one in the morning."

There he was again. This mind thing he had that could see right through her. Another pot shot that just happened to be right. "It might be what you're wishing for, but you'd be well advised to remember the distinction between fictional and factual."

"Samantha speaks like a true attorney. If you let Sam talk, what would she say?"

"That you're full of shit."

Every Wednesday during the summer months, Front Street in Hamilton closed to vehicles and became a gathering spot for locals and tourists alike. The Harbor Nights Festival was larger than the street festival in St. George due to a larger population. Sparkling lights, lively dancers and food vendors offered tasty Bermudian fare to keep you fed. A variety of things to keep one entertained. And the opportunity for fun.

Sara talked her into getting their faces painted with a tropical design and they enjoyed live music and local acts to the captivating beat of the local Gombey troops dressed in colorful festive attire. Then they drug her by the hand and forced her into a melee' of dancers on the street who welcomed them. Put flowers in their hair and wrapped their waists in festive sarongs.

They wouldn't be deterred even when a slight drizzle of rain began to fall, they weren't fazed in the least, even when it started to rain harder. They laughed, held hands, and raised their faces up to be cooled and never stopped moving to the beat of the music. Sam was so totally relaxed, all of her cares and thoughts thrown elsewhere as she danced down the street. Her laughter filled the night air like a sweet song.

When she happened to glance toward the sidewalk, she saw Carter there, and she hesitated for a brief second. Their eyes locked in the short distance between them and she couldn't turn away from his smile. Hadn't realized she stopped dancing until Nikki grabbed her hand and pulled her along again. When she turned around he looked so boyishly adorable as he leaned against a light post, his white shirtsleeves rolled up with sloppy abandon. Hair unkempt. An easy smile with a strange look of contentment, as if he knew something no one else did.

CHAPTER 13

Their last full day in Bermuda gave everyone a sense of excitement and disappointment at the same time. The week was almost over, and no one would be prepared for it to come to a close. A few of the group gathered by a pre-designated waiting spot outside the port.

Carter and Michael stood together talking, now watched together as Sam approached. Michael looked to his friend, had been concerned with the direction he headed.

"Don't set yourself up for too hard a fall."

Carter's eyes remained on Sam. "It's too late for that. Besides, my heart has already been broken, she can only break it into smaller pieces."

Michael's voice held sadness at what had become of them. "I worry about you Carter, I know where you're headed. I was there the day you fell in love the first time, remember?"

"The only time Michael."

Carter knew the day he spoke of, he'd said it often before. And he himself had thought it was that day on the dock when he dove in to meet her on her very first visit to the Cape, but as he thought of it now, he could never remember a time he wasn't in love with her. So it was actually the first day he laid eyes on her from a distance on the college campus, and as he watched her approach now, nothing had changed.

Carter sighed, still hadn't taken his eyes from her. "You were also there the day you had to pick up the pieces. Maybe that's why I'm throwing myself in full force now, I know you'll be there again if I need you to be. And if I miss this chance, I'll never have another. How can I not take the risk?"

Sam thought she was going shopping for last minute treasures but she saw plans had changed when she approached and everyone waited. They all mounted their mopeds, Sara on Richard's, Nikki on Blake's, and Shawna, of course, on Michael's.

"We had a change of plans, Sam." Sara called out to her. "Some things got cancelled and it ended up to work out we could all spend the day together, so we thought we'd take advantage of it."

Carter waited patiently for her. "Come on."

"You're awfully presumptuous aren't you? How do you know I'm riding with you?"

He looked around to all the others getting on their motorized bikes and joked. "Doesn't look like anyone else wants you. I'm all you got."

"Maybe I don't even want to go."

"You do." He said and waited patiently.

A few days ago she would have thought nothing of it, now she was hesitant, tried to stand her ground. He held the ability to scare her and she was afraid to be with him. Carter took it as the good sign it was. Knew her barriers weakened.

"Get on the bike Sam."

The others had already started to pull off. Again she heard that little warning in her head, the one that kept at her, the one she didn't listen to. Sam got on.

They followed the others and she was quiet for a long time. Still contemplated going back, but how foolish was that? Couldn't she enjoy the day with everyone? All eight of them together. There was safety in numbers.

"I think this was a set up. I thought all you men were doing something else and we were supposed to be shopping."

"Think of it as saving Trenton money."

"I have my own money thank you." She pinched his sides in retaliation.

"But isn't it much more fun to spend his?" Carter took a turn a little harder than he needed and she had to squeeze him to hold on.

"You did that on purpose."

"Yeah, I did." He admitted without hesitation.

"Where are we going?"

"Does it matter? You're in Bermuda, on the back of my bike again. What more could you want?"

"You're awfully arrogant today, or should I add even more than your usual self." Then she added. "What happened? Get lucky last night?"

He didn't answer her question and for just a moment she wondered if it was because it was true. Mindy was only one who would keep him company, there were many he could have chosen from, but she quickly dismissed the thought.

"Do we have any sort of plan? It looks like they know where they're going." It was easier to be off the bike and not have to wrap her arms around him.

"I can't hear you." He leaned back slightly and she moved closer to his ear, repeated the words but he still denied he understood. "I still can't hear you."

This time she was so close her lips almost touched skin and she screamed the words.

"Where are we going, do you know?"

"You'll have to say it one more time." This time Carter couldn't help but laugh and she caught on to him.

"Now that you've had your fun, do you know where we're going?"

"All I know is Richard insisted last night that I be ready to leave bright and early." He finally answered.

They soon found out when Richard led them to a place called Kenny's Kitchen. Although it was Thursday, he ordered what was traditionally a Sunday breakfast for Bermudians. Codfish Breakfast, for all.

"Okay, I'm always pretty open to new things but this sounds a little strange." Nikki was the first to almost object. She didn't of course and went along grudgingly. "I guess cod fish and potatoes sound somewhat close to normal fare, not actually for breakfast, but what scares me the most is the garnishments. Avocado pear, ripe bananas, okra's or a boiled egg on the side or with a sauce. Quite an interesting range."

"It's all about new things, I'm on a mission today." Sara smiled and held Richard's hand tight underneath the table.

"And we all have to be dragged along because you had a craving for codfish? Are you going to tell us you're pregnant?" Shawna grinned from ear to ear, sure she'd guessed a secret, but was disappointed in the denial.

"No craving. No pregnancy. We're off that kick, I think Richie is enough for right now."

Richard pretended to agree. "Sometimes more than enough."

For one brief second Sam glimpsed something in Sara's eye she perhaps was not supposed to, but it quickly disappeared and no one else seemed to notice. A strong friendship carried with it what could be considered a blessing and a burden. One knew when something was out of whack about the other, but gut instinct revealed only that. Not what the problem actually was.

A blessing because you could guess something exciting was about to happen. A burden when you knew it was merely something about to happen. In this instance, Sam considered it a burden, and it caught her at breakfast and wouldn't let go.

"Are you going to enlighten me?" Carter asked while they put their helmets on to leave.

"What?" She looked up but was unsure of his words.

"There's something wrong, are you going to tell me what it is?"

Like reading Sara, Carter too was affluent in her own silent language. She answered honestly. "I just... there's something wrong and I don't know what it is. There's something wrong with Sara, do you know anything?"

"I haven't been told anything if that's what you mean, but I don't notice anything off about her. She's been having a great time all week."

"I had this feeling the other day also, but I thought maybe it was my imagination. This morning was different. I guess because she sat directly across me, I was closer to her and could see... I don't even know what I saw. Maybe it's nothing." She said it more to convince herself.

Although Carter tried to reassure her, the feeling wouldn't leave. There was something ahead of them, she didn't know what, but she was almost positive it was something she didn't want to face.

The port city of Hamilton served as the capital of Bermuda and it bustled with people and traffic. All the girls on the back of the bikes waved to the man clad in Bermuda shorts and knee socks in the 'Bird cage' on Front Street.

Then just off Queen Street they found Par-la-Ville Park. A small garden park of trees, shrubs and flowers and one of Bermuda's famous Moongates, a limestone built arch that brought good luck to lovers and newlyweds who stepped through it. It was also said if lovers stood beneath and made a wish they'd be granted eternal happiness. They'd all casually stepped through not knowing the meaning.

Off again, they drove down Church Street. Aptly named because more churches were located there than anywhere else. Sam lost count as they rode along. She leaned close to Carter so he could hear above the small engine noise.

"Some English settlers ended up here because they were lost on their way to Virginia."

"I think you made that up," he said.

"It's true. It was in 1609, and did you know Bermuda is about one third the size of Washington D.C.?"

"Lot's of reading time with Buster Brown, huh? I could think of much better ways for you to spend your time."

"Trenton. Trenton Spalding Edwards."

"He doesn't work into the equation of a much better time." He took all the jabs and pinches she gave at his teasing.

City Hall was topped with a bronze replica of the Sea Venture, the wrecked ship of the English settlers she spoke of. Further down, fourteen saints flanked the Lord at Cathedral of the Most Holy Trinity. Inside was a replica of a pulpit of one in St. Giles, Edinburgh, Scotland. Treasured history of Bermuda spread before her from the back of a motorbike.

Heading east on Victoria Street, left on King Street and a left at Happy Valley Road led them to Pembroke Perish and Fort Hamilton. An imposing old fortress, complete with a moat on the eastern outskirts of the city. It was erected during a period of rising tensions between Britain and the USA, with 18-ton artillery pieces capable of firing 400-pound cannonballs through iron hulled vessels that had never been used. 64-pound riffled muzzleloaders, underground passageways cut through solid rock by Royal Engineers in the 1860's, but it was outdated even before completion and never fired a shot in aggression. Had it been a Monday they would have been treated to bagpipers and a Skirling Ceremony.

Now the Fort served as a wonderful standpoint. Like a postcard, Bermuda's botanical beauty was evident in a splendid view of the capital of Bermuda and its harbor that stretched to Gibb's Hill Lighthouse.

Back in Hamilton they took a break off the bikes to meander through several stores and when Carter couldn't be found Sam insisted they not wait. Sara circled a meeting place on the map for her to guide Carter to Elbow Beach and they would catch up.

"Where have you been?" Sam questioned with pretend sternness when he finally did show up.

He didn't answer, only smiled mysteriously, and strapped his purchases on before they set off. Once they met up with the others, they rode the South Shore Road from Elbow Beach in Paget Parish through Warwick Parish, and the marvels they found there. Stopped at Astwood Cove with its steep cliffs and watched a flock of migrating seabirds and saw a few Longtail's, Bermuda's national bird.

"Hey Sam, you and Carter turn around." As they stood along the water edge Sara beckoned from behind them with her camera.

"You're going to need a new computer when you get home, yours is entirely too small for all the digital pictures you've taken." Sam tried to avoid it but couldn't.

"Put your arm around her Carter, smile Sam."

As she encouraged their pose, Sam found herself not wanting to deny her. It was Sara's day, she decided. For whatever reason she didn't quite know yet, she'd claimed it Sara's day.

"You can move your arm now Carter." Sara had gone and there was no reason for him to, but he kept it there.

"She might be back, don't you want to be ready? If we wait long enough I think she'll be back and ask us to kiss for the next shot."

"That would be difficult since you don't want to kiss me." She reminded him of a moment he wouldn't.

"For reasons I'm questioning myself for now, maybe morals have no place here."

"With or without won't get you anywhere. My wedding day is fast approaching."

"But there won't be one."

"There you go mixing fictional and factual again."

Sam found herself just as content on the back of the motorbike in glorious open air as she'd been on the water in a boat the previous evening. No matter how you looked at it, Bermuda was beautiful at any angle as they explored the island's outer reaches.

Drove past beaches and viewed them from the road, and sometimes stopped at a few pink coral one's for closer inspection. Warwick Long Bay was the longest stretch of prime beach and they practically had to drag Nikki away, pacified her with a mussel pie and a Bermuda fish sandwich they shared from a lunch wagon. There were many other beaches in between. Jobson's Cove, Stonehole Bay and in Southampton Parish there was Chaplin Bay and Horseshoe.

As the wind whipped through her hair and sun warmed her face, Sam silently vowed to one day return and explore them all with closer inspection. Perhaps even paint them, one by one. Maybe at some point in her life she'd be ready to paint again, something she hadn't thought of in years. But with so much undeniable beauty she had the urge to put it to canvas and capture it.

Now she could only try to burn it into the depths of her mind, embed it there. Didn't want to forget, but knew that one day, this too she would have to let slip away with all of her other memories.

They stopped briefly at Gibb's Hill Lighthouse, the oldest cast iron lighthouse in the world. Then just past Church Bay the road turned inland and gave clear views over the Great sound. Sara was anxious to get somewhere so they didn't stop for quite a while and arrived at the West End and the Royal Dockyard just in time to prevent her from having a meltdown.

"Leader Sara, do I have time to go to the bathroom before we go to whatever it is we're late for?" Shawna stood like a little girl, her legs crossed as if it would hold back the flood, and they laughed at her need to ask permission.

"Only if you hurry."

The sign read Bermuda Maritime Museum and no one suspected exactly what was in store until Blake finally asked. "We're late for a visit to a Museum?"

"We're swimming with dolphins." Sara stated it as fact and continued her march towards their destination.

"Oh no, you're swimming with big fish, not we, you, you all, but not we." Sam quickly tried to make her escape but Sara grabbed her hand and pulled her along as she continued to march.

"Yes Sam, you too are swimming with dolphins."

"You know I don't do well with large wild animal things. Every one of you were there when I was almost swallowed by a whale. Right there in the boat just as scared as I was, but I was the only one in the water."

They all laughed at the memory. It was at the Cape. They'd taken a boat out and idled in the water, just enjoyed the day of sun. Sam decided on a quick dip to cool off and only swam out a little way but as she was headed back, out from the deep of the sea, a Finback whale, the second largest animal on earth, breached the surface. The mammoth creature splashed down and was so close she felt the ripple of his wave.

Felt terror inside every bone in her body, it was a fear she wouldn't soon forget. Since then she'd never gone into the mysterious sea again.

"It was just a little whale." Carter teased, it had actually been the largest one he'd ever seen. A newborn finback was normally around twenty feet, and they could grow to lengths of 85 feet. That one had probably been closer to the latter.

"I peed myself, and I was in the boat." Blake admitted.

"I'll play with chickens or goats if you want. I'm the one who's a shark out of water, not in it!"

Like a mother dragging a reluctant child to the bathtub, Sara held on and wouldn't let her go. Objections fell on deaf ears.

"Dogs or cats." She rambled on but there was no one to save her. "I'll be the bravest thing you ever saw with dogs or cats, but I'm a chicken when it comes to other things. You know I'm a chicken when it comes to other things. Fish. I'll go snorkeling, but small fish. Not big, dolphin, wild animal fish."

They were briefly instructed before they stepped foot in the water but everything they'd told her disappeared. Although the water temperature was warm, Sam shook from fear on the shallow water platform. Carter held her hand underneath the water's surface but even that was little comfort.

As a dolphin approached for attention, with much encouragement from both the group and the instructors, she finally reached out to it. As she did it splashed her as if on queue and nearly made her pee out of fright.

It took her longer than the others to become comfortable enough to at least swim out a little ways from the safety of the platform. Sleek, smooth dolphins came for play and she could laugh at herself as the others had when two dolphins jumped over their heads and she covered her face and squealed.

By the end of the encounter, although she hadn't relaxed completely, hadn't fully overcome that slight fear, Sam had to admit it was one of the greatest things she'd ever done. They were magnificent creatures to be both admired and respected. She admitted, only to herself, that Carter was a great help in squelching some of her raging nerves.

"Don't think because I let you hold my hand it gives you free reign." She smiled and threw her wet towel at him when she'd finished changing into dry clothes. The others, of course, had left Carter to wait on her.

"I help you through the most fearful, horrific moments of your life and that's all I get?" Carter wrapped the towel she'd thrown at him around her neck and pulled her close to him. "I think it was a very heroic effort on my part. That dolphin could have charged and I'd have been willing to throw myself in its path for you."

"That probably could have happened." Sam moved her face as close to his as humanly possible without touching. "But it still wouldn't have entitled you to free reign."

Carter could feel her breathe sweep ever so lightly across his lips. Smell the sweetness of freshly showered skin. Skin that didn't actually touch, wasn't connected in any way, but he could feel it.

"Where is everyone?" Sam said in a normal tone.

"Don't act as if you don't want to kiss me."

"You said morals had no place here, even if I wanted a kiss, which I'm not saying I do, all I would have to do is wait. You'll kiss me."

"I lied." It had to be her, she had to kiss him, he wasn't sure why it was so important to him but it was.

Sam stared at him for a long time. His eyes pulled her in, his scent and feel beckoned to her deep senses she buried as if they knew instinctively how to reach her. On the verge of betrayal to Trenton, and the fence she straddled wasn't made of sturdy wood.

"No one's here, we're all alone. What's stopping you Sam?" Carter whispered.

The saddest part was, she didn't even know. Desire coursed through her veins, desire that fed off the distant memories she'd locked away. By doing so and being dormant for so long, it gave that desire more substance and it only became stronger with each second. But as much as Sam's heart wanted him, Samantha's skilled brain talked her out of it.

The Frog and Onion Pub at the Royal Navel Dockyard sat directly across from the Maritime Museum and it was the farthest Michael could get before he thought he'd faint from hunger. He'd been begging for hours for food.

Housed in a former warehouse with a decor of stone and wood, the Frog and Onion Pub resembled an old English Pub. Made one feel they were in a different era in time with its limestone ceilings and thick walls. The massive fireplace could possibly have fit the eight of them inside.

Several hearty English Pub fare dishes were offered and they decided to try several to share and get a sampling of as many different items as they could. Fresh fish always seemed to be a staple on the menu's around the island. Along with fish and chips they tried the Argus Bank fish sandwich, conch fritters and bangers and mash were also among their choices. All of that along with a Bermudian favorite, the classic Dark and Stormy, which consisted of an interesting combination of Bermuda's own Gosling's Rum and Ginger Beer.

The men could now imbibe in a few since they would be taking the mopeds on the ferry back to St. George's. Much laughter emitted from their table as the group fell into comfortable banter among themselves, even with other people around them.

They were fun people, people who seemed to have so much in common and yet sometimes nothing at all. The mix just the right combination. Mingled among them various personality traits that when in connected unison was just the right blend to always keep it interesting and more than entertaining. So many years ago when they were college kids, now as they sat as adults and every moment in between, each complimented the other in so many various yet distinct ways.

Nikki would begin to root through her purse and Richard, Sara's husband, would remind her to wear her watch on her wrist and not put it in the bottom of a seemingly endless bag. The innocent act of Carter as he played with just a small corner of a paper napkin signified to Sara that he was impatient about something, either wanted to contribute something to the conversation and patiently waited so as not to butt in, or edgy about something else. Sometimes Blake and Sam would complete each other's sentences or if Sam didn't, Shawna sometimes would. At times, when Michael looked for his keys or a lost item, Carter would know exactly where to find them.

They all knew each other's hearts, each other's souls, were bonded together as if they'd taken a vow as a group for better or worse. Maybe that's why as the meal wore on Sam couldn't let go of something in Sara's eyes. This time it was accompanied by a feeling of impending doom. Thought that if she got up right then and left she could avoid what lay before them, even though she didn't know exactly what it was. It was as if she could see a tornado building in the distance and it headed directly for her.

Sam's eyes locked with Sara's but neither spoke. The others chatter carried on around them. Sara stared directly back with eyes that tried to promise hope but fell short. She raised her glass into the air.

"I can't thank you all enough for sharing this day with Richard and I. I'd like to make a toast. To old friends." Sara clanked her glass against each and every one.

The others repeated her sentiments and added their own. 'To old friends... Can't we say young at heart friends?... I think she's actually rubbing it in she's the youngest here... Speaking as the oldest, something we don't need to be reminded of... To forever friends...'

Sam finally dropped her gaze when Sara turned away. Tried to lighten the gloominess she felt. "Well, I feel duped, I was told we were going shopping and then got stuck with Carter all day. And I'm sure all of ya'll thought it was just great, but you've never ridden on back of a moped with him. He does all he can to come as close to the edge as possible."

"I wanted to make sure you were awake."

"Oh, she was awake." Michael laughed. "I could hear her scream and we were in the back of the pack, I think it just floated in the air."

"And you were no help, egging him on to race that teenage ninja turtle." Sam couldn't think of another thing to call the young man with his bright green and yellow moped painted up with what she thought to be ninja turtles with swords.

"I want to know why it took you guys so long to catch up to us when we left that one place in Hamilton."

"Sam wanted to spend hours in that one store, I had to drag her out." Carter playfully fibbed.

She slapped him across the arm. "You lie. I wasn't even shopping, you were. He disappeared and I waited for him at the bike for half an hour. I was almost going to rent my own and leave him."

"I've seen you on a regular bike and you needed training wheels, there's no way Bermuda would survive with you on a moped."

"You didn't even show me what you bought, I waited in the hot sun for all that time and I just remembered you never even showed me why."

Carter leaned back and raised his eyebrows as if he spoke the truth. "If you're going to complain about the hot sun, maybe you shouldn't have been laid up on that bench tanning yourself."

The others watched them banter back and forth. With every second that passed the smiles grew broader.

It was Nikki who commented on it. "I feel like we're back at Casey's Brew House on Buchanan Street."

Their first unofficial date passed through Carter's mind, the first day he'd been able to get close to her. They were a long way from Casey's Brew House.

CHAPTER 14

After lunch they all dispersed their separate ways to meet up later. Bermuda was an important Royal Base from 1795 to 1953 and the dockyard became a key British military dockyard around 1815. A hilly site considered Ireland Island at the western tip of Bermuda, it was used among other things, as re-supply depot for ships heading between Nova Scotia and British West Indies. Nearly 10,000 convicts quartered in barely tolerable conditions on prison ships stationed in deepwater coves were responsible for the labor.

It became a base for the British navy to launch a raid on Washington D.C.. Now stretches of concrete replaced with trees, shrubs and green lawn catered mainly to tourists along with serving as a cruise ship terminal. The dockyard was home to favorites such as a Maritime Museum, a craft market, a Gallery and Arts Center, a snorkel park and water sports center.

The men appreciated its history, the women went in search of other things. Sam had been wandering through a few stores when Carter found her, took hold of her hand and led her away.

"You've had enough shopping for one day, come on." He held onto her hand and led her to a secluded grassy area along the shore.

"You're going to get arrested for trespassing. How do you know this isn't someone's property?" Sam looked around at the beautiful lush green grounds full of Bougainvillea. It was someone's garden she was almost sure, though there wasn't a house to be seen.

"You mean *we're* going to get arrested for trespassing." He corrected her and produced a bottle of champagne from a bag and two plastic cups.

"We shouldn't be here, and especially not with a bottle of champagne."

"I can't think of any a more perfect place to be on our last evening in Bermuda than right here overlooking the sea and toasting the sunset. How can I create a romantic memory without champagne?"

"I shouldn't be here." She continued her protest but he simply ignored her as if she weren't talking at all. "We shouldn't be here."

"You know, there's many a women who'd love to be in your shoes right now."

"Then maybe I should go get one of my better pairs so at least she'll have something decent to wear when she shows up."

She reluctantly settled on the grass with the cup he handed her, knew she shouldn't be there but did nothing about it. It wasn't as if he handcuffed her to a tree, forced her to stay, yet she continued to protest. Even as she made herself comfortable.

He threw the bag of mystery he'd purchased in Hamilton that morning in front of them but didn't say anything else about it. When he was in the middle of talking about something trivial she could take no more and curiosity made her ask.

"Are you going to tell me what's in the bag?"

Carter looked straight ahead and smiled. "No."

"So it's just going to sit there like that? Couldn't you have left it on the bike?"

"Didn't want to." He leaned back in the grass and closed his eyes as if he could relax and forget about it.

Sam fidgeted in the silent agony. With his eyes closed, she moved her foot slightly to try and jar it open then realized it was stapled shut. Adjusted its angle a little where she could try to see through a tiny slit, but even that didn't work.

"Open the bag Sam." He stated without moving.

"If you insist." She quickly snatched it up, ripped the top and dumped the contents between her legs.

Out of it flowed beautiful hues of oil paints in the most magnificent colors. Vivid sapphire and turquoise of the ocean dotted with sailboats. Pastel gingerbread houses that lined the streets. Lush green grass and the flamboyant color of prominent Bougainvillea and Lantana. There were glorious pink sand beaches and gray/blue rock formations that lined the shore.

She even envisioned the China plates with many different patterns in the store window of that cute establishment in Hamilton. The soft color of the town hall in St. George's square and the flags that waved above, the eye pop yellow of the business at the beginning of the road that led to Tobacco Bay, and the crisp blue, yellow and pink houses that sat in silent welcome along the shore as one sailed through the channel. She didn't see mere oil paint, she saw Bermuda in all its glory. All spread before her in the colorful tubes.

"Some brushes, sketch pads and canvas have been delivered to your stateroom." Carter spoke without opening his eyes.

"Why did you do this?" She finally asked.

"Because I know you Sam, I know you like no one else does."

They both remained quiet and still. The only thing that interrupted the silence was soft, slow music from somewhere in the distance. An outdoor cafe'? Someone's home? A boat in the harbor?

She hadn't painted in so many years, hadn't the desire. But earlier that day, and now, as she took in Bermuda with every movement of her eye, every inhale of breath, the stir of a long lost aspiration to sit on a cliff like this at the break of dawn and not leave until she'd covered canvas would have consumed her had she not been so skilled at blocking it out.

"Don't do this to me, Carter."

"Don't do what? Remind you of who you are? If you'd listen to your heart I wouldn't have to."

Her words were said in a flame of frustration over a struggle that went on inside. "My heart? I don't think I have one. If I do I don't want it. Maybe I'll rip it out and leave it right here."

"You're going to get arrested for littering." He said with all seriousness.

"And don't do that either."

"I'm just laying here minding my own business, I'm not doing anything. But if I were, what did I do that time?"

"You make me want to be so mad at you and then you say something and take it away, stop that, let me be mad." She tried to sound stern but it was impossible.

"Be mad, but be mad down here beside me."

He reached up and pulled her down, cradled her to his side with his arm. She rested her head in resignation on his chest.

"And don't do this either." She said softly. "This is crazy. We've been acting like Nikki said, as if we were college kids again. Sitting at Casey's Brew House instead of two separate people who have nothing to do with the other. I don't even know how this happened."

It was natural between them. They hadn't meant to act a certain way around one another, or not act a particular way. It was the way it was. They'd been through anger, indifference, avoidance, and back to friendship. Now had arrived at this strange place that didn't even have a name.

Shawna's words came back to her. This must be at least a little part of the 'might have been'. She felt both blessed and cursed to see a small glimpse, a small taste for just a little while, then she would do what she'd learned to do so well. Convince herself things were otherwise, tell her heart things it needed to hear to get back on level ground.

Sam rolled off him and lie flat on her back, looked up to sky but he positioned himself on one elbow and hovered over her.

"It didn't happen this week Sam, it happened a long time ago. You act as if it disappeared when it's been right here all along. What more proof do you need? You're laying in the grass with me on a cliff overlooking Bermuda and I didn't force you here. You weren't tied to the moped."

"I should have been today, I thought you wanted me to flip off the back and over the cliff."

"That was only a fantasy in the early days after you'd left me."

"I didn't leave you, you left me." She corrected.

Sam liked the emotional place they'd arrived at. How it happened, she wasn't sure but it felt natural, real. Did it mean anything? If she thought it could, like everything else she swept the thoughts away to somewhere deep.

"I still haven't figured out what's wrong with Sara, but I know there's something going on and whatever it is, it isn't good."

"If it's anything important, you'll know when she wants to tell you." Carter softly placed his right palm on her cheek, caressed her lips with his thumb.

"Carter, I..."

"Shhhh..." He wanted desperately to replace his thumb with his lips. When he was closer, inches from her mouth, he urged her to do so. "Kiss me Sam. Just once. One little kiss is all I ask."

Sam could feel the deep yearning stir within her. A hunger that went unfed for so many years. It would be so easy and natural for their lips to come together for even one second, but knew she would need another lifetime to forget the feelings that would instill. His kiss the other evening already enough threat to her stone reserve.

"We'd better get back, it's almost time to meet the others." Sam wanted to rise but couldn't, even knowing the dangerous place she was in.

"We can catch another ferry."

"I think it might be the last one."

He laid his face on hers, lips not touching but she could feel them on her cheek. "We'll drive back, we have a moped remember?"

The electricity that shot through her wasn't new. She remembered well the natural smell of him, his skin as it touched hers, the way his hair felt between her fingers when she put her hands through it briefly then just as quickly pulled back again.

"This isn't fair, you use Champagne and Bermuda sunset as weapons and expect me to resist."

"And gifts, I bought you a gift remember? But I use them for you not to resist." He lowered his mouth closer to her ear and brushed his bottom lip against her skin.

It stung his senses with fire and he took a deep breath as her hand found its way to the back of his neck, and although she held him close she turned her face away so their lips wouldn't touch. When it began to rain slightly, the suddenness of the water shocked her senses to return and she quickly pulled away and rose.

But it wouldn't be her escape. He pulled her into his arms and they slow danced to the faint music from somewhere unknown as sun melted into sea and a soft glow surrounded them. She'd been comfortable with Carter. Until then hadn't felt fully threatened or in too deep a turmoil over what seemed to be between them. Harbored the notion she could cast anything she felt aside.

Now she was embraced in strong arms that surrounded her, felt safe and warm as they danced in misty rain. His touch thawed her skin and her reserve slowly melted as she easily fell into a place from her long ago past. Where nothing could touch her. A world without pain and sorrow that encircled her.

"Kiss me Sam." Carter's words pleaded, it wasn't a matter of want, now he desperately needed her to.

A slow release came and her barriers crumbled, it surprised her how effortless it felt to not try to hold onto it. She didn't want to think about the price she'd pay afterwards. Her world was right there, a past, a future, absolutely everything. It all looked complete as their souls connected through their eyes to make one, a complete union that was bound together and always had been.

As the rain began to come down harder and harder, she pressed her lips to his and lost total control of every emotion. Any power she thought she could hold onto melted completely. There she was, in between crystal clear azure waters of the sound and the Atlantic Ocean, as if she'd waited so long just for this one more moment with him. It was difficult, but she finally pulled away to keep what little she had left intact.

"It's out of your hands now Sam, just give in to it. I still see it there in your eyes. You try to hide it and you do a damn fine job, but you can't anymore."

"It doesn't matter, Carter, it doesn't mean anything."

"It means everything. It means you should come home."

"I can't do that."

"Hold onto me Sam, and hold on tight this time." Carter's voice was a throaty pleading whisper, a promise that if she could do that, they would find their way.

"It's more complicated than that." How was she to explain what she'd dedicated her life to? Something he could never understand.

"It doesn't have to be. What is it going to take? What do I have to do, you name it."

"It isn't you, Carter, it never was." Sam could feel her insides literally turning back to stone. As if with each breath she took it filled her with the hardness she needed to resist any temptation.

"Come home with me."

"I can't." Her breath caught at the words her soul didn't want to say.

"Then let go of my heart." There was pain in his whisper.

****

The rain stopped by the time they met up with the others outside of the ferry terminal and Nikki and Shawna compared shopping bargains.

Michael proudly displayed his, a golf shirt with Port Royal Golf Course embroidered on it. "I'm wearing mine. If I couldn't get to my dream course, I could at least pretend. I tried for months and couldn't get a time on that course because of a big tournament."

"Then what did you cancel for? I thought you were supposed to golf today?" Carter asked.

"I didn't cancel. Trenton cancelled this morning."

Carter had assumed Michael cancelled to spend the day with them. He'd run into Brian Phelps early that morning who couldn't brag enough he was golfing at Port Royal with Trenton. He made an honest mistake when he asked the simple question, but as he looked to Sam, then to Michael, he took the opportunity when that door opened. She had to open her eyes, had to see things clearly, even if it meant he had to help her along.

Carter had to force his words out. "Trenton went golfing at Port Royal today, with Brian Phelps."

Sam looked from Carter to Michael, just as confused as any of them. Michael's smile faded ever so slight at the knowledge. He shrugged his shoulders casually as if it wasn't that big of a deal, but she saw the edge of disappointment.

What was she to say? She felt foolish and could feel reddening in her face that had nothing to do with the heat of the sun. There was an uncomfortable silence among the group for a brief moment. It was the first time Sam ever felt discomfort in their presence, the first time in the years she'd known them she felt like she didn't belong among them.

"I don't know what anyone wants to chase a little white ball around for anyway" Shawna broke the silence and the others easily and quickly followed suit.

"A beautiful day like this with all of Bermuda to see. Watching a tiny white blur sail through the sky doesn't sound very appealing to me." Richard put his arm around Sara. "We have a little more time, how about one more, a toast to the end of the day."

"I don't know, I may be toasted enough." Blake laughed.

"Blake can't have anymore. He's been hanging out at the bar while Nikki's been shopping and I'm afraid the ship may be overloaded if she buys anymore." Sara pointed out her bags.

They quietly and easily began to disperse. When the others either made one more stop for something or boarded the ferry early, Sam wandered off alone knowing Carter would follow. Took the first opportunity she had to let out Montezuma's revenge. They stood in beautiful surroundings, a poignant setting for the rage that was let loose.

"You did that on purpose. You, who profess to care so much about me wanted to make me look like an ass in front of everyone."

"No, Sam, I didn't make anyone look like an ass. Your fiancé' is the ass, and I wasn't the one to make him so. He does that all on his own."

"And you just couldn't stop yourself from proving a point. For what purpose?" She screamed.

"What the hell are you so mad at me for? I'm not the one who did it, I'm just the one who exposed him for what he is. Why aren't you over there on the golf course giving him hell? I'll give you a ride, I'd love to see it."

"It was embarrassing, Carter. You stood there and opened your mouth without regard to how it would make me look or feel. You embarrassed the shit out of me." Sam shouted the words, didn't care if anyone heard, the red of her face was a blaze of anger.

"You're not embarrassed by anything in front of your friends. It wasn't embarrassment Sam, it was shame. You are ashamed someone you're going to marry and spend the rest of your life with would treat Michael with such blatant disregard."

"I don't know the details and neither do you."

"The details? He made plans with Michael to golf, then cancelled to golf with someone he felt was more in his league."

"Why do you have to jump to conclusions and think Trenton is to blame for something here?"

"Maybe because Trenton is the only asshole who did something here." He expected her to be angry, even a little angry with him, but he didn't expect her to overlook the obvious.

"There's got to be an explanation."

"Then explain to me, Sam, I'm listening."

"I don't know." She threw her hands in the air, exasperated and confused.

"Want me to enlighten you?"

"Your enlightenment is far from impartial since you want me in your bed."

Carter's eyebrows rose with an incredulous look. "Is that what you think this is about? If that's all I wanted I didn't have to go through all this. This isn't some egotistical man thing, this isn't me against Trenton, this is about not wanting to watch my best friend ruin her life more than she already has."

"You don't know anything about my life. I have a damn good life."

He huffed with sarcasm. "Sam's perfect little world."

"Quit being so condescending about things you know nothing about."

"Let me guess and you can stop me anytime I'm wrong. Designer suits and imported leather briefcases by day and Gucci dresses and Tiffany jewels at night. You socialize with all the best people and before you consider adding any new friends to the guest list of parties the first question is what business they're in. It's how you equate acceptability. I bet the wedding guest list only includes the finest of society."

Sam was taken back to conversations with Harriet about the guest list. She'd given over control, so it was Harriet's doing that he was right. Wasn't it?

"Don't group me with your opinion of a certain class of people."

Carter couldn't stop the words from coming, everything he held back seemed to flow with no control. "Samantha Durham Edwards. You'll have the perfect little name too. Those highbrow types always introduce with a wife's maiden name so everyone will know they didn't marry beneath them. Does he ever just say your first name? Does he ever just call you Sam?"

"That means nothing, so he knows proper etiquette." She continued her defense.

He tried to keep his voice to a certain amount of calm. "The right genes. The right name. Someone emotionally unattached. Look at you Sam, you are your mother."

Sam's eyes blazed and it looked as if she were going to smack him. "How the hell did she get into this? You didn't even know my mother."

"I know I wasn't good enough for her. Tell me I'm wrong."

Sam didn't lie to him. "My mother had twisted notions. Yes, she thought I should be with someone else, but that didn't have anything to do with what I felt."

"What did you feel Sam? You never told me." Carter's voice boomed. "You lay in my bed, pretended to have a life with me, talked about a future. And at the same time kept me away from who you really were. Obviously I was never good enough for you just like I was never good enough for your mother."

"Our problems were entirely different Carter, it had nothing to do with it."

"Maybe that's what you wanted me to believe. That it was because I couldn't live in your world and you couldn't live in mine. That made it easy for you didn't it, because you never had to own up to the truth."

Nothing had been easy for her and it angered her more for him to think so, she'd been tormented by memories that drove her to madness. "Don't make up excuses, you walked out on me Carter. You walked out and I never saw you again."

"Face it Sam, I was never good enough, and Michael isn't good enough. Like you, Trenton wants to socialize with the proper people. Obviously Brian Phelps passes through to acceptability and Michael just doesn't have it."

"This has nothing to do with me, I didn't snub him."

"You might as well have, you're making excuses." Carter saw the hurt in her eyes but couldn't stop. "Was this all part of your plan? To start snubbing your friends? Are they the last to go to make your parents proud?"

"What are you talking about?"

"You've destroyed everything you were for them. So intent on making your parents proud and they're not even here. They're dead Sam..."

The harsh words spoken so loud they seemed to echo across Bermuda. He was angry, frustrated, and completely lost in trying to scream sense into her he didn't even care what he said anymore as he continued.

"But oh how proud they would be. Your father because you're exactly what he wished for, someone just like him. Your mother because you'll be marrying the type of man who can provide a lifetime of income and has the right name. It's a bonus he's an asshole. You've given your entire life over to people who never gave a shit for what you ever wanted."

"I was a young college girl, I didn't know what I wanted. Most people do what's natural and move into adulthood and accept some responsibility. And you can't understand that because you haven't done it yet, but don't make me feel guilty for it."

"You've been feeling guilty since your parents died, that's why you're trying to live the life they wanted you to. You may not have figured it out yet, but I have. You're doing it for them." Carter wondered if his words were sinking into her. He was so intent on getting them out, everything he'd always wanted to say to her, but she shielded herself at every turn.

"What makes you so sure I'm not doing it for me?"

"Then say the words, Sam, tell me you love him and that you're happy. Just say it out loud."

"I don't have to prove anything to you, you're not part of my life anymore." She continued to lash out just as he. Her heart beat so loud she could barely hear her words as everything inside her shook.

"And I never want to be part of that life. I love the girl with the flower in her hair who likes to dance in the rain. The one who can get up on stage and belt out a song to a cheering crowd or spread her arms wide and laugh like a child while flying downhill on the back of a moped. That's the girl I want in my life. But if you can sit there and try to rationalize, make excuses for Trenton for spitting in Michael's face, then I'm afraid she may be lost forever..."

The onslaught of emotions that spilled out couldn't be stopped.

"Inside you're looking for excuses but there is no reasonable explanation Trenton would go with an asshole like Brian, some stranger he just met who has six children he doesn't pay child support to but has a garage full of imported cars worth half a million dollars. For Christ sake, it isn't only the fact that Michael is one of your best friends, Trenton sat at his kitchen table and drank his wine. A particular wine Michael went out of his way to find because he knew it was a favorite. And not because he liked Trenton, but because that's the type of man he is. One of the best people anyone in the world would be blessed to know..."

"The facts are, Brian is Wall Street wonder boy and Michael is a blue-collar worker from Rhode Island. If that's not the stink of shit I don't know what is."

Sam continued to search for reason, until she talked to Trenton, she wouldn't know. Couldn't believe he'd be so insensitive but Carter's words, all of them, reverberated in her mind. Pounded her senses until she could take no more and turned away, didn't want to hear anymore as she tried not to let his words sink in.

"What's the matter Sam? Am I saying things you don't want to hear, or am I just confirming the ugly truth you already know? Trenton is nothing but a fucking self-serving bastard. And all you can do is stand here and tell me that's what you want for your life."

Carter too wanted to turn away from it all. Maybe he shouldn't have opened his mouth but she had to see what she was doing and he took a chance. A chance he now suffered the wrath for. He loved her too much to ignore his instincts, not only with a lover's passion, but as a best friend and it tore through his soul like fire.

"You've sold out Sam. If you hadn't, you'd be over on that golf course cursing him until there's no tomorrow instead of trying to find excuses. You don't need to explain it to me, I don't give a shit anymore. Look Michael in the face, someone who's been a brother to you, and tell him he isn't good enough for your kind." With deep aggravation that couldn't be resolved by screaming at one another, he walked away.

The day of companionship ended with isolation and Nikki's words rang through her head that things would change once she married Trenton. Although she tried to brush it off before, it was now painfully evident that's the way it was going to be, and she didn't have to wait for her wedding day to see it. From a distant point, she watched them all board the ferry together while she sat alone. No longer part of their group. They would slip right through her hands and be lost to her. This was the beginning as she watched it happen and felt powerless to avoid it.

CHAPTER 15

"I can't believe we left her." Nikki paced back and forth.

They stood underneath the cover of the port entrance building, the rain pelted down but the lightening had stopped. By the time they realized she wasn't on the ferry they were halfway across the sound. The others thought she boarded with Carter, Carter assumed she'd followed him after he left her. She had plenty of time, but never boarded. Now Nikki and Carter waited for her safe return with the others waiting for the first word inside.

"You should have gone back to get her Carter." Nikki looked half crazed with worry.

"Not only the fact she would have been gone, she has someone else for that. It isn't my job." He leaned against the wall. The ferry's had stopped operating for the night so his eyes peeled to every person who ran in from a taxi or across the way from a bus.

"Yeah, well, when I told Trenton she didn't come back with us he isn't worried at all. Said she goes off on her own all the time and comes back when she's ready. He's too busy to worry about her because he's up smoking a cigar somewhere and bragging about his wonderful day of golf. He's such a..." Nikki stopped herself, she didn't have to finish her sentence.

"But that's her choice, Nikki."

She swung her head around and stared at him. "That we both know is the wrong one. You, me and everyone else know exactly who she needs to be with."

"That isn't for us to decide, is it?" He still raged inside from the confrontation. In one moment she held him in her arms and he could see and feel everything that was meant to be. In the next she pushed him away and pretended her life was the way she wanted it to be.

That afternoon reminded him of the enormity of the agonized torment he'd lived with and his inability to love her enough for her to let go of her guilt. The frustrating part of it all was that he knew the truth. Knew she loved him and there wasn't a damn thing he could do about it.

Nikki looked at her watch, her voice desperate with concern now. "Carter, it's almost ten o'clock. Maybe we should call someone? Police? The hospital? Who do you call in Bermuda? Do they have 911? Missing persons?"

"She's fine, Nikki, why don't you go back inside and I'll wait."

"I'm scared, I'm scared for her to be out there somewhere by herself. What if..."

"Don't." His voice was strong and adamant, he didn't want to think about 'what ifs'. As angry as he still was, he'd never forgive himself if something happened to her.

She stayed for another hour of waiting until Blake came out to reassure her everything would be fine and drug her back inside. Nikki only agreed with promises from Carter that she would be the first to know when Sam returned.

It was after midnight when the rain finally stopped. Carter sat alone on a wall ledge in the open air, blocked by the shadows of night. She didn't see him, and he didn't make himself known when she stepped from the cab, paid her fare, and went onto the ship. Only when she was long gone did he finally go inside himself.

The rage she unleashed on Trenton was tenfold what she had that afternoon with Carter. One thing she determined in her time alone was that Carter had been right about a few things, one being it made her feel ashamed. And it was a feeling that had no place in a relationship.

"Michael even asked me how it was, he was fine with it, why aren't you?" Trenton tried desperately to defend himself but found it difficult with no viable excuse.

"Because it isn't the point of Michael being the decent human being he is, it's the point of you being an asshole and decided a stranger would be more beneficial to you in the long run."

"I told you, the others met Brian the other evening and suggested he come. There were only two spots open."

"You had plans with Michael, you could have said you had someone else to take or refuse the invitation if that wasn't an option."

"Do you know how difficult it was to get spots?"

Sam glared at him, a tangible rage surrounded her. "Golf spots. You defend yourself because being able to play there was more important than insulting someone."

Trenton sighed. No matter what he said it wouldn't help, he knew he'd been insensitive, but didn't know it would cause this kind of reaction. "I'm sorry, Samantha. I wasn't thinking."

"You said you had to screen your choices better. I assumed you meant because of their skills, I didn't know you meant the size of their wallets." Sam was so enraged she couldn't stop moving about the room, from one place to the next as she screamed.

Trenton calmly retrieved his Armani jacket from the chair. "Maybe I should leave for awhile until you calm down."

"That's going to be so long other passengers will be booked in this room by the time that happens."

It made her even angrier he wouldn't stay and fight and she picked up a pillow and threw it at the door when he left. It just happened to be the closest thing she could get her hands on, probably should have been thankful it wasn't anything breakable. But she wouldn't have cared if it was.

It didn't matter what he said, it was still wrong. And he made lame excuses. What bothered Sam most was that she felt no different than him. Didn't she do the same with her friends? Make excuses for the way he was at times?

Sam didn't like herself anymore than she did Trenton at that moment. There was sad realization that deep down, she knew it wouldn't change things between them, things would go on as planned. If she didn't marry Trenton her heart would be left exposed and vulnerable. Sam couldn't let that happen.

Carter sat at a far table in a quiet lounge. He watched undetected from shadowed darkness as Trenton came in, sat at the bar, and ordered a drink. He stared at him for a long time before he decided he had nothing left to lose.

"She's wicked when she's mad, isn't she?" Carter pushed his empty glass across to the bartender and refused another when offered. He wouldn't share a drink with this man he despised.

Trenton didn't look up when he spoke, his voice was hard, cold and knowing. "So we've both experienced it, don't mistake that to mean we have anything else in common."

"One thing is more than I want."

"I didn't realize until a few days ago you and Sam had so much of a past. If I were the jealous kind, I guess I would have let that bother me." Trenton sipped his drink casually.

Carter's words were flown with just as straight an arrow. "She doesn't love you and you know it."

"I'm secure with myself, I can live with that." He paused and looked into his glass, the amber liquid void of the distraction of ice and yet it didn't seem to be strong enough. "You don't think she loves you, do you? Sam doesn't love anyone."

"What if she does and you're keeping her from it?"

Trenton laughed. It was a mocking sound. "She doesn't love you."

"Why don't you let her go and we'll see." Carter spoke with a hint of challenge in his voice. It was far fetched to think it would happen, but it would be his only hope.

Trenton remained quiet as he finished his drink and asked for another, a double this time.

"What's the matter, not feeling so secure about yourself now?" Carter jabbed.

"What purpose would that serve? Even if I let her go, she wouldn't go to you."

They both knew it was probably the truth, whether she loved Carter or not.

"Do you know why she's marrying you?"

"I told you it didn't matter to me. I want Samantha in my life and I don't care her reasons or why's. I just know she wants to be there too." Trenton didn't look at him, had yet to look him in the eye and hadn't planned to. His focus was straight ahead or into his glass.

Carter looked at him for a long time. Thought it sad not because of him, but for Sam that he didn't know or care why she'd made the choice she had. He himself knew not only every physical detail but also every emotional haunt she suffered that made her do things she did.

"You're what her parents wanted, she wants to make two dead people proud because she didn't think she did that when they were alive. It's all she can think of, it consumes her to this day." If Carter thought he would get a reaction, he was wrong. Trenton's face never wavered, never changed.

He smiled then, more like a half smirk. "Then doesn't that make me the lucky one? I'm the one who can fulfill those needs."

Carter left before he resorted to physical violence. Couldn't look at Trenton and his smugness without wanting to slap him off the stool and that wouldn't solve anything. He debated doing it anyway.

He spent the night awake in a wet lounge chair underneath the stars. Couldn't bring himself to go back to his room and face the dark, felt suffocated and alone. By the time the sun rose, Carter was long gone on a moped driving around Bermuda as the colors formed to create a new day and he wanted to absorb it. Take it all with him when they left that afternoon. It was all he would have.

What hurt most was when he'd come to the conclusion that maybe it actually was what she wanted. A life with Trenton and all that life offered her. It wasn't her at one time, and in the beginning it probably wasn't her intention to change, but she lost herself somewhere in the process. Melded into it over time. Grown accustomed to the role she played both as Samantha Durham and soon to be Samantha Durham Edwards. All the years he thought of her as one person, not realizing it was possible for her to truly change into another.

What he thought were the deep psychologically rooted reasons that placed her there in the first place, to make her parents proud, had evolved into the person she now was. One that moved on to a different life without him, and it was difficult for him to face it. Being apart always made his heart feel better when he thought she loved him. And he had to think she truly did in her own way, but he wasn't what she wanted or needed now. Maybe at one time, but not now. Sam had moved on. It was time for him to do the same.

At noon that day, he stood on deck against the banister as the ship left St. George's harbor bound for home. Carter said goodbye to Bermuda and goodbye to any notion that she would find her way back into his life again. There was pain, but there was also a freedom as an invisible weight lifted. A smile of resignation crossed his lips. He'd fought a good battle, still loved her and always would, and his smile was for her. She'd won.

"That kind of smile makes me think all is well in your world." Nikki stepped next to him as they watched the square of St. George diminish in the distance as they sailed through the small channel bound for open sea.

"Finally, I think it is."

Nikki's heart lifted. "Does that mean what I think it means? You and Sam come through yesterday all in one piece? See, I knew all you both had to do was hash it out once and for all. I knew if you just..."

Carter stopped her quickly. "Maybe you're right, but not in the way you think. Maybe all we had to do was hash it out once and for all, to put it behind us."

"Behind you?" Her voice shot out.

"This is it, Nikki, this is the end for me. All of you can stop trying to intervene on our behalf. There will never again be a Carter and Sam. No more setups, no more secret planning's of surprises when I'm at your house and you'd forgotten Sam was coming in for the weekend. I know it means things will change, and maybe they have to. I can't live the rest of my life waiting for Sam, none of us can."

"But..." Nikki shook her head, couldn't believe what she was hearing.

"We'd do ourselves justice and leave the past where it belongs and move on. She has, why can't we?" Carter looked to her with sad satisfaction within himself.

"But she hasn't, she's just being stubborn, she's just..." Nikki didn't want him to stop fighting now, not when they were so close. She'd seen it, felt it between them.

"It's over, Nikki. You'll always have her and I envy you that. But I have to realize that I won't, and I'm finally to the point that I have to be okay with that. I think I am."

"You're just going to give up?"

"Give up what? I can't give up something I don't have. I lost her a long time ago and she has the life she wants. Now I have to find mine." The finality in his voice couldn't be denied. It hurt him to say the words but it gave them credence to say it out loud to someone else.

Others slowly joined them at the banister. There was sadness in the air between them. They all knew whatever happened in Bermuda to bring them all together, would be left behind in Bermuda, they couldn't take it with them. All of them watched the island fade into oblivion as the ship pulled further and further out to sea until you could see it no longer. As if it never existed.

CHAPTER 16

The last day on the ship was a full day at sea, it gave them time to relax and enjoy being with everyone for one last day. There was no outward sign of the previous day's incident. Except that Sam couldn't stand to look at Trenton's face so he made himself scarce.

As a group they took advantage of the short time left. Participated in various activities offered or nothing at all, just spent the little time they had left with one another. Including Carter and Sam, who joked and teased back and forth in their normal way. There was no anger. No animosity. They were the friends they always would be in a comfortable circle that still had changes to get through, but in the meantime, they would enjoy it as it were.

Thirty or so alumni classmates gathered in the very aft of the ship for casual dining that evening on pizza, hamburgers and light fare. Watched as yet another sun set into the sea and sat around the tables for hours. As the ship bound for home and night moved on, no one wanted it to end. They all mingled together to exchange addresses, promises to keep in touch, and talked of the next time, someone was already planning another. Even Mindy joined in the fun. None of them had seen her since the night she threw herself at Carter but embarrassment stopped her from even talking to him now.

Sam hadn't had an opportunity to be alone with Michael that day, so she approached him through the crowd when he stood across the other side of the deck. But he would accept no apology from her.

"Don't apologize. I'll never hold you responsible for anything Trenton does." To assure her, Michael put his arm around her, pulled her close. "Besides, I wouldn't have missed that day for anything. Probably the last time all eight of us will ever be together like that again."

She couldn't deny he was right. For the longest time she remained there in his arms, in the warmth of friendship, brotherhood, he offered.

"Hey you two, people are going to start talking if you don't break your little love fest up." Nikki called from across the way and they all laughed.

"Sara?" Carter called to her teasingly. "You'd better take a picture, I don't think you have one like that."

Sara was before them with her always ready camera, had been a fanatic that evening as picture after picture was taken.

Michael talked through gritted teeth. "When we get home I'm going to look like a cartoon character to Amy. A big mouth and teeth. I think it's permanent."

They both burst into laughter. The picture Sara got was of two people who laughed naturally, it would become one of her favorites.

"I can't wait to print out all my pictures." She took one more of the group, one of many she'd taken over the week. Then she handed her camera to Richard. "Take a picture of all the girls, Richard, the four of us."

"I like this job a lot better than taking a picture of Blake or Carter." He stood and waited for them to gather.

Carter looked offended. "I didn't hear you mention Michael's name, why not him?"

"That's a given. That bald head of his puts out too much of a glare for the flash."

Carter looked on as the four women laughed and smiled, playfully fought and scrambled over who would stand where. When Sam looked up he caught her eye and there was laughter in them. It was here, among these people, where she was the happiest. He could see it, could feel it, but stopped himself from pretending that she ever would. She would forever be able to cast him even the smallest of glances that sent his heart reeling. His smile faded as he reminded himself of his decision.

Sam and Shawna had been standing by the rail and Nikki and Sara joined them, and after a few moments of playfulness, they finally settled into a position. All their arms were around each other, their smiles and laughter genuine and not posed as Nikki whispered her breasts were bigger than the others and the camera flashed.

"What kind of paper are you going to be using, Sara? Be sure to let me know so I can buy stock in that company." Sam moved her head closer to Shawna as yet another flash went off.

"I have some beauties on here. We'll all get together and have a picture party when I'm done with them." Sara looked at her camera she'd become so attached to, glanced through the most recent pictures taken.

"A new reason for a party? I'm always game for that." Shawna commented quickly.

"You have enough that by the time you print them all out it will be great to see what we all used to look like. I can marvel at myself in a two-piece bathing suit! By that time I'll probably be too old to wear one at all."

"I'll have them done by the time we get to the summer rental house."

"Why don't we come back here next year? We could rent a house on the island, the kids would love it."

They started talking about their lives, summers together and parties to view the pictures. Things she would miss, things she didn't feel a part of. Sam would try to hold onto them for as long as she could, maybe the girls would get together for an occasional weekend or two, but she wouldn't be on their family vacations. Wouldn't share a house at the ocean every summer, or join in their Christmas parties.

When she discreetly moved away from the crowd, no one noticed when she left, no one but Carter who followed her up the stairs to the top deck where the laughter from below could still be heard in the otherwise quiet night. It all went on without her. Just as it would.

"Kind of hard, isn't it?" Carter said, knew exactly what she was thinking and feeling. "I feel it too. It's hard to be part of something for so long and know you really aren't anymore. We have no children to share birthdays and we won't be going on summer vacations to the beach. It won't be us they call when Richard Jr. gets his drivers license or someone has their first date, first prom, goes off to college. Think we'll eventually be the one's who get the Christmas card every year?"

She was surprised he'd felt the same. "You'll always be part of it, it's me that won't belong. We all know Trenton isn't the type to sit in a rowboat on a lake and enjoy it. He's not 'one of the boys'."

"Neither one of my wives fit in, and I don't imagine I'll find anyone who will. It's difficult to bring an outsider into something like that, all kinds of things someone on the outside just doesn't understand." Carter looked out to sea, couldn't quite face her.

"I think others feel jealous, threatened by it somehow. It's something unique not everyone can share."

Sam knew it, would miss it. In the back of her mind still harbored hope it would always stay just as it was, but knew better. The winds of change that blew across her face solidified it. But she wouldn't turn any of it over completely until forced, Sam didn't know that was just about to happen.

"Odd isn't it? The first two, from the very beginning, and yet we're the one's feeling the outsiders." Carter said.

It was as if the common ground that bound them all together, crumbled beneath them. But the others had built up a strong foundation without them and would be spared the fall.

"Do you ever wonder what would have become of all of them had we not gotten together?" It was something she'd thought of before but would never truly know the answer. "I mean, they all pretty much met because of us. Shawna was my friend, Michael yours. We rented the house and needed roommates and that's how the others came along."

"Maybe that was the only purpose of us being together, just to bring all of them together. Pawns in the hands of fate." It could possibly be true, and they'd finished their task long ago and he just held on long after his time. If that were his only purpose, it still didn't make it any easier to let go now.

"Carter, you said a lot of things and..."

"None that I'll apologize for if that's what you're getting at." He teased.

Sam laughed and shook her head. "I didn't expect you would, and that's not why I brought it up." She paused and spoke again as if she asked for forgiveness for her actions. "I've come to see that you understand more than I do. Maybe I'm doing it for reasons that don't appear normal, but I don't have the courage to do it any other way."

"I knew a girl once who had the courage to visit an angry old man who sat in a fish hut all day and called her names."

"Skippy McGee." She said softly, hadn't thought of him in a long time. "How is Skippy?"

"Older but still just as mean. Funny though, I'll see him sometimes on the pier and he looks at me different. Doesn't look like he wants to throw a fish knife at me anyway. As if he understands what I was going through when it was obvious you weren't coming back. I never thought I'd share anything in common with Skippy McGee, but I guess I do. Guess those stories of the only woman he'll ever love leaving the Cape, are true after all."

Sam was quiet for a while before she spoke. "I might have had the courage then, but I surely wouldn't have the courage now to go back and see him. Not even my chocolate cheesecake muffins would do me good. He always said I didn't belong, I've proven him right about me, haven't I?"

"I guess you have." Carter's statement held a tone of acceptance. He wouldn't argue it didn't have to be that way, wouldn't try to make her see things she didn't want to see.

Sam didn't expect him to agree with her. She watched his face as he looked out towards the water and noticed an odd change in Carter. A distance about him. Almost as if she could actually see him pulling away from her. She didn't like the feeling it gave her, all of a sudden there was a desperate need to pull him back from where she felt he was going.

In an attempt to avoid it, she tried to joke. "I guess if I ever find myself back at the fish hut he'll be throwing those fish knives you always worried about at me."

"That won't happen." He paused then wanted to make it clear what he meant. "You'll never find yourself back at the fish hut to worry about it."

In that moment Sam knew she was right about what she'd seen from him a moment ago. He was letting go and it scared her, she could almost physically feel him leaving her, and they weren't touching in any way. When he finally turned and faced her she knew before he even said the words.

"I've come to a decision, Sam."

"I'm not sure I want to know what it is." It wouldn't make a difference, she wouldn't be able to avoid the words that would come.

"I'm giving up." He sighed deeply. "You win."

"I think we got carried away with our emotions in that argument and it got out of hand. It certainly wasn't a battle anyone could win. You were right, I should have been mad at Trenton more than you and..." In a nervous chatter she wanted to ramble on but he stopped her.

"The argument has nothing to do with it. It's been a battle for me since I walked out of that door in Virginia when your parents died. A battle of me against the new Samantha who I refused to believe existed. I've been trying to find something that isn't there. Maybe I never wanted to see the truth, that was my fault, but I do now and I can't do anything about it. So I'm saying goodbye."

"You make it sound so final."

"Rather than be rushed at the port tomorrow it's why I followed you. I wanted to explain why you wouldn't hear from me again. And tell you to do the same. I don't see any need for us to ever contact each other."

"We'll see each other." The fear was present in her voice as she refused to believe his words.

"I can't, Sam."

"Why? We're friends, Carter. Friends call each other, why can't we just go on like we've always done?" She couldn't accept it, wouldn't accept that he was walking out of her life completely. "We'll see each other at Michael's, or Nikki's, or when..."

"No, we won't. I can't do it anymore." Carter pulled her to him. They were face to face, his voice a whisper of finality. "Don't look behind you this time, Sam, I won't be there."

"What if I call you anyway? Would you hang up?"

"You've gone on with your life, just let me go on with mine." His voice reflected the sadness in his eyes. "It's time for us to say goodbye."

Sam reached up and touched his face. Familiar skin that seamlessly blended with hers and she noticed he still had that tiny freckle just in front of his ear. She ran her thumb over the small cleft in his chin and noticed it wasn't as pronounced as it used to be. There were so many things she felt desperate to see, touch, and feel so she would remember it forever in case he stayed true to his word.

She always took for granted he'd be there. Somewhere. Even if only in the background, but always within reach. Was she ready for him not to be? Was she so selfish to think she'd have a choice? He meant every word and it scared her, too many things were happening at once and she wasn't prepared. She couldn't say the words, wouldn't say goodbye.

"I can't understand this, I can't let you do this."

"It's the only thing left for me to do. I can't break down that wall you've built up to block me out, all I can do is accept the person you've become. So I'll walk away from you, but this will be the last time."

Sam brushed her fingers across his mouth. How desperately she wanted him. Needed him. Would for the rest of her life. "Why this drastic solution, what's wrong with staying the friends we are. How are you going to remember to send birthday cards?"

"I'll figure it out on my own."

"How are you going to pick out the kids presents on your own?" She worried about every little thing. He couldn't do those things on his own, she always called him and reminded him, told him what kind of gift to get and where to get it.

"I'll manage."

He tried to pull away and she wouldn't let him. If this were the last time she'd ever have him in her arms she wasn't letting go so easy. Though she didn't know how hard she was making it for him.

Sam couldn't stop the tear that escaped and Carter kissed it softly away. The feel of his tender lips consoling and she reached behind his neck and held him there to her cheek. No. She screamed to herself. Don't let this be happening. Don't let this be real.

"Oh, Sam, when you get to where you're going, I want nothing but happiness there for you, you know that. But don't think you're going to walk down the aisle and find something worth having at the end of it. Don't marry Trenton. Find that girl again who can dance in the rain, that's all I'm asking of you, but find her for you, no one else."

"She only comes out with you, you can't just leave me hanging. How am I going to find her on my own?" She sounded despondent and felt immediately cold and alone when he pulled his face away from the closeness of her cheek where it had given her warmth.

"I wish I knew." Carter felt the softness of her face, his voice just as desperate. "God, I wish I knew."

"Don't leave me, Carter."

"You left a long time ago, and as much as I've prayed and hoped, you're not coming back."

"I love you." She'd finally said the words, whispered them in frantic desperation. Isn't that what he always wanted to hear? Wouldn't that make him stay close to her, even if only on the outskirts of her life?

Hearing her speak the words was bittersweet. At one time in their lives, he thought hearing them would get them through anything, but this was a different time in their lives. Carter knew in his heart he couldn't help her. And that's what hurt the most.

"The saddest part is, I know that. But loving me isn't enough for you."

"Can't it be enough for you?"

"Not when it means knowing the woman who loves me is spending her life with another man. You merely want our lives to go on as they have. Me calling every now and then about something stupid just to hear your voice, you calling for the same reason and pretending you have a viable excuse. The whole time you're married to someone else, sleeping in his bed, having his children. No, Sam, your love isn't enough for me under those terms."

Carter pulled away from her. It would take nothing for him to fall back into it all over again just when he arrived to the point of moving on. His reserve could melt away in seconds.

"Wait, Carter, not like this. I'm not ready for something like this." She felt as if she were going to have some sort of panic attack. Her heart raced as her mind tried to race faster to know the words that would make him stop what he was doing.

"You'll never be ready for something like this and I've come to see I can't force you to be ready for anything else. I can't stop you from going in the direction you're headed. I can't do it, and I can't keep pretending that one day you'll miraculously come to see things differently."

"But you gave me no warning, you can't just spring this on me. Can't we say in a month we'll go our separate ways? Six months? A year?"

"This is it, Sam. This is where we go on with our lives, and its two different paths." He kissed two fingers and placed them on her cheek as he left. "I've got to go, there's a long road ahead of me."

****

When morning came she heard Trenton's muffled sounds of conversation on his cell phone but didn't open her eyes. Sleep eluded her all night and she'd only fallen into it lightly at the normal time she woke. Now as the rising sun started to seep into the room, and she woke fully, her heart ached with pain. She immediately wanted that feeling of limbo in Bermuda back. Somewhere in between reality of her past and reality of her future, it lay there in the Atlantic Ocean and she couldn't reach far enough to grasp it again.

"Okay, I'll see you later then." Trenton said to someone unknown.

"Anxious?" Her voice held a smart tone as she rose, didn't want to face the day, or him.

"Needs to be a much stronger word, anxious doesn't do it justice. We'll be called soon, are you going to get up? We have an early flight and mother is expecting us this afternoon when we get in."

"I'm not going to your mothers."

Her statement was direct. She didn't want to deal with Trenton that morning, certainly the last person she wanted to see was his mother. He watched her back as she disappeared into the bathroom.

There were many hugs, kisses and tears as they gathered outside the doors after disembarkation and said their farewells. Trenton was quick with a few handshakes while it took Sam much more time.

She'd kissed all the others and held onto Sara longer, her feelings of something amiss still plagued her. "It's been a long time since I've come to visit, why don't I call you in a few weeks and I'll come for a weekend."

"We're always there. Come anytime, Sam, you know that."

Sam hugged her again. Sara was the smallest of them all, a tiny petite thing that felt like a child in her arms. "If you need me before then, you call."

If Sam had any doubts Carter would stick to his word, they disappeared when he said goodbye to the others and began to walk towards his cab. Not even a backward glance in her direction. She couldn't stop herself from going after him, called to him when he was just about to open the cab door and he sighed deeply and turned to her slowly when she reached him.

Sam looked into his eyes and wouldn't accept it to be the last time ever. "I don't know if I can do this. I don't know if I can just leave it like this."

"Then get in the cab with me, it's your only other option. I'll take nothing less." He knew by the look in her eyes it wasn't going to happen. She would leave her past right there on the dirty cement of the port and go on, just as she always did when she left him.

Only this time, he would too. What they shared had vanished. He could no longer fantasize of the possibility of ever getting it back so he gave up the fight. Carter nodded over towards the limousine where Trenton paced.

"You'd better go, Edwards is waiting."

Sam looked over and saw the obvious impatience then turned back to Carter. Ironic it was the same thing he'd said so long ago at the Durham Estate in Virginia when he'd left. Only that time it had been Trenton's father who waited for her. That moment changed their lives, just as this would, her second chance, her last chance. As much as her heart ached with searing pain, she would walk away knowing she loved him.

There was so much in the air between them. A kiss, an embrace, something more than either of them had the courage for. Sam searched his eyes for hesitation and saw none. He gave her no hope he would change his mind.

"I meant what I said, Carter, I do love you."

"If that were enough we wouldn't be standing here like this saying goodbye for the last time."

"I won't say it," she said softly, "I can't."

"Then I will." He paused as the word came slowly. "Goodbye."

He turned away and she stopped him once more. Prolonged it, couldn't let him slip away so quickly. Her voice portrayed the hurt she felt.

"After all these years, all we've meant to each other. How can that be so easy for you? You tell me you're leaving my life forever, never going to see me again, and you say it so casually."

"It's easy for me to say goodbye to Samantha. I lost Sam a long time ago." To him, she was two separate people. Carter summoned up all he had, knew it would only make it worse on him to taste her love one more time. He placed his hand on her cheek and pulled her slowly to him. Didn't kiss her directly on the mouth, instead touched her soft cheek with his lips and lingered there. Afterwards he moved to her lips, placed the softest of kisses there, as gentle as the breeze that blew around them. "That was for Sam."

She watched as he got into the cab and never looked back.

PART THREE

The Long Road Home

CHAPTER 17

Sam stepped back into her life. Trenton was comfortable to be home and back to work, Sam unsettled. Not even a grueling work schedule would calm her, it was the only thing that ever had, but it wasn't enough now. The more she took on, the unhappier she became. It used to fill her mind, fill her life, now it filled nothing but time and it seemed there was so much time to fill. Twenty-four hours in a day, seven days a week, was quite a bit to find something to occupy her mind.

Even to have Max Maines, Pig man, in her office, only gave her a little satisfaction. Her mind was so wrapped up, the reward she felt was minimal. And she'd performed and negotiated the best she ever had, could almost see her father beaming at her ability to triumph. And it had been so easy.

She insisted on meeting with him alone. Spalding, Trenton, and all the others who would normally gather around a conference table were banned. As luck would have it, she had two things at a major advantage. The first, she was a woman and he trusted her, he was confident he would be lucky and get the deal he wanted, because she couldn't possibly know what she was doing. The second factor, he desperately wanted, needed, the real estate holdings she offered.

He had two things to a major disadvantage. The first, she couldn't stand the sight of him. The second, he caught her at a bad time. She could have been kinder, could still have negotiated a deal more beneficial to her side and been satisfied with that, but she wanted more. She went for the jugular.

In order for him to complete the deal, he would need to purchase it in portions. For what he wanted, it amounted to over ten million. She told him she wasn't sure, but they could probably come to an agreement and work it so that he could purchase it all now, with her company holding onto a portion.

They talked for almost five hours behind closed doors. Of course she had to disagree with things and pretend it was tough, and they rewrote it several times and he had to get information faxed in. By the time they were done he thought that everything there had actually been his idea. The deal she offered was exactly what he needed.

She had all the documents prepared immediately. Of course, she had the authority to ratify the contract, but she pretended it wasn't a good idea that he sign it right away, she should probably get the others approval. And he should probably get his lawyers to look it over. He was so afraid of losing it if he waited, he couldn't sign it fast enough.

Max stood up and stretched. He assembled his papers together that had been all over the conference table, and then he was ready to leave. In his mind, he wanted to find more stupid women to do business with.

"Well, you weren't as tough as all the talk I've heard, guess it takes a real man to face you. Now that I've cracked that hard nut, do I get the sweet meat inside?" He laughed. That disgusting laugh and snort as his belly shook, like a pig that found the gem of an apple in the mud. And Sam just smiled on the inside. "But don't worry, a little more time and you'll get better."

"I call it practice." She answered with an odd smile. "You might want to remember those words. Just so you know that the next time we meet up, I might be a little tougher."

As she watched him walk out the door, she was content to know that he didn't even know what hit him and she would love to be there when he found out. By the time she was done, now the contract ratified, she basically owned him and everything else he owned. Plus the fact, in the long run, he would pay ten times more than what the real estate holdings could possibly be worth in ten years time.

It was a couple days later when Trenton walked into her office. Her head was buried in papers and she didn't look up when he walked straight to her desk, his voice agitated and nervous.

"What the hell did you do?"

"What the hell are you talking about?" She said calmly as she continued writing.

"Max Maines just called and he's screaming, said he feels like he sold his soul to the devil."

"Devils a good name. At least he won't call me sweet meat anymore. And I didn't buy his soul, I don't want it."

"He's threatening to sue." Trenton leaned on her desk now, tried to get her attention but she still didn't look up.

"I'm thorough in my work, there are no loose ends here Trenton, it isn't like I have his signature on a napkin. Not only did he sign a contract, he has no grounds."

"Says it was done under duress."

"Let him try to prove to a judge and jury that I held his big Pig ass down and forced him. Besides, he won't sue. It would be too embarrassing for him to admit in court he was merely beaten at his own game by a woman." She flipped over the page of her yellow pad and began writing on another.

"Do you think we should meet with him?" The call made him nervous.

"I don't want to play with him anymore." She finally looked up. "Is that all? I'm a little busy here."

He left her office. She looked calm, and it had been her deal, he had to trust her. This wasn't his territory, but he was going to go over the contract to find out what the hell was going on. All she'd told him was the deal had been made and Max was more than happy about it when he left.

By the time Spalding returned from a trip and walked into her office a week later, she was more willing to let Pig man's balls loose.

Spalding came in and sat on the corner of her desk. "Trenton tells me you've been a bad girl, said you haven't been playing well with others."

"You know better than to believe that." She said it with feigned innocence.

He laughed. "As much as I love this deal, and would be a fool to pass it up, I have to say, it's even more over the top than I could have ever done. A little tough to say the least."

"He had a great disadvantage, I don't like him."

"You know I stand behind you and your decisions 100 percent, anything you do, and this is just my opinion, but I have to go with Trenton on this one. Maybe we should consider renegotiating, we wouldn't sacrifice anything, but the decision is entirely yours. Will the contract stand up in court? Probably. Is it worth the hassle?" He left that question unanswered and waited for her reply.

She waited a few moments. "I guess I've had what fun I could." Sam finally consented. "But I won't do it, he isn't much of a challenge and he'll bore me now. I'll draw something up to take myself out of it and give you the power to renegotiate. You can decide what you want to do and I really don't care what it is."

Satisfied, he walked to the door, and then stopped before he actually walked out. His voice was only half teasing. "Samantha? About that paper? No offense, but you don't have to draw anything up, I'll get Peter to do that."

"You wouldn't have anything to worry about, I like you Spalding."

"This is proof of why I pity the men you don't."

She thought it would be enough to bring her out of her slump but work still frustrated her, and the wedding plans with Harriet became unbearable. Sam let her have her way on most things, but when she said she'd planned for a white netting on the ceiling of the church with lights underneath, Sam lost her cool.

"Cancel it," she stated.

"I can't. It's being done as a favor, I practically had to beg for it."

"I don't care if you got down on your knees to beg, I'll not get married in a circus tent." Sam's voice rose in protest, she put no thought into being more tactful, Harriet wouldn't have listened no matter how she formed her words.

"Think of how beautiful it will be, Samantha, like clouds that..."

"If I wanted clouds I'd get married outside. It's already over the top, if you have a circus tent you might as well have a hotdog cart and clowns. Maybe that's what I want." Sam had enough of the entire thing.

Harriet threatened to make her do the rest herself and Sam knew she was bluffing, couldn't imagine her giving up control, even to the bride. If she did, Sam would take over and do just that. Hotdog stands and clowns just for spite.

Before Sam had the opportunity to call Sara and plan a visit, Sara called herself with news, she revealed her doctor discovered possible breast cancer right before they'd left on the cruise.

"Oh, Sara, I knew something was wrong, why didn't you tell me?"

"We wanted to wait until it was confirmed. No sense everyone worrying about something we weren't sure of ourselves."

She explained the process she would go through, an operation then chemotherapy and radiation afterwards. The prognosis for a recovery was unknown yet, they would know more after they operated. Sam knew what she needed to do and didn't hesitate.

"I'll be there. Someone needs to take care of you, someone needs to be there to help. I'll come."

"Sam, I wouldn't ask you to do that."

"I know you wouldn't, that's why I'm doing it anyway." It was easy for Sam to take an active role in her care. Sam decided it's where she needed to be. "I'll come for as long as you need, doesn't matter how long."

"You have..."

"I have to be there, nothing else matters right now."

It wasn't an option Sam had to ponder over, there wasn't a question in her mind as she made immediate plane reservations and began to pack.

"How long do you plan on being gone?" Trenton asked when he saw the large suitcase being packed instead of the small one she always packed for short trips.

"I can't say. A week, a month, two months, maybe more."

"I can understand you feel like you have to be there, but why can't any of the others help? Why does it have to be you?"

Sam talked as she went into the bathroom to get her personal items. "They'll be there at times, but they have families, Trenton, their own kids, jobs, it isn't as easy for some people to stop their lives no matter how badly they want to."

"It isn't easy for you either."

"Easier than most." Sam stepped into the doorway and stared at him. "I'm not that imperative, we pay hundreds of thousands of dollars in salaries to hundreds of people, surely I won't be that missed at the office."

"That's a ludicrous statement, you know…"

"I know what I have to do, and the office and work is the last thing on my mind. If it can't survive without me, when I get back I'll fire all those hundreds of people and find people who can run a business when one person is missing."

Trenton still didn't understand why she couldn't go for a few days and return. "What about the wedding plans? Things have to be decided."

"And we both know your mother is very capable of handling that job. More than capable and she prefers to do it on her own anyway." She placed more things in her suitcase and glared at him. "Why are you trying to fight me on this?"

"Of course I'm not trying to be disagreeable, I understand why you feel like you have to be there. I'm not that callous." Trenton walked over and took her in his arms. "No more questions, you go, and return when it suits you. Let me know how it's going."

Trenton was as understanding and patient as he could be, on the outside anyway. Thought it was important she perceive him that way because he'd noticed the difference in her since they'd returned. She threw herself into work just as hard, if not harder than before, but she was restless. An agitation of some kind he couldn't figure out. It worried him, but he said nothing else about it.

CHAPTER 18

Sam moved into Sara and Richard's home for the duration, whatever that was going to be, and everyone came to be there for the operation. Including Carter, who said not one word to her and only stayed the day while the others stayed a few. Then they all returned to their own responsibilities of their own families. It was great comfort for them to know Sam would be there to stay for follow up of chemo and radiation treatments.

As for the prognosis, nothing was guaranteed and she still had a fight ahead of her. So small and petite, Sara always seemed to her the frailest of them all. Sam prayed for the best but often wondered how she was going to fight something of this magnitude, but Sara would expose a side she would never have guessed.

It didn't take long to settle in. Only took them a few days to get into a routine that worked for all and things began to flow as smoothly as they could under the circumstances. All of them sat down with the doctor as he explained the process and they all knew what to expect as Sara got weaker and weaker from aggressive treatment. But Sam had never seen someone so brave. No matter how she was feeling, she always had a smile on her face when someone walked in the room, an especially large one for a young five year old son who was confused by what was happening to his mother.

"Come here baby boy." The words came slowly, Sara's throat a burn of fire.

Richie had been standing in the hallway merely peeking into the crack of the door when she'd seen him. He crept in to stand beside her and it took her a few moments to hold her hand out for him.

"Hey mommy. Were you sleeping?"

"Just resting." Her voice a throaty rasp, her smile not forced but it took great effort.

"Aunt Sam and I are going to the park when daddy gets home. She said she'll throw ball with me, said she used to be able to throw a ball just like Cal Ripkin."

She huffed with a small air of laughter, Sam had never picked up a baseball in her life, but she didn't reveal that to her son. "Don't be surprised if she's a little rusty."

"Can you come today?"

"Not today baby." She answered a son who was fanatic about the sport of baseball. Wished it could be her in the park but it would have to wait.

"Richie?" Sam's whisper came down the hall then entered the room when she saw the open door. "I'm sorry, Sara, I'm getting the hang of it but I lost him again."

"He's fine."

Sam could see she would sit there awake for the rest of the night if it would make her son happy. Richie didn't like to see her sleep, it scared him.

"Richie, let's go get ready for the park and let your mom rest. Your dad will be home in just a little while and she'll need some energy to visit with him too."

Reluctantly, he would leave. With great care he stepped on his stool next to the bed and kissed her gingerly on the cheek.

"I love you, mommy."

"I love you too, Richie."

Although she'd offered however much money they could want, pride wouldn't let them accept a dime.

"I'd take all you had if it would fix this, but it won't." Richard told her when she made the offer. "You being here helps us so much, that's all we need."

With good medical insurance they would be fine financially. And his company was very understanding, very generous in giving him liberal leave to use whenever he needed, which he used to take Sara to doctor's appointments and a few days here and there when he just needed to be home with her.

Sam always took care of Sara until early evening came when Richard returned from work and wanted to take over. Other than that, she took care of the household and Richie who surprised her with something new every day. Never being around children for any length of time, in the beginning Richie intimidated her. Boisterous and outrageous he was merely being a five year old little boy with boundless energy. And knowing how important a child's attitude and vision on life was, she didn't want to say or do the wrong thing. She also knew she was being ridiculous about the issue when she had to correct him or discipline him and constantly worried if she did it the right way. If she didn't, it could affect him later on in life.

Sam knew she was being overly sensitive. Would he suffer later because she wouldn't let him have cake for breakfast? Then he taught her it wasn't so bad to have cake for breakfast. Why not? She had no logical explanation so one evening a week they would make a cake. Complete with icing, sprinkles, whatever they wanted, and eat it for breakfast the next day.

They became an unlikely pair. He as important to her as she was to him. Sam came to know every little detail about him. Little signs of when he was tired or hungry, bigger one's like the way he'd become anxious when Sara was asleep too long, or angry while playing sometimes and she knew he needed to see his mother. Even if Sara were sleeping they'd peek into the room quietly, it would pacify him until she woke.

He too seemed to know her in an odd way. Like in the evening when Richard came home it was a little relief to have the break and she'd sit on the porch and read. It was the only time of the day Richie was quiet and still. Would entertain himself beside her with a coloring book or another toy.

A few times when he'd walk into the room quietly, and she hadn't known he was there, she suspected he'd seen her guard down for just a moment. He'd come to her and pat her hand. Repeat words she often told him.

"Have to be happy, today is a good day, Aunt Sam."

She'd pull him into her lap and hold him there so close to her. "It is a good day, isn't it?" It was always a good day when Sara was alive.

They came to know and trust one another. Depend on one another. The situation gave them a need for each other and they formed a lasting bond that would be with them for many years to come.

Sam had been there from the very beginning, so the gradual change in Sara's appearance was something she'd seen happen. It didn't affect her like it did the others when they visited. Nikki was shocked and broke down the first time she saw her a few weeks after the operation. They'd had a nice visit and waited until she was alone with Sam before the tears came.

"She looks so sick. Sam, she looks like death."

"The outside fools you. She's strong on the inside and that's what counts. She's going to get through this." Sam held her tight for the comfort Nikki needed, she was always the one who appeared strong, a role that fit her well.

"You and Richard, even Richie, you all walk around and joke and laugh as if it's nothing, and she looks like she's on the verge of death."

"Normalcy is what helps us get through this. Living with it day in and day out, you have to laugh, you have to joke. If not, you'd completely break down. And you know me, I'm good at putting on a great outside face when the inside is falling apart, it's my area of expertise." Sam commented with honesty. "In fact, I pride myself on my chameleon talents."

Nikki chuckled as the tears flowed down her face. "I wasn't surprised when you decided to do this. I know it wasn't your reason, but I know it must help to keep Carter off your mind. Blake told me he's been working hard, bidding on some major projects, even in different states."

They all knew what Carter's position was. He told them all at great insistence so they would take him seriously and not try to force the two together as they had in the past.

It was just as difficult for the others to see Sara and the changes she'd gone through. They saw what Nikki did. Someone who appeared to be on deaths door and they could only think the worst. Sam found herself always cheering them up before they left, everyone but Carter.

When Carter came to visit he sat in Sara's room for the whole day, took Richie out that evening to a ballgame and not spoken to her once. There wasn't even a simple greeting of 'Hello'. Carter treated her as if she didn't exist and Sam stayed out of his way.

She escaped to the front porch as he was saying his goodbye's. A mixture of anger and understanding flooded her emotions as he stepped out of the front door, glanced in her direction, then descended down the stairs to the sidewalk. Halfway to his car he turned and came back and stood quietly before her. Sam waited for words that finally came.

"Thank you for everything you're doing. Sara needs you. As much as I love both Nikki and Shawna, they aren't strong enough for this type of thing. Hell, I wouldn't be strong enough for it. I know how hard it must be on you."

"No, Carter, you don't know," was all she answered.

He looked to eyes that held nothing but hope and faith when she was around the others, but he could see beyond that. Could see what it was doing to her. For his own survival he had to walk away, even though it killed him to walk away from her when she needed him so much.

On his following visits it wasn't repeated. He never said another word to her and she gave him space with Sara. Afterwards he would spend time with Richie and most times they went to a baseball game, one evening Richie wanted her to go with them.

"Please, Aunt Sam?" Then he looked to Carter. "She can go, can't she?"

Sam answered him quickly. "I really can't, Richie. Maybe we can talk your dad into going."

Carter always asked Richard to go with them, but he never did, this time Sam talked him into it. Insisted he go, knew he needed the distraction of fun even if it would only be for a little while.

"I'm glad you're here, daddy, but I wish Sam could have come too." Richie settled into his seat between Carter and Richard. "She really likes baseball."

"She does?" Richard raised his eyes and looked to Carter, they both knew it wasn't one of Sam's favorite sports.

"Yeah. Her favorite is Cal Ripkin, just like me." His voice was serious when he spoke again. "I think I'm going to marry Sam."

Richard looked to Carter again who held back his laughter, and then he looked back to Richie. "Have you asked her yet, son?"

"Not yet. I have to talk to mom first but I don't think she'll mind. I wanted to marry mom, but mom has you. And Sam doesn't have anyone, so I guess I'll marry her."

"Good luck little buddy." Carter ruffled the little boy's hair. Envious he'd grabbed a true piece of her heart and could hold it forever.

When they returned, Sam could see the look of relaxation in Richard's eyes and he thanked her later when they sat at the kitchen table talking before going to bed. He cut a piece of the chocolate cake they'd had for breakfast and sat down opposite her.

"I only went because you threatened my life if I didn't, but we really had a good time. Thanks for forcing me."

"Shame for doubting me, Richard, I knew what was best for you after all. Admit it."

"I'll never doubt you again. It was good to distance my mind for a few hours, and always good to spend time with Carter." He paused before continuing. "This is hard for him. Other than you of course, he's always been the closest to Sara. Takes his role as the brother she never had very seriously."

"I can remember how worried he was when he realized you'd stayed over at the house that night you met Sara. Did I ever tell you I saved your life that morning? He wanted to kill."

Richard burst into laughter. "I never knew that."

She didn't want to remember that other time, didn't want to talk about Carter, but would patiently wait until he finished his cake before she went to bed.

"Did you remember to stop and get Richie those juice things he wanted for his outing with Bobby tomorrow?" She asked to change the subject.

"One of every flavor. By the way, he's decided he wants to marry you since Sara is already taken."

"If I wasn't already engaged to Trenton, I can't think of a better man, even if he is a little man."

"How is Trenton?" Richard asked out of courtesy. "Getting by without you?"

Sam laughed. "He has his mother and his maid, that's basically all he needs for survival."

Richard brought up a subject he knew would see resistance. "It's hard for me to imagine you and Carter like this for the rest of our lives. You two don't talk, you don't look at each other, I can't see it staying like this, something has to give."

"It's his choice, I didn't see anything wrong with the way it was."

"Didn't you?" He pressed even more.

"There's nothing to be said about it. Carter has chosen to exclude me from his life, I'll live with that if I have to, but I don't have to dwell on it." Sam rose and cleared the plates from the table and began washing them.

"He isn't budging, you aren't budging, I guess it's easier to ignore it?"

"Nothing is easy anymore, is it? That's a fairytale statement in itself."

Richard stood next to her and dried the few things she washed. "I guess it's just as well life takes us down different roads at whim. I'm not sure we can prepare for things even if we know ahead of time what's coming."

"Most things that happen are for our benefit to toughen us up so the blows we take further down the line don't seem so enormous. It's all planned, the surprises around every corner are meant to keep us paying attention. Without them, we'd become stale and placid."

Richard laughed as he looked at her with raised eyebrows. "Did you prepare God's contract?"

"Had I done that, I would have put in a few extra clauses."

"Whatever the surprises are for, I'm fully alert." Richard began putting the few dry dishes in the cabinet. "If God wanted my attention, all he had to do was tap me on the shoulder a few times."

Sam took his hand in hers. "We'll get through this, Richard. We're all going to come out of this."

"Are you talking about Sara or Carter?"

"Both. Sara much sooner, but Carter is being stubborn. I can't make any calculations on how long it will take him to realize he can't function without me reminding him to buy a present. I imagine the first birthday he misses he'll be reaching for the phone."

"I'm not so sure this time, Sam."

She shrugged her shoulders and wiped the wet counter around the sink. "Then I guess I won't have to worry about live lobster delivery anymore, will I?"

Richard saw the casualness in her eyes, and heard the light sound of her words, it was the only kind of relationship from Carter she would accept. She wanted nothing but their friendship back, still couldn't see beyond that, or wouldn't see beyond it. For the first time in many years, Richard wondered if perhaps Carter had been right about Sam moving beyond him, or if she was truly a master at disguising what she truly felt.

****

It always seemed there were so many different directions to go into, so many things to be done at once. Her life in New York was the same, except she could schedule those things, had appointments. Now she flew off the walls. Richie didn't let her know when he would go through three sets of clothes a day so she could prepare time for the laundry the next day. Or that he was going to bring a frog inside who proceeded to jump out of his hands and they destroyed the kitchen trying to catch him.

She ended up feeling frazzled as all kinds of things kept her from an orderly day. Always prepared for orderly chaos in the business world, but Sara's world knew no such thing. Or at least Sam hadn't figured out how to do it.

"I can say without a doubt you have the hardest job of anyone I know." Sam told Sara as they waited for Richard to come home to take her to her doctor's appointment. Richie was at a neighbor's birthday party she would meet him at that afternoon.

"Hard, not very profitable, but very rewarding."

Sara looked good that day. It was their appointment day to discover if she would be in remission or if there was nothing else that could be done. Sam didn't look worried but saw fear in Sara's eyes.

"Everything is going to be fine, Sara. I know it, I feel it." Sam took her small hand in her own.

"I haven't thought about it this whole time. I've just kept fighting away, but I'm scared today. It's like judgment day, maybe I should go to church and confess my sins first before I go."

"You have no sins to confess. You're the good one out of the bunch."

Sara's smile was a hint of mischief. "Don't let the good one's fool you, they're the one's you have to watch out for."

"I thought that was quiet one's."

"Them too." Sara looked across the street and waved to the neighbor and then her voice became softer. "I have a good life, I appreciate it more today."

"You'll have tomorrow."

"Are you promising me that?"

She'd made a promise of tomorrow once before, that was to Carter. She certainly knew it was something that wasn't guaranteed. "No Sara. I can't promise."

When they left for the appointment Sam walked down the street to the birthday party. A yard full of young boys and girls all running in different directions and Sam had a hard time keeping up. Her eyes scanned the crowd and she finally saw him.

She scooped Richie up in her arms when he ran past her and he laughed, his high melodic pitch that was music in her ears. A child's laughter was untainted, unpracticed, the most natural of all, a sound of pure joy and innocence.

"Hey Superman."

"Spiderman, Aunt Sam. I'm Spiderman today."

"I knew that." She set him down again.

He then reached inside her bag she'd set on the ground. "I'm getting a piece of gum, okay?"

The hostess of the party spotted her and held out a piece of cake. "I saved you a piece. I'd offer you punch but there's things floating in it at this point."

"I don't have clean up duty, do I?"

Sam looked around the yard that looked like a giant piñata exploded and they stood in the middle of it. They talked for quite some time but her mind was on the doctor's office, on Sara. Then it went back to the yard as she tried to keep her eye on Richie but kept losing him.

"He's fine." Sara's friend assured her.

"How can one child disappear so fast? I look in one spot and he's right there, I turn my eyes for one second, look back and he's gone. It's like a magic trick."

"Relax, the yard is fully childproof, he can't get out or hurt himself with anything."

"I've never worked so hard in my life, no wonder there's so many working mothers." Sam laughed, had come to fully appreciate motherhood.

"When it's your life it really isn't that hard. You just kind of go with it, whatever comes along." The woman stopped a young boy who ran by, took his ice cream stick away then off he went again. "You're getting married soon, aren't you?"

"Yes." If she asked exactly when, Sam wasn't even sure she would be able to conjure up the answer immediately. It had been the last thing on her mind lately.

"Having children right away?"

"No. I doubt there will be any at all. We're both pretty career oriented. I'm not sure we'd have the time to conceive them, much less raise them." Sam didn't mince words. No matter how hard she looked at her and Trenton's relationship, she couldn't see children there.

The woman looked at her with a sadness but didn't delve further. Sam didn't remind her of a woman whose priorities would be work over children, but there was obviously something more to it.

"Aunt Sam, daddy's on the phone." Richie ran up and held up her cell phone to her, Sam hadn't even known he had it.

"Where did you... How did you..." She was flustered but he didn't answer, just ran off again.

The woman next to her laughed. "It's another one of those magic tricks."

Sam's eyes remained on Richie in the distance and took a deep breath as Richard spoke.

"I would have waited, but Sara insisted we call now. Everything is gone, Sam. No more treatments, she's in remission. She dialed, and wanted to talk herself, but she's crying now and couldn't speak." Richard laughed and his voice cracked also.

The news she waited for and she released the air she'd been holding inside, air that had probably been there since she'd originally heard of the illness. Sam looked around the yard full of kid's. The laughter. The friends of Richard and Sara. The wonderful life they'd created together would continue as planned. How lucky they were.

"Sam, are you there?" Richard asked, thought maybe they'd lost the connection.

"Okay, so I'm just a little depressed I'll be fired soon. I'll be losing my job." Then she took a deep breath to hold back her own tears. "But it's the most wonderful news. It's a good day today, isn't it?"

When she hung up the phone, the sky looked brighter, the laughter of the kids rang more clearly in her ears, and Sam thought everything around her came more to life than it had been just moments ago. As if their lives had literally been put on hold and was released now. She looked to Richie in the distance, the small tears that escaped were for him, a young boy who wouldn't have to suffer a devastating death so soon in life. A young boy who would be blessed with the love of his mother for a long, long, time.

****

"Can't I just stay here in your life? I like your life." Sam sat next to Sara and folded Richie's clothes. "And I've been doing a pretty good job, haven't I?"

"You think you know your friends completely, and although I would suspect you to be the one to do something like this, I certainly didn't expect you to do it so well. Such a good job that I'm afraid when you do leave, I'll never be able to live up to the way you've been running things. You have the business world you're queen of, now you come and prove you're domestic goddess too?"

Sam put her fingers over her mouth. "Shhhhh... Don't tell Richard but I cheated, I've had a maid coming in. I quickly discovered that Richie is about all I can handle."

"I should have known." Sara laughed so hard it hurt.

"Even with her coming in, it was still a never ending cycle. And to think, our company hires from the best business schools in the world, I'm hiring full time mothers from now on. They're the one's that know how to run things. If you ever want a new career, all you have to do is say so."

"Not me. I have all I can handle here, and hopefully more to handle soon. I think it's about time we start adding to the family now."

"You're going to try to get pregnant again?"

"As soon as possible." Sara felt sure there were at least two more in their future, she wasn't done quite yet.

"And you'll have more time to spend with a baby when you do have another. I've already arranged for the maid service to continue. Richard can't stop her, or you. It's a gift from me."

"Sam, I can't possibly..." Sara began to object.

"You can't do anything about it, if I can't use my obscene amount of money on my friends what would I ever do with it."

Sara looked at her with gratitude, for everything. "I'm certainly going to miss you."

"I can tell you with every ounce of honesty I have, I'm going to miss being here more than you'll ever know. Trenton's mother can't wait to tell me all about the plans she's made. I've not any vague idea what I'll see when I walk down the aisle. Are there going to be dancers? Maybe some jester's with funny hats and pointy shoes? How many bands she's going to have is anyone's guess. One certainly wouldn't be enough. I think probably a symphony orchestra with at least 50 instruments, and that would just be for the ceremony." Sam rolled her eyes to emphasis the circus she thought it had become.

"She's that bad?"

"Worse than bad. I'm overdue in choosing my wedding dress and she has three appointments set up with of course all the best designers who will rush the alteration job. As you can tell, I'm not looking forward to going back to New York."

"That's because you don't want to go back to New York." Sara stated and looked with sadness at the path her friend had taken.

"It'll be fine. I'll pick out a dress, of course it will be one she's already pre-arranged for me to try on. I just hope it isn't too gaudy. All I can see is some humongous contraption that will take a team of at least six to help me into. Probably a train as long as the aisle itself and maybe even electric. Lights underneath that will cause a blackout in New York City. At this point, I'll probably wear it anyway. And I'll get married, and who knows, maybe I'll live happily ever after just like you and Richard."

"Don't do it, Sam, don't go back."

Sam stopped folding and looked at her. "And where do you suppose I go?"

"Your life is in Cape Cod, right where you left it. Go back for it Sam, before it's too late." Sara's words filled the space of the room, time was not something that was guaranteed, and she'd found it a precious commodity that was not to be wasted.

"You're delusional Sara, that was a long time ago, and besides, Carter dumped me again, remember? As a friend this time, but he still dumped me." Sam teased with a smile to make it light.

Sara knew everything about her and Carter, if Carter didn't tell her Sam did. There were no secrets. And it tore at her still that it had come to what it had. "He hurts, he's trying to be stoic but giving you up isn't easy."

"He didn't make it look so difficult." Sam stopped herself from sounding bitter by saying it lightly. "Carter's a big boy now, I think he's fine."

"When Richard called him with the good news, he was packing to leave for California for the next few weeks. Said he was going to stop by on his way out but decided to wait until after his trip now that he knew everything was okay, and he'd spend a few days then. I know it was because he didn't want to see you again and figures by the time he gets back, you'll be gone."

"Only because you're forcing me out and won't let me live with you." She continued to fold the clothes, concentrated on every meticulous crease.

"He won't say it, but I know he was putting off a decision because of me. Waiting to see what would happen with my health condition."

"What decision?" Sam stopped folding but only momentarily. "Don't tell me, let me guess. He's getting married again."

"A big renovation project in California, some old historical house that's a dream for a man like him. If he takes the job he'll be moving there."

Sam finally spoke when Sara just waited for a reply. "I didn't mean to run him off the east coast."

"What you should do is run after him."

"I'm not sure Trenton would understand that trip." Sam countered.

"He held on for as long as he could, it was your engagement to Trenton that took away his hope. Without that, he had no choice but to let go. Sam, are you going to make the biggest mistake of your life and let him?" Sara watched her, didn't take her eyes from her dear friend.

"I can't stop Carter from moving to California." She continued her task and remained calm, as usual, it was a calm on the outside.

"When I first heard the news of my cancer, all I could think about was death. What if I died? How would Richard cope with it? How would my son get along in life without a mother?"

Remembering her feelings bought her the same pain even though the danger had passed and tears formed at the thought as Sara continued. "After those fears, the main thing that stood out in my mind was what had I not done in my life I wanted to do? Was I leaving something unfinished? Then I realized I'd done everything I was meant to do. Love Richard and my son, nothing else was important. It wouldn't matter that I'd never planted that garden I always said I would. Or paint the garage. None of that meant anything."

"After living the kind of life you have, it's no wonder you never got the garage painted. But we don't have to worry about those things you didn't do, they'll still be on your list and you'll have a lifetime to get to them." It was more, so much more but Sam tried her best to keep the wall up, to not let the words penetrate, but she could feel the crack when it took place. A crack that continued to get bigger the more Sara spoke.

"And I'll still never paint it." Sara took her hand and wouldn't let go. "The point is, this kind of thing makes you think about your life. And I was satisfied, no matter what happened, I'd done everything I was meant to do. And that was to love them."

Sara squeezed her hand and held tight, her next words were a mere whisper but they resounded through the air. "You loved your parents, Sam, and that should be enough, for you to know that. Don't punish yourself for the rest of your life because you think you have to prove it."

"I have to, until I feel like they'd love me too." It was the first time she'd ever spoken the words out loud to anyone. Words that pounded her senses in the quiet of the lonely nights. Words that pushed her forward whenever she wanted to quit. And Sam didn't know when the feeling would ever stop, or if it ever would. It was always there to drive her. Everything she ever did was for that reason.

Inside, she was still the little girl sitting alone on her birthday, only Bea to light the candles and sing. The child who begged her mother not to drink but she didn't love her enough to listen. The girl who waited by the door or phone time and time again only to get another postcard, and another lonely night. She could still hear her silent cries in the dark of her room, they sounded the same now, and she could have been that child as she began to weep.

"Oh, you poor thing," Sara pulled her inside loving arms, held her with all the compassion she did her son when she told him she was sick. Her voice was a sad laugh, as the two began to cry. "Honey, they didn't know how to love you."

In that moment, a weak frail woman who battled against something Sam didn't think she herself would have been strong enough for, gave reason why her heart was still left so empty. And it would never matter what she did.

Sara continued in a soft tone and held tight as she could with her thin arms. "Stop the madness, Sam."

"How? I've been pushing myself in one direction for so long, I can't stop, I don't even know how to."

"Forgive them."

CHAPTER 19

Sam was emotionally and physically drained. So much had gone into taking care of Sara and Richie and all with a smile of courage. Bravery she didn't feel sometimes but never let her guard down once. They never witnessed how difficult it had been for her, all they saw was the valiant front, never the terrified side that got up every morning and prayed she'd walk into the bedroom and find Sara alive. Prayed she wouldn't be faced with having to sit side by side with a little boy and explain why his mother was dead.

As she sat alone in the airport, she thought about them at home ensconced in their wonderful life. Wondered if they remembered Richie liked cinnamon toast now for breakfast, on the days they didn't have chocolate cake. Had she told Sara they had chocolate cake for breakfast? She began to worry because she knew she'd forgotten to tell Sara that Richie had a little crush on Kelsey Weaver down the street. And had she told them he was fascinated with the Discovery channel now? Preferred it to cartoons?

The neighbors down the street were having a party the week after next, had they gotten the note on the bulletin board? Had she mentioned it? Richard had to pick up the dry cleaning and there was a package waiting at the post office.

She stopped herself from picking up her cell phone and calling to make sure everything was okay. It was their life, not hers. She'd put hers on hold, waited for it to begin again just as she waited for the plane that would take her back to New York.

When she thought of it, it only added to the strain of her emotions. Harriet's voice echoed in the back of her head... 'I think the flowers are perfect the way they are'... 'You don't want ribbons on the end of the pew, it's tacky, we want flower sprays, big flower sprays'... 'Keep all these numbers handy, after you're married and begin entertaining, you'll need them'...

Then Spalding's face loomed in front of her imagination... 'Business is in your genes'... 'Your father would be so proud'... 'If he were alive today you couldn't make him happier'...

Trenton's face came also... 'We're going to have a great life'... 'I'll give you everything'... 'The kind of life your parents wanted for you'... 'Once we have children you'll settle down'... 'things will be different'...

Through all of that, came Sara's soft voice that rose above everything... 'They didn't know how to love you'.

Sam laid her face in her hands as her elbows rested on her knees and the voices rang out loud and clear. Sam didn't want to listen to them, didn't want to hear them. She was so tired, exhausted, didn't even know if she had the strength to get up from her seat when they called her plane. When they did, she didn't move, remained there as if she were going to have a complete breakdown.

The stress of living with life and death in the air caught up to her in that one instant, and immobilized her to the point she had nothing left to give anyone, not even herself. Drained and empty she couldn't cope with the simple task of rising from her seat and boarding her flight to New York.

Trenton awaited her. The wedding. Hundreds of people looked forward to a celebration of their marriage in just a few short weeks. The life she set up for herself was about to unfold before her eyes and she was having a panic attack. It was all before her now, everything she'd planned, everything that should have made her relentless feeling that plagued her subside. Wasn't she on the threshold of relief? Wasn't this where she should feel satisfied? The point where her parents would feel satisfied and she could feel she'd accomplished something for them?

Anxiety. That's all it was, Sam told herself. Normal wedding jitters that any bride experienced. Everyone went through it, but yours was being enhanced by what you'd just been through. Get up. Just get up and walk, you'll feel better. Find that place in your mind, that place you take yourself to where that driving force moves you. The one that got you through moments of weakness and vulnerability. As hard as she tried, she could think of nothing to calm her. She needed something, needed someone, but had nowhere to turn.

"Do you need some help?"

The words came from a distance, somewhere far off. Sam wasn't even sure if she'd heard them at all.

"Miss? Do you need help?"

It took her a few moments to realize it was reality and someone was talking to her. "What?" She asked confused when she raised her face.

"Are you sick? Do you need some help?" The kind woman's face showed concern.

"I... uh... I think... no..."

Sam wanted to scream she desperately needed help but had nowhere to turn for it. Had no family and couldn't go back to her friends when they all deserved to spend the future elated and happy after what they'd been through. They didn't need to be bothered with someone who felt like the world was crashing down around her. And she couldn't see finding comfort in New York. Sam had no one, a sad lonely soul who felt isolated and deserted, the knowledge and realization only made her anxiety worse.

"Should I call for help? Do you need a doctor?"

Sam's eyes were dazed and confused which frightened the woman more. "I'll be fine." She managed to whisper.

"You look pale, do you want some water? I…" The woman held out a bottle of water. "I haven't opened it yet."

"No… no, thank you." She still had a hard time focusing on the woman's face, everything seemed to spin around her in a haze.

"I think you missed your flight. Were you going to New York?"

She looked to the closed door then through the window as her plane taxied out to the runway. "No." She stated in a much stronger voice. "No, I'm not going to New York."

****

The sight of the beautiful Inn as she drove up the long drive was one she could only recall in her dreams. It was still here. Hadn't changed at all and just looking at it, outside of her dreams, made it real again. After she parked, she didn't go inside, instead walked around to the grassy area overlooking the immense sea that spread before her.

She breathed deep the air, let it fill her. Remembered clearly how different it was here. How happy she'd once been. Safe and secure with pressures of her parent's miles away, at one time there were no pressures of any kind here. Nothing but her happiness.

Sam wasn't sure what she thought she'd find now, but she couldn't stop the need to be there. It had called to her tattered and torn soul like a silent sweet lullaby. And she'd followed the sound. Standing there now, she could have been back in her dreams. Wasn't even sure of the journey there or the physical steps she had to have taken to bring her back.

In one instant, along the familiar bluff when she took her shoes off and walked barefoot in the grass, she felt a part of the family who lived there. Felt one of them even still. Somehow knew in the back of her mind they wouldn't hate her for running out on them. And as afraid as she was to come, she felt it the only place she needed to be.

"Would you look what the wind blew in?" Pop said from behind her, his voice a soft sigh in the breeze.

Sam hadn't heard him approach, now quickly turned to face him. Carter's father was a large man with the same deep kind eyes she remembered. But his hair was completely gray now and he walked with a cane, so much slower than he used to be.

"Hey, Pop." Sam said meekly as her voice cracked.

"I don't care how old you get, you'll never be too old to greet an old man with a hug." He held out his arms and she easily moved into them. "I knew it was you from the third floor but I couldn't believe it, had to come see for myself."

She embraced him. Immediate tears formed and her heart took a jolt. All the barriers she had years to build up, took only seconds to fall to pieces around her. Sam cried like a child as he held her, comforted her, she stayed for a long time in protective arms that promised her solace.

Everything she kept balled inside seemed to flow out in the form of tears. Her childhood, her parents, her guilt, and the shame of leaving Grace and Pop behind to find something that was impossible to find anywhere else. The turmoil of her life seemed to peak in that one instant and all washed over her like a wave that left her gasping for air. He said nothing until she calmed enough to find the strength to speak.

"I think I've made a mess of my life," she said.

"Well, you done the best thing to come home to right whatever is wrong. We've been waiting for you."

She'd run out on them just as she had everything else that had been real in her life. But they weren't angry with her, didn't question why, and didn't question what she was there for now. They did what they always did, simply made her feel one of them, one that needed to be taken care of in a time of need. Would nurture and protect her. Love her regardless the decisions she'd made in the past or any she would make in the future.

It was the reason she'd found herself there. In the back of her mind, no matter how many years it had taken her, Sam knew she could always go home. Always return to this place and find the same comfort she always had. The same love they'd always given her, even if at times she questioned if she deserved it after her years of silence.

"Oh Sweet Lord." When Grace saw her, she dropped the pot she'd been drying, embraced her and she too cried.

As she held her, Sam smelled her sweet scent. Freshness she'd never been able to find anywhere else on earth, no matter how hard she tried. The softness of her hands as she wiped the tears from her cheeks and smiled in that way that said all was right.

Grace touched her wet cheek tenderly. "What has this world done to you, you look exhausted child."

Like a small frail child who lost her way, like a sick child who needed to get well, Grace took her to her old room and insisted rest was what she needed first. Everything else would come later.

Nothing about her room had changed. As if she'd stepped back in time to her past she lay across the plump feather bed, smelled the familiar freshness of the blue and yellow quilted cover. Ran her hand along the softness. Her bag was made of the same material and with it, she thought she'd be able to carry this feeling with her, but she hadn't. Couldn't truly feel it, or place it in the bag and carry it around. This feeling of safety could only be found here. In this home.

With the soothing sound of the water's surf that floated through the window Grace opened, and as the movement of white gauze curtains mesmerized her when the breeze filtered in, Sam quickly drifted off to sleep as if hypnotized. By the time Grace returned with a tray of food and tea, she was already in deep slumber.

****

Sam woke at dawn. The sun just slightly above the horizon changed the room and a soft glow surrounded her. In sleepy dazed state, she couldn't remember exactly where she was. As her mind cleared, adjusted to being awake, she recalled the previous day. Recalled where she'd come, where she was now, and smiled.

It was afternoon when she'd arrived, now the following morning. She'd been asleep for more than fifteen hours, probably more in that one night than a week in New York. She lay for a long time and continued to watch the color of the room change, listened to the calm surf, the birds as they too woke. All the morning sounds that indicated a new day awaited.

After a shower she dressed quickly. No make-up and hair still wet, she passed no one as she made her way outside to the shore that called to her like a sweet whisper of her name. She buried her toes in sand and felt warm water wash over her feet. Sam's mind held nothing. No stress. No chaos. It seemed an instant blank canvas. Calm relief to be alone on the banks of New England.

The soft breeze soothed tired, aching muscles, just by crossing softly over her body. She walked slowly, absorbed in taking in the familiar beauty. When she looked up she realized she'd walked all the way to town.

In her bitter torment over the years she'd pushed the memory of her life on the Cape away. Now on the outskirts, she watched from a safe distance as it came alive with morning. Wondered if Mrs. Banner from the bakery had ever married. Or how many kids Beth and Gerry would have by now, she wanted a dozen at one time. And the Parker's who owned the bookstore, now probably run by their children as they were an elderly couple. Were they still alive?

Friends, people who once included her in their lives, and she'd run out on all of them. Left them all behind. Who would be as forgiving as Grace and Pop? How would they greet her? What would they say?

Then she looked to Skippy McGee's fish hut on the old pier that looked as if it would fall into the water at any moment. She could hear his words as if he spoke them from beside her... 'You don't belong here'... 'Get out of town now'... 'You'll leave one day, outsiders always do'... She wondered if for once, the town would stand behind him this time. Perhaps her reception would be quiet nods from old friends. They would whisper. People would gawk and point to the girl who shunned them. Sam wouldn't blame them if they turned their backs on her, ran her out of town just as Skippy McGee always wanted to do.

She returned home. When she entered the back door to the kitchen, Grace's relief was evident with a heavy sigh and a broad smile.

"You look better. Child, you worried the fool out of me yesterday. So pale you were I was afraid you'd taken sick and I almost called the doctor." Her tender hand pressed to Sam's forehead for any indication of fever.

"I think my body just shut down." She felt her words were true. As if she'd had a breakdown of sorts, like a computer crash from overload. The last few days like a hazy filtered dream. Neurotransmitters of her brain moved her physical body forward, but her brain halted function.

Grace took her hand and sat her at the table. "And when was the last time you ate?"

Sam thought seriously about her question and truly couldn't remember. Purchased a wrapped sticky bun when she stopped for gas but couldn't remember if she'd eaten it or not.

From the oven Grace produced a stack of blueberry pancakes, one of Sam's many favorites. "I was keeping breakfast warm for you."

"I didn't mean to be gone so long, I was going to help you with breakfast."

"Please, you're not here to work. Besides, I don't do it by myself anymore. I'll introduce you to Arty as soon as he gets back from the market."

Arty had worked there a few years. Heard about Sam, but never expected to meet her. He was glad she truly was real. Sometimes thought the mysterious girl was someone Grace made up in her mind. She didn't talk of her all the time but comments came out of the blue.

'Look at that sunrise, Arty. In the dead of this winter, Sam would be out there on the bluff all bundled up in Robert's parka trying to put that on canvas as quick as she could... our girl Sam would love these new pancakes with orange sauce, she'd probably put ice cream on top... where do you suppose she is today, Arty?'

Somehow, he always knew the last comment had nothing to do with her physical location. Thoughts spoken out loud that she didn't expect an answer to. And even though she never said the name, he always knew who she spoke of, their girl Sam. Robert didn't say much but Arty often thought he searched for her on the expanse of the cliff edge. He could see him watch from the window at times as if he truly expected to see her out there.

Sam jumped up immediately and helped Arty put the groceries away, and afterwards they all sat with a fresh pot of coffee. They filled her in on all her old friends on the Cape when Sam asked about them. Beth and Gerry were still married and had five children. Mrs. Banner from the bakery had married and divorced. Decided at fifty-five years old she was too independent for a husband. And yes, the Parker's from the bookstore had passed away.

Pop joined them and they sat for a long time talking of everything and nothing. They made her part of their lives as they always had and asked no questions. Sam herself didn't know why she was there or when she would leave. Only knew it was where she needed to be to clear her mind. And there were years of clutter to be filtered out.

Carter's name wasn't mentioned. Sam hadn't come because of him, but in search of comfort. Relief from chaos her mind battled, to find a center, something to ground her and get her back on solid footing. Grace and Pop sensed that. Sam didn't feel a need to bring Carter's name up, felt as if there were a silent understanding between them. It would be tested later that afternoon.

She was sitting on the porch when the phone rang and Grace answered, Sam could hear clearly without trying.

"Waterside Inn, how can I help you today?"

"Hey, Mom." Carter's voice crackled and spat over a bad cell connection.

"Hey, son, I've been waiting to hear from you again."

"Service isn't very good here."

"How's California?"

"Big. Busy. Bearable I guess. It's not too bad." Carter leaned against the car, faced the 150 year old historical building that screamed for someone to save her. "How's New England?"

"Small. Easy lifestyle. More than bearable I guess."

"Is that a hint it's better than California and I shouldn't move here?" He cared what his parents thought about his decision, wanted their input.

"I'm not going to tell you what to do."

Sam thought it ironic, odd their lives ran parallel to each other. She at Carter's home on the east coast trying to figure out her life, he on the west coast doing the same.

From the hood of his car, Carter flipped through preliminary pictures. "I haven't delved into specifics much, I'll be doing that next week. I'm waiting to get my first look inside now."

"What do you think about it so far?"

"It's a beauty, no doubt about that. It would be a minimum two year project just on first impression. Probably longer, old homes, especially one this size, have a way of hiding surprises behind old walls. Never know what you'll find, so two years is a minimum guess."

"New England was here two years ago, and it will be here two years from now." Grace remained neutral with her words.

Carter couldn't expect help from his parents, they wouldn't tell him whether it was right or wrong. Since he was a child they had always been good at letting him make his own mistakes.

One of the biggest concerns he had about leaving was their age. They were getting up in years and he worried about them. But it wasn't as if they were ill, both in top shape other than a few slight kinks here and there. So it really gave him no legitimate worry. He already had an excuse in his mind, using it as reason to possibly turn down the job and go back to the Cape. And to what? What awaited him there?

When he finished the short conversation with his mother, his thoughts were somewhere far from the old house before him when he was interrupted.

"Carter Stevens?" The woman approached him and held out her hand. "I'm Anne Banks with the Historical Society."

"The woman with the key." Carter shook her hand, a soft one that lingered longer than necessary.

"I hope I didn't keep you from something. I was across town when I was told I needed to get here to let you in."

"Someone else was supposed to meet me, but I was stood up."

"On behalf of the Historical Society, let me apologize for that. As a matter of fact," she said the words with obvious attraction. "Let me make it up to you by offering dinner this evening."

She was quite direct. Carter guessed it came from confidence. Short blond hair, hazel eyes, a shapely figure accented by a form fitting simple dress.

Anne Banks was the opposite of everything he'd been attracted to previous. That would be anyone who resembled Sam. Maybe it was time he went in a totally different direction, after all, wasn't that what all this was about? Moving to California? Getting her off his mind? A fresh start?

He went to dinner with her that evening. Afterwards, he called a real estate company and made arrangements to sell his house on Ocean Lane. A home he'd rebuilt for Sam. Even if she hadn't known about it, it was created to her exact specifications. One to share their lives, grow their family. A home she'd never live in. A family they'd never have.

Carter set into motion his clean slate. Nothing before him now. If he decided after two years to move back, he'd buy another, one that wasn't haunted with a life that never was.

CHAPTER 20

After only a few days, Sam found it difficult to button her jeans, mentioned it at breakfast after her walk. Every morning when she entered the kitchen Grace presented her with a huge plate piled high, and more at lunch. Sam wasn't used to eating at all most times, always too busy.

"I'm either going to have to stop eating, or buy new clothes. It's taken me years to get the weight off from your good cooking, and now I'm starting over again."

Grace handed her a filled plate. "There was never anything wrong with your weight. You looked healthier than you do now. Your city life refrigerator probably holds what? Diet soda and eggs?"

"I think there's a few tubs of ice cream in the freezer."

"I've no doubt it's something with chocolate and brownies." Grace knew her well.

With Arty doing just about everything in the kitchen, and two others hired for the bedrooms, there was little for Sam to help with. Occasionally she'd organize the desk or the bookcase. Found odd things to do here and there but mostly she'd talk with guests when she wasn't out alone.

One afternoon she found new guests sitting on the front porch when she went there to relax. An older couple sat at the table and they encouraged her to join them.

"You must be Sam, why don't you come over and sit down. I feel like I know you." The gentlemen pushed his stray newspaper aside to give Sam room.

His wife smiled. "We just checked in this morning. Grace was beside herself telling us about you coming home. We've been coming here for five years now and I know we've never met, but I feel like I know you through your paintings."

The man offered some of their iced tea. "Please tell us you've come back to paint. We've tried to purchase your paintings but they won't part with them, not one."

"I'm afraid I don't paint anymore."

"A talent such as that? But you're back now, surely you'll paint. I beg of you, let us know what you'll have for sale. We're not picky about what it is, even if they sold us one, I'd never be able to choose."

"I really don't..."

"Just keep us in mind, will you?" The woman didn't want to hear the negative and her voice was hopeful.

"Of course." Sam's answer was the noncommittal easy thing to do.

Nothing about the Inn had changed. Not on the outside, nor on the inside. Not even her paintings had been moved, still hung proudly for display. One by one she walked through the rooms and viewed them, recalled the feelings they'd stirred then, and now. As she stood in the sunroom, before the first one she'd ever put to canvas, the simplicity of it almost made her laugh out loud. Beach, water and sky.

It was the beginning of Sam, the independent being disconnected from her parents. An entity of her own. Where was that person now? Was she lost like Carter believed? She'd been suppressed for so long, felt only a small part of that person had survived the years. A small part buried deep inside, hidden behind the guilt and shame.

Grace watched from the doorway a long time before she spoke. "Every time I come in here, that painting has always made me feel like you were home again."

Grace had never known Samantha, she spoke to Sam. She couldn't know there was little left. Only a small sliver of hope survived after Samantha's destruction of her but there was a tiny piece of that girl she knew that clung to that small sliver of hope for dear life.

Without hesitation, her words came. "I don't know if I'll ever be able to come home again, Grace. Not fully. As much as I love being here, as much as it feels like home, I feel guilty. As if I should be back in New York."

Grace misunderstood. "I know you're getting married Sam, but there's nothing to feel guilty about. Carter isn't here, it isn't as if you're doing anything wrong."

"It isn't that." Sam walked to the window and let the view of the sea calm her. It enabled her to go on as she began to talk of things she'd never spoken to anyone about. "I loved my parents. All I wanted to do was make them see, make them understand what I needed from them..."

She found herself confessing to Grace all the things of her childhood, all the fears of a child who only wanted to be loved. Told her the reasons she kept her identity to herself, the reasons she only wanted to be Sam, and keep the two worlds separate. She concluded with the horrific argument of hateful words in New York, the last time she'd ever seen her parents alive.

"So, they died thinking I hated them. Thought I'd found something else, and I did. But that didn't mean I didn't need them. I just needed them to love me too."

Grace sighed with deep sadness. Put her arm around the young woman who looked a lost child still. "And you've had to live with that all these years."

"I just wish..." She didn't finish her sentence, there was no use wishing. "I know how foolish it must sound."

"Never foolish. They're real feelings. Someone else's death has a way of making us all take stock in our lives. Things we did. Things we didn't do. And the longer you hold onto thoughts like that, it festers inside and becomes something very real."

"Mine's had years to fester." Sam accepted the tissue Grace offered.

"I know my telling you isn't the same, but I know they must have loved you, Sam. I can't imagine they truly didn't."

"I tell myself that. And maybe if I'd had proof, I wouldn't have spent the last ten years willing it to happen. How ridiculous and pathetic am I? I want two dead people to prove they loved me, before I can be happy."

"I bet if you looked deep, you'd find something."

"Can you see love? Maybe I could have the bodies exhumed and the hearts examined. Maybe there's a picture of me stamped on them," Sam said.

"Not that I would encourage that, but I know from fact you're stamped on many hearts."

Sara had been right, they didn't know how to love her. But knowing that didn't make Sam's need any less. She still needed to feel it, still yearned for it just as that small child she once was did.

Cape Cod had become once again a place she could be who she wanted. As before, there were no expectations of her. Days spent walking the shore or sitting along the back hill watching the boats in the harbor gave her a solitude that enveloped her, but she didn't feel alone.

Without reminders of her other world of New York, she discovered more and more pieces to that person she'd left there. Tiny pieces, but there was more hope than before. Alongside the guilt that hadn't gone away. There was still that part of her that would always need something she would probably never find, but enough of it subsided that she at least knew marrying Trenton was no longer in her plans.

****

That morning when Sam stepped onto the kitchen, Grace and Pop greeted her with a knowing look.

"It's time for you to go?" Pop asked.

"I have to. I've probably been here too long as it is." Her bag was already beside the front door.

Grace touched her face with a mother's tenderness. "I know it's not the same, but we love you Sam. And with or without Carter, this is your home. I hope you know that."

"I may never be back again." Sam's voice didn't want to say the words, but she wanted them to know.

"The porch light's been on for years just waiting for you. It will always be on for you to find your way."

She wanted to turn back. It was so hard for her to leave them behind once more, to not know when or if she would ever see them again. It was home to Sam. She felt like part of the family and they treated her as such. But it was also Carter's home first, and she had to respect that.

Sam didn't know what would become of them, if anything, and knew the more time that passed, the bigger the risk of losing him forever. And he gave signs that she possibly already had. Called and extended his trip to California a few more weeks. Put his house on the market for sale and he had called Grace to help. Told her it didn't mean he'd come to a final decision, but he wanted to sell the house regardless, asked her to call someone to clean it well and for her to arrange for the agent to have the key.

Sam accidentally came across paperwork with the address and only then did she find out about the house on Ocean Lane. Grace explained all the work he'd done hadn't been for an absent owner, Carter purchased the house. It had been for them, a surprise for Sam. She'd never known.

So Carter stayed true to his last words to her. Taking necessary steps to put her behind him, erase her from his life. As much as she wanted to think he would always be there he'd proven he cut her out, needed to be free to find his way elsewhere, and she understood.

She wasn't the girl he fell in love with but one still burdened with regret and anguish over death. One who hadn't found her way out of the guilt that plagued her and didn't know if she ever would. She wanted desperately to be the girl he loved but that meant finding what she searched for, or let the feeling go. She had to resolve uncertainties, the fears that prevented her from loving completely.

Until then, she truly wouldn't belong in Cape Cod or with Carter. No matter what happened, he would always be the one she truly loved. And she could only pray she would find her way back to him. Sometime. Somewhere. Someplace. Maybe she could give him the promised tomorrow. Until then, she placed no blame on him wanting life elsewhere, when Sam didn't have one to offer him.

The ordeal with Sara, of feeling on the verge of life and death, added with the freedom to clear her mind, had given her the perspective to know she wouldn't be able to drive herself any longer. Wouldn't be able to pretend that what she'd been doing was living. To do so, to go on with the false pretense of life took something away from Sara who'd fought so hard for the real thing.

She didn't know if she had a future with Carter, but she did know it wasn't with Trenton. And she discovered that driving herself further and deeper into the business would only get her there, further and deeper into the business.

It was her first major step. It wasn't as difficult as she thought to put closure on her life in New York, closure on her parent's world. Plans were put into motion to sever ties with the company, which stunned Spalding Edwards who was openly upset but supportive.

"Everything will be taken care of, Samantha. It will certainly be an adjustment without you around here."

"You always did make me seem more important than I actually am."

"That isn't true. You've been an integral part of this company, we wouldn't be where we are today had it not been for you." Spalding never would have imagined so much was to be gained from the young lady he'd met so many years ago, and the young woman who stood before him now. She'd changed over the years, but one thing still remained. A hollow, cold, emptiness in her beautiful eyes. He could only hope he would see them filled with something different one day, but he doubted it. The determined look in her eye now told him she would never come back into this life. If they were ever filled with something different, he doubted he'd ever see it.

"You'll manage quite well without me, I'm sure."

"Won't be as exciting." Spalding rose and walked her to the door. "How did Trenton take it?"

"I haven't told him yet, this was my first stop. I called him, he's going to meet me at his place." Sam paused and looked at her watch. "In a half hour, so I guess I'd better go."

Spalding embraced her. "What will you do? Where will you go?"

It was only then she'd thought about it. Sam knew she had to put closure on New York, but she hadn't thought of what came afterwards. She laughed lightly. "You know, Spalding, I honestly don't know."

"I know I've said it before but it's always worth repeating. Even in his absence, you made your father proud."

She smiled, the words taken to heart. "If he were alive today, I think I might have been able to give him a run for his money." She did know that now, but it still wasn't enough to satisfy her completely. There was still the cry inside of a young child who needed his love.

"No question of that. Whichever way you want to look at it, having the pleasure, or punishment, and that's a compliment, I had the opportunity to work with you both. You're father was at the top of the business world, but truth be known, I think you even topped him." Spalding hugged her close, said the words for her father who couldn't, and for himself who truly felt them. "You made me proud, Sam."

There were times when you knew you were faced with a departing point, knew you'd never see that person in your life again. Sam knew it was one of those times but had no regrets when she closed the door behind her.

It was only slightly more difficult to face Trenton. He'd been somewhat prepared, had suspected there would be a drastic change of plans when she didn't return from Sara's and he hadn't heard from her in weeks. All she said was she needed space, and he'd given it to her, now as she slowly approached him he knew it was over.

He protested regardless because he didn't want it to be. Maybe there was a small chance. "I'm glad you're home Samantha. I've missed you."

Sam returned his hug but didn't linger, pulled away quickly. "I can't do this anymore. I'm finally being honest to myself, and to you. I can't pretend we're happy together."

"You've had reservations, but everything will be fine. Our wedding is just..."

"No, Trenton, there will be no wedding. I'm not what you need, I can't give you what you deserve from someone."

"I accept that, Samantha, I always have." He knew she didn't love him, had always known, and he was okay with that.

"It's easier to spend the rest of our lives together with someone like an old comfortable blanket than it is to actually put any emotion out there. But I can't live that way anymore Trenton, and if you're honest with yourself, you shouldn't have to settle for it either."

"Why didn't you tell me this from the beginning? Why did you say you'd marry me then you're doing this?"

Sam touched his face, whispered the words. "I never said yes. When you asked me to marry you everyone was excited, people started talking, toasts were being made. You kissed me and put the ring on my finger, but I never said yes."

"But you went along with it."

"Because it was easy to. But how sad is that? I went along with it, and I would have gone through with it, because it was easy." She could see both acceptance and denial in his face.

"Have you been with him? Is that what all this is about?" He had to ask. "Have you been with Carter?"

She looked at his face and didn't ask how he knew of their intense relationship. She was completely honest with him, owed him that. "I can truthfully say this has nothing to do with him. It was something he encouraged, he knew I'd become someone I wasn't over the years, and he encouraged me to find myself again. But that's the extent of his involvement. This isn't about you or him. It's about me, if you can understand that."

"You? I don't even know who you are anymore." Trenton was now a little angry, didn't want her to just walk out, just leave.

"That's the point. You never did." Sam moved over to look at the city spread both at her feet and towered above. So many people, yet no one really knew anyone did they? "You know the person my parents wanted me to be, the person I was out of obligation and guilt. I gave my entire life over to that. But after watching Sara fight so valiantly for her life, I can't take it for granted anymore. Life is too important to pretend to be someone I'm not."

"What are we going to tell hundreds of people? How am I going to explain this?"

Sam walked over and stopped in front of him. "It isn't important, tell them what you will, blame it on me, make something up. I don't care, I'll never see those people again."

Trenton saw the finality of it. Had seen it the moment she stepped in the door and now lived through its final moments. He was almost envious she'd escaped from the trap, which was much more difficult to do than it was to just accept the life you were expected to live.

"I'm sorry, Trenton."

He sighed, pulled her to him with understanding. "Don't be sorry Sam. I love you, as difficult as this is, I've always known you weren't happy. The least I can do is wish that for you."

****

Ending her relationship and future with Trenton had been an easy decision, it was her next step that was difficult. She did decide the city wasn't where she wanted to be and prepared to sell her apartment. After that, with no job and no home, she didn't know what she would do.

Sam didn't call her friends and tell them the wedding was off, it would be obvious when they didn't get an invitation. She was afraid they would see the cancellation as something more than it was, they'd see it as opportunity for her and Carter. So she didn't contact them.

There wasn't much from her apartment to keep. She decided to sell it furnished so all she had to do was remove her things and turn it over to be sold. Her wardrobe boxed up and shipped to her assistant, a young girl about the same size who'd always admired her clothes. So she shipped them off with a note and a very generous check.

Certain pieces of furniture, jewels and such were arranged to be sold at auction and the money given to charity. It's what she'd done with most of her parent's things after their deaths and the things she kept fit into two suitcases. Sam didn't own many personal items, her only real memento she considered special was a box of old postcards. They were the only things she found worthy of keeping.

At one time she took them for granted because they always came, she'd never given any thought to the day they would stop coming. It had been a long time but Sam opened the box before placing them in the suitcase. She had placed them into the box as she received them, so the top was Monte Carlo where they spent some time their last summer alive. Scratched on the back with a quick hand... Having a lovely holiday, we miss you.

Sam chuckled lightly to herself. Her mother always said it was 'holiday', as if she were European. Most of the postcards said the same thing or a variation of it, generalized greetings that could have been meant for anyone. Sam wondered had they got the chance, what the last one would have said, the one from Italy. Postcards always came the first few days of their departure as if her mother wanted to get it out of the way quickly before she forgot. Between the time of their argument and the accident, there would have been time to send one, but they hadn't.

The reason was obvious to Sam, she'd hurt them deeply. Had to understand they wouldn't send a postcard to a daughter they believed didn't love them. One they believed wanted nothing to do with them. In the back of her mind she thought about what it would say if it had been sent. Would it be more than the general greeting that was always scribbled on the back? Or would they have acknowledged her feelings she'd exposed?

In her mind she conjured up the latter. It didn't make her feel better, she had no proof they would have sent one that finally professed their love for her. Only a dream to think she had stirred her parent's emotions, had at least made them think about things. And maybe they did think about things, possibly on the short ride to the airport, but once they boarded the plane thoughts of her would have disappeared.

What if they had sent one? What if one had been mailed and she never received it? Could they possibly have mailed one right before their deaths? It would have gone to her school address, but she hadn't been there, had never gone back. The school would have forwarded it to Virginia. In the chaos after their deaths it could have been overlooked.

Sam put it to the back of her mind. One little postcard wasn't going to solve her life's dilemma. One little postcard that could possibly have been sent, yet more than likely hadn't been.

But as Grace said, the longer one thought about something, the more it festered.

CHAPTER 20

"Isn't it about time for lunch?" Anne entered the dirty construction trailer and found Carter over a set of blueprints.

He didn't look up, his full concentration on the plans spread out on the metal table, and she had to repeat herself.

"Hello? Isn't it about time for lunch?" She touched his shoulder and realized he hadn't even known she was there. "Talk about concentration. I work hard but I at least know when there's a beautiful woman in the room."

He only gave a quick look, then back to his plans. And she'd worn her sexiest work outfit.

"I'm a little busy right now, Anne."

"It's lunch time though. I'll buy."

"Can't." Putting the pencil in his mouth he flipped the large sheet of the plans over then leaned down on both elbows and began marking.

Anne took her hint to leave when he said nothing else. They hadn't really moved past being friends, she tried to get closer to him but there was something that stopped him still. He needed to move at a slow pace. He was trying to let go of something in his life and receive something at the same time. But on that day his concentration was not on Anne or his work, he couldn't seem to get past the phone conversation with Sara that morning. Didn't want to think about it but it filtered through anyway.

"Carter," she hesitated. "I don't know if I should be worried or not, and I thought maybe you could help. Sam's missing."

"Missing? Define missing." He didn't want to go with his first instant reaction of fear, calmed himself and decided not to jump to conclusions.

"I haven't talked to her since she left my house. Neither has Nikki or Shawna. She doesn't go this long without talking to at least one of us," Sara paused. "We've left messages. You haven't talked to her by any chance have you?"

"I certainly haven't heard from her. The wedding's coming up, she's busy."

"And that's another thing. We should have received the invitations by now."

Carter didn't want to think it was true, but maybe he'd been right when he told her in Bermuda she would distance herself from her friends. The hard side of him that shut her out believed it.

"Maybe no one is invited Sara."

"Of course we'd all be invited."

He didn't want to tell her he had his doubts. "I can't help you, but I wouldn't worry about her. You know how she is, probably off somewhere on one of her solo journey's and wasn't considerate enough to at least let you know so you wouldn't worry about her."

"Do you have to be so angry at her?"

"It helps."

It took him a few days of work, but he was able to push the conversation to the back of his mind. Hard manual labor helped tremendously. And when his real estate agent called with the news someone had made an offer on the house, he saw it as a positive step.

"It's above asking price. They've offered fifty grand more to buy it furnished and be able to settle right away."

"When do they want to settle?"

"Saturday. I've shipped some papers to you by express, you should have them this afternoon."

Carter heard his words, but that was only four days away, certainly he didn't mean this Saturday, but he had. And Carter had to make a decision. He stood at a window in a lonely hotel room, could see a little of the Pacific Ocean in the distance. It was so quick. He thought he'd have more time to get used to the idea, thought he'd have more time in his home. But for what? To make excuses to hang onto it? To talk himself out of it?

"I didn't wake you, did I?" Carter asked when his mother picked up the phone after a few rings.

Grace smiled broadly on the other end of the phone line. "I didn't expect to hear from you this late, and no, you didn't wake me, I was just on my way to bed."

"I'm glad I caught you then. I got an offer on the house, they want to settle Saturday."

"This Saturday? That's four days away."

He picked the paper up and read the date as if he needed to verify it. "They're anxious. Offered over the asking price and want it furnished."

Grace was quiet. He called for her opinion, she didn't want Carter to sell his home, but knew he'd been especially unhappy there since his return from Bermuda. And knew how difficult a choice it was for him. Grace decided to reveal Sam's visit, but not all they talked about, Sam's confidences weren't to be shared.

"Carter, Sam came to visit not long ago, just after taking care of Sara. I think she came because she was completely worn out and didn't have anywhere else to go."

Carter could understand that. When he'd seen her at Sara's he knew how difficult her role as caretaker had been and knew the toll it took. "It was difficult for her, but she did it without complaint. I don't think anyone else would have been up for it. I'm assuming the Cape did her some good?"

"I think it did. I'm glad she came."

Carter began to think about what her visit had meant, if it had meant anything. Before he could read anything else into it, his mother continued.

"When she left, she said she may never be back again."

Carter looked out of the window to the street below and watched the people scurry about. Everyone with someplace to go, everyone busy living their lives. It wasn't something he wanted to hear, but it was something he had to face. "I did what you said, mom. I gave her my whole heart."

"I know you did son, I know you did."

If he needed a more solid sign to get on with his life, his mother's words hit the mark. Carter signed and sent the ratified contract. He would leave Saturday morning, but return Saturday evening a California resident. Between work and Anne he thought he'd have a very good chance at his new start.

"I'm tired of being turned down for lunch, so it's dinner this time. My treat." Anne smiled to coax him. This time had gone out and bought a new sexy outfit, but this one wasn't work, she was dressed for dinner.

Carter had been cleaning up the desk and looked at his watch, then looked up to her, noticed how attractive she looked. He would get this behind him and notice more when he returned.

"It's tempting, but I have a flight out this evening."

"You're leaving? You didn't say anything about leaving."

"I'll be back tomorrow evening. I put my house on the market and it's already sold. The buyer wants a quick settlement, very quick. So we settle in a few days."

"And you'll be back? Does that mean you're taking the position?" Anne looked excited and hopeful. News she'd waited to hear.

"It means I won't have a reason not to. I haven't fully committed yet, but with this house behind me, I can."

He'd given her no real positive sign, but Anne would remain optimistic. Maybe he hadn't wanted to get involved until he was sure he would be there. Very respectful, but very frustrating for her. She wouldn't have cared, would have taken the casual encounter if that was all he was willing to give, but he hadn't even given her that. And she wanted something before he left.

"When you get back, I think it's about time we get to know each other a little better, don't you?" She put her hands on his hips, pressed herself to him.

Anne liked the feel of him close to her. When she kissed him, his lips felt just as she knew they would. She moved her hand up his strong chest, felt the muscles underneath his shirt. Wanted him to have something to know she'd be waiting for him.

****

After she left New York, with an analytical mind Sam had deduced her choices down to Preston Burke or Bea. Bea turned out to be the one to possibly help when she called her and the woman revealed she'd been holding something for her.

With nervous hesitation Sam waited while she opened a drawer of her china cabinet and pulled from it a large envelope. Like the child whose mother dangled hope, only to snatch it away, she wondered if she wanted to reach for it. Was it wasted emotion to think she'd find anything?

"You'd gone. I tried to send it on to Mr. Burke, but it was returned. Then that office in New York, but... I just kept it, thought maybe one day you'd come back."

Sam didn't want to set herself up for disappointment, but her heart pounded as Bea reached inside then pulled out a smaller white envelope and handed it to her.

"It was forwarded from the school. It isn't the postcard you're looking for, but it's from your mother."

Sam's fingers, hands and arms shook as she opened the envelope. The postcard was inside, scribbled on the back was her mother's normal, simple, greeting. But there was a letter there also.

'My precious Samantha... I am sober this moment. My version of being in rare form. I will not offer you excuses for myself, there are none, your words were true and I haven't been there for you. But it has never been because I didn't love you, never doubt my love for you. It was because I didn't want you close to me. I didn't want you to see the ugliness of my life, the ugliness of this disease. Wanted you exposed to as little as possible.

I was afraid. I wanted so much better for you, so I did buy you things, because those things were so much better than what I could give of myself.

My name is Joan Durham. I am an alcoholic. I want to say those words. So I have asked your father to find me a center here in Italy. The next time I see you I want to be the mother you love. For you have such a pure heart, you can even love a mother like me.

Please forgive me... I love you.'

Afterwards, Bea held her for a long time. It was everything she'd searched for. In an old woman's arms, Sam felt every stone reserve melt as her heart filled with her mothers love. It's all she needed, it was all she ever needed.

When she calmed, Bea handed her a folder she'd found while cleaning out her fathers desk. Sam opened it to reveal child drawings of scraggly trees, crooked houses, people with no arms. All the pictures she'd done as a child underneath his desk. All in order as she'd done them, just like her postcards in the order she'd received them. Proof she'd meant something.

The last thing Bea pulled from the envelope was a small item wrapped in tissue paper. A small gold ring with a little diamond chip that represented her promised tomorrows. When she moved to New York she saw no need to take it with her and didn't feel Carter wanted it back either.

"I found it on your night table. It looked like it meant something, I saved it just in case." Bea rescued it after Sam left.

"It means a great deal." Sam laughed and wiped her eyes with the tissue she handed her. "You know Bea, all the excessive wealth, people motivated by greed for more. More money, more houses, more jewels. Everything, absolutely everything has been given to me, and there's not anything on this earth that's worth more than what you pulled out of that old envelope."

It was as if she held her parents in one hand and Carter in the other. It had been the dividing line between their lives many years ago, now she was presented with it again. There was no question which one she was going to let go this time.

****

After Virginia, Sam went back to Cape Cod but didn't go to Waterside Inn, she went directly to Skippy McGee's pier. When everyone else welcomed her, he wanted to know why she was there, mistrusted her. She didn't belong in these parts, an outsider, he said to fit in perfectly you had to have its blood.

Just as before, he never glanced up to look at her and didn't say a word as she sat down on the old rickety chair next to him. And just like his old dog used to, a younger version of the same meandered over and plopped its head on her leg.

"Good day today, isn't it Skippy McGee." She set her meek offering of purchased cookies down on the table, almost embarrassed she didn't have his favorite of chocolate cheesecake muffins.

It was a long time before he spoke, his hands and attention concentrated on a piece of wood he scratched something into. "What you come back for?" He stated with his gruff voice, but still didn't look at her.

"I think I wanted to see if I could paint again."

"You *think* that?"

"I want to paint again." She changed her answer.

"And can you?"

"I don't know."

"For a slick city girl, you don't know much do you."

Sam took a deep breath. Her voice a strong statement, adamant with her words as if she dared him to challenge her. "I know I belong now."

Why she valued the opinion of this old angry man, she didn't know, but her heart stopped a beat as Skippy finally raised his head and stared at her for a long time. Steel gray eyes confronted hers. So intense was his gaze she almost turned away but couldn't, faced him eye to eye.

He then lowered his head again and went back to his task. "You know, sometimes things ain't what they appear to be. Take ole' Daisy for instance, looks just like my old dog but she ain't."

Sam took it as confirmation. Without saying the words directly she knew he accepted her now. As she left, Sam stopped at the door with her usual farewell.

"I'll see you another day, Skippy McGee."

He never turned around so he couldn't see the smile that beamed across her face. His voice was soft, as if it was a moment he too had waited for, as if it were about time.

"Welcome home, Sammy."

CHAPTER 22

Carter spent his last night in his home with a bottle of wine and a fire, wondered how a person could miss something they'd never had, but even then he yearned deep for it. Maybe the people who were buying his home could fill it with what he'd envisioned. In the lonely quiet of the still room, he raised his glass in the air in silent toast and wished them luck.

The next morning, when he woke up in his home for the last time, the first thought on his mind was Sam. It was her wedding day. How fitting they would each begin their lives anew on the same day. When he closed the door, he bid both Sam and the life they'd never had a silent farewell.

His mind was on California, it had to be, and although he would have liked to have met the people who were buying the home he'd built with his own two hands, an attorney represented them instead. They signed all the papers and concluded with rapid speed.

The attorney shook his hand. "Mr. Stevens, It's been a pleasure."

Carter wouldn't have used his choice of words. It had been quick. "I hope they enjoy it."

"So now you're a homeless guitar player."

He stopped and hesitated before the man with an odd expression, an odd sensation. "I... I don't play the guitar."

The lawyer continued. "A guitar was there when the house was shown."

A homeless guitar player. The words repeated in his mind. "Ah. I've tried to strum something on it, but no, I don't play." Sam had sent it years before as a joke.

Carter stood in the parking lot a few moments before he finally left for the airport with the odd sensation still. He'd already told his parents he would be leaving right away, said he'd be back in a few weeks to visit. Strange, he would visit Cape Cod now, no longer lived there. He was homeless.

Early for his flight, he stopped into a coffee shop, one he could see his boarding gate from. He thought about whoever was sitting in his home, having their coffee with a view of the ocean. It wasn't your home anymore, Carter. You're homeless, remember? He had some humor left to joke with himself, told himself he'd never even learned to play that guitar to collect change in a tin can if he needed to. His mind began to wander back in time until he took a deep breath to clear it. Think of California ahead of you, that's all you have to think about, your mind didn't need to wander, he told himself.

There was no fear of being late and missing his flight, but he felt anxious and didn't know why. Was he anxious now to return to California and get started on his new life? Maybe it was all he had before him, he could now delve into the project full force, could find a permanent place instead of the hotel. But was that what he was thinking of? His mind seemed to be working in irrational order, as if it were trying to tell him something, something he couldn't quite grasp. Was he forgetting something?

When his cell phone rang he picked it up and heard Michael's voice. "Today's the wedding day," he said.

"I thought you were one of my best friends, you have to call and remind me? Or did you call to ask if you should wear your red tie or blue one." Don't start thinking of her Carter, keep your mind focused on where it needed to be, and that wasn't on Sam.

"Today's the wedding day and we still haven't heard from Sam. No invitation. No call to say it's cancelled. We've left Trenton messages but no return call. Carter, she's still missing." Michael looked to his wife who paced the floor.

Carter's first instinct was concern, but he quickly pushed it aside. "I wouldn't worry, Sam's good at taking care of herself."

"Shawna, Nikki and Sara are frantic, and I'm beginning to think they might have something to be frantic about, but I'm not sure what to even do. I would think if she called off the wedding, she would have called someone. I was assuming maybe you."

"And maybe that's why she didn't tell anyone, she didn't want anyone jumping to conclusions."

"You have a point."

"If she called off the wedding, it wasn't because of me, Michael. She visited my parents just after taking care of Sara, said she may never be back again. That doesn't sound like she has any intentions of calling me." Carter didn't want to worry about Sam, but it crept in. "You know how Sam is. She's taken off by herself before, does it all the time."

"Not this long without someone knowing where she is. Her apartment phones been disconnected, her office says she can't be reached at that number any longer, and as of a few days ago, her cell phone no longer works either. We have no way to find her, unless she calls."

Carter didn't want to admit it was strange but he had to put it logically in his head in order for it to make sense. He didn't want to believe it was true that she would pull away from her friends, but like his anger towards her, the thought made it easier to deal with her rejection. Don't start worrying Carter, not now, he told himself again.

"She was planning to get married so she probably sold her apartment. And as for her office, maybe she got a more private number and they don't give it out to just anyone."

"Could be." Michael's voice was still uncertain.

It was as if they needed to counter and balance and make sense of it, but Carter couldn't make sense of it, didn't have an explanation. He was almost out of it, on the verge of finally beginning a life she didn't want to be a part of, he couldn't be pulled back in, wouldn't let himself be pulled back in where life was painful.

Carter listened to the announcement of his flight boarding, now looked to the boarding line that dwindled down. "Sounds like she doesn't want to be found, she has some things to deal with Michael, money hasn't been able to buy her peace of mind."

Michael knew he was right. It wasn't unusual for Sam to do such a thing. "Maybe you're right. I just hope nothings happened to her."

Carter didn't want to think of all the possibilities. Was she sick? In the hospital? Uneasiness made him shift in his seat, made him think the worst and he stood up and walked a moment to calm his rising fears. There was so much going through his mind he couldn't think clearly, an anxiety that still made him restless and fidgety.

Inside, he could feel his gut wrench with apprehension and the beginnings of terror as he thought about something happening to her and it was possible they would never know. Trenton wouldn't think to call any of them, and she had no family that would contact them, all she had was their close group of friends.

Had something happened to her? Before he got carried away he had to stop himself. No Carter, he told himself. Stop thinking like that. So she didn't get married but that didn't mean anything. She went off for a long break and she could have gone anywhere in the world she wanted. Could spend the rest of her life lost in Europe. Disappear. Dissolve completely into oblivion. And maybe that's what she wanted, what she needed.

If she had gone off she would get settled and send them all a note or call and tell them what a wonderful time she was having. There was nothing to be concerned about. All that concerned him was California ahead, not Sam, he had to believe she was safe somewhere. He couldn't be pulled back in when he was so close to getting out. Carter knew he couldn't spend his next ten years like he had the last, was sure it would kill him.

"I'm at the airport, Michael, my house is sold and I'm moving to California." He paused. "I don't want to seem callous, but I can't help in this. You understand, don't you?" Carter picked up his small bag and headed for the gate. "Give her a few days, I'm sure she'll call."

When he disconnected, the phone remained in his hand and he took a moment to look in his appointment book and dialed Anne's number.

"Anne? This is Carter."

"Are you back in town? I didn't expect you till this evening."

"Just about to board my plane now. I've tied up everything here and there's… well, there's nothing left on this end." He paused and took a deep breath. This was it, this was the life that lay ahead for him. "I was wondering if you could pick me up at the airport. I get in at three this afternoon, your time. I'd like to spend some time with you this evening, maybe you could help me out. I'll need to find a place and…"

****

Sam had been anxious all day as she made it through the long morning wait and into the afternoon. Her fear was, maybe he hadn't picked up on the hint. Though her attorney was sure he'd seen a strange look, was sure Carter would realize the clue he'd been given about being a homeless guitar player. It was very distinct. How could he not have known?

She expected him to run home to her, take her in his arms, and they would finally resume their lives together. But the day had passed, then evening came, followed by midnight that approached as she walked around their home on Ocean Lane. She listened to the waves outside the open doors, the ticking of the clock on the mantle in the still room.

Her fear of him not knowing it was her there had intensified and changed. A fear far worse had happened, he did know, and it didn't matter anymore. It had been months. His distance from her at Sara's, his extended stay in California, and her attorney mentioned he'd planned a move there. She'd only made a confident assumption to think he wouldn't have fully let go. But she had to see it, Sam lost him, Carter wasn't coming home, he'd found another.

It was time for her to give up the useless wait. Put an end to the longest day of her life and begin another tomorrow. Maybe she'd go somewhere. The Caribbean, back to Bermuda, she could go anywhere in the world she wanted. She had no one to answer to, no responsibilities or obligations. She'd wanted it to be a surprise, so no one knew where she was. Not even Grace and Pop, she hadn't seen them since her last visit, and she wouldn't now. She'd send her friends a note not to worry about her, and she'd travel. Get lost somewhere for a few years, maybe see all the places depicted in her postcards, visit all the places her parents so loved.

Pawns in the hands of fate, perhaps that's what they were forever meant to be. The magnificent home Carter basically built with his own two hands, out of love for her, would remain quiet and bare. She'd had all day to conjure up visions of their future together, children they would have to bring it much laughter. Pictured herself in the kitchen that overlooked the sea, as they all made cake for breakfast.

She imagined the loving look on his face when she finally offered him everything, the promised tomorrow he'd always wanted. Now she knew it was something he no longer wanted and the pain of knowing that had all day to intensify. Carter wouldn't be in her life, in their home. It would stand empty. There would be no children to bring it laughter, there was no one but her, and she couldn't stay in this lonely quiet house with nothing but visions of something that would never be. It was never intended for that. It was built to be filled with life. Now it was only a reminder of the life that never was.

CHAPTER 23

Long past midnight, she'd stopped listening to the ticking of the clock. Didn't need a reminder that she'd been too late, a reminder of how important every moment in a persons life was. Sam stood alone and watched the ocean, listened to the surf roll in, the only sound in the stillness of a dark night, one that seemed darker than usual. Then the breeze came, a wind that seeped into her skin.

From somewhere within, she sensed the moment the car turned into the drive and as she walked to the front door, saw headlights fast approaching. Sam was a silhouette against the warm light from inside as she waited at the open door. When she saw Carter's face, it held many things. Great relief, question, confusion, and then his smile came as he slowly approached.

It was her answer, her own relief to her question and confusion about where she would stand in his life. That one boyish grin was all she needed to know she hadn't lost him after all. Sam waited until he reached the top of the steps and onto the porch before she spoke.

"Where have you been?"

"Boston to California, then California back to Boston is a long trip. Especially when you hadn't planned it and weren't prepared with a return ticket and have to take what you can get. The most frustrating part? I'd realized it just after takeoff, before the plane had flown out of Massachusetts. And there wasn't a damn thing I could do about it."

Carter stepped closer, immediately noticed eyes with that glimmer of long ago, that enthusiasm for life that had gone missing for so long. Sam again. But this time there was no fear or hesitation, not the slightest hint of something buried deep like there had been in her secrets of the past. She'd found what she needed to finally be free from her silent haunts that plagued her. Ready to give herself fully to him, ready to give the promised tomorrow, for he noticed on her left hand the small diamond chip of a ring.

"A little presumptuous, aren't you?" His heart was almost unable to stay within the confines of his chest. "You think you can come right back here and take up where we left off?"

"I think it's about time, don't you?"

"If you're sure you want this homeless guitar player."

She stepped over the threshold, and slowly moved into his arms. "Are you ready to settle down? You've been married twice."

"They weren't you."

"You're not very responsible."

"When we have kids you can be the responsible one, they need at least one irresponsible to be the fun parent." He could hear the sound of the ocean that carried her in with the tide and washed her up on his doorstep.

"Why can't I be the irresponsible parent?"

"Because you're out of practice."

"It shouldn't take long to get me up to par, by the time we have kids I should be back in rare form."

Her hands moved to his back to feel familiar muscles, his strength, immediately felt safe and secure once again in his arms. Protected, loved. Never to be cold and alone again. Palms pressed hard against him to pull him closer still, the feel of him a final link to fill her, only now whole in his arms.

Her world was right. She'd found what Sara spoke of, that special place those faced with death discovered much more easily than people too busy living. Where she knew she was only meant to love him and the children they would be blessed with. What freedom to know nothing else mattered.

Perhaps with a premonition of her own death, Joan Durham discovered it too. Her long sought after words of love almost on the eve of her death, was Sam's last connection to her. It was as if her parents had given Carter back to her. One last gift. This time one of love.

"I love you, Carter, I belong here now."

"You certainly took the long way around to figure that out. Remind me to buy you a map to keep with you at all times. A GPS system will be even better."

Sam touched his face, knew she'd never be lost again. How lucky she was to have been given a second chance, how lucky she was that he truly still loved her after all this time.

"Why don't we go inside, this house has been empty far too long and we have quite a bit of time to make up."

"Welcome home, Sam."

The touch of their lips solidified the connection that could never be broken. Two souls bound for eternity, neither time nor distance could alter it and they'd never be tested again. A light breeze crossed the porch, winds of change blew in. This time there was nothing to fear as it circled, for it carried with it the promised tomorrows neither thought would ever come.

Carter and Sam stepped inside and closed the door.

EPILOUGE
Six Years Later

"Skkiiiiipppppyyyy..." Miranda screamed as she raced across the grass and bounded down the pier. Black curls bounced everywhere, her child's delightful laughter rang out.

"Skippy McGee, don't..." Before Sam could finish the words the old man turned around and scooped the little five year old girl up in his arms. He never listened to her anyway. "You're going to hurt your back."

"I may get old one day, but it ain't today." He grumbled and smiled at the little girl now in his arms, then looked to Ryan, almost three, who squirmed to get out of Sam's arms. "Come here, where's my muffins?"

"My muffins." Ryan giggled and practically jumped to the old man with his bag of chocolate cheesecake muffins.

The old fish shack had changed over the years. The children had made him things he hung proud, both inside and out. A haphazard assortment of neon painted pots full of red plastic flowers, painted fish, painted signs. An old wreath to which there was glued several crayons, an eggbeater, a pencil cup and a few mittens. They also painted portions of the shack itself. Trees, suns, flowers, there was a mix of colors everywhere. It had become quite the tourist attraction, and her painting of it one of her gallery's best sellers, she couldn't keep stock of the eclectic print.

They couldn't stay long that day but the kids were content to know they'd see him for dinner in a few days. When she asked him to come on Sunday, he grumbled, as he always did, but he'd be there, just as he always was.

"Can I come back and fish tomorrow, mommy?" Miranda looked into the water in anticipation. She never kept what they caught, always felt bad and threw them back into the water.

"We'll see, but we have to get home now, daddy is home with Elise all by himself and Lord knows what kind of trouble they're in."

Skippy handed over Ryan and teased with his words. "Then you'd better hurry."

"Carter may bring Miranda back tomorrow, but I'll see you on Sunday."

"Like I ain't... fancy dinner... don't need nothing but a simple meal..." He grumbled more to himself as they made their way off the pier.

Miranda was constantly on the lookout in the water and Ryan continued to wave to the old man who smiled and waved back, would for as long as it lasted, and most times until he couldn't see him any longer.

Traditions were important to Sam, even if it was as simple as visiting Skippy McGee every Friday and taking muffins, or a Sunday dinner at times with an old man who sat in a fish shack all day. She'd created many traditions for their children, and the ones on the way Carter didn't know about yet.

They ate cake once a month for breakfast, spent Christmas Eve at home, no matter what. Carter read to them every evening, and even if it was the smallest of things, it was a constant in their lives. Sam's hesitations about being a good mother were dispelled as soon as she'd given birth to their first child, sweet Miranda. She'd had no lessons in motherhood, no good example as a child, but she knew what love was, and how to share it. That's all that mattered.

When they returned home, she laughed when she saw Carter on the ocean edge with their one year old daughter Elise. She in a diaper, he fully clothed and sitting in the sand and water. When they joined him, not only did Miranda and Ryan take the opportunity to play in their clothes, but Sam also sat down in the surf next to him. Elise giggled to see her, climbed over Carter to get into her arms and it didn't bother her that the child's hands were full of muddy, wet sand as she kissed her. To anyone else they would look like a family of fools. A family of wet fools.

"I think she's going to swim before she walks. I ended up here because she insisted." Carter leaned over and kissed Sam, Elise climbed back over to him.

"You're so easy." When she revealed her news, his shock amused her. "You'd better hope she's walking before the other two come along. It's twins this time."

The sound of his laughter boomed loud, told everyone who could hear, that life was good, and Carter pulled her to him. Elise giggled, wrapped her sandy hands around them both, then Miranda and Ryan joined in, they didn't quite understand two babies at once, but laughed anyway.

"We wanted to fill this house. At the rate we're going, I might have to add an entire wing."

"Or two." Sam added. Yes, life was good. A home filled with everything, and cake for breakfast too.

NEW RELEASES COMING SOON BY BON VOYAGE BOOKS AND...

ALISA ALLAN

AFTER MIDNIGHT:

A television reality show on the premise of 'opposites attract' throws two completely different people together. Strangers marry sight unseen and live under the scrutiny of cameras to create a show that will reveal to the world a clash of souls. From the beginnings of a honeymoon aboard a cruise to the Mexican Riviera, to an ending of their ordeal aboard another cruise highlighting Canada/New England, America will watch as two people collide in a blaze of differences. But an unexpected love finds its way through the near impossible.

In the beginning, the payoff of money drives them both. In the end, when choices have to be made, it's the unpredicted payoff of love they find. But for the first time in his life, Drake Hudson learns the lesson of true sacrifice, when he must let go of a woman that is bound by other loyalties. A loyalty that doesn't give her the freedom of choice.

ANGEL MIST:

Things were happening to Morgan Bailey, strange things she couldn't explain. She tried to convince herself things were coincidence, but signs were appearing, odd reminders of her past. A past she didn't want to be drawn back to, one she escaped from. But when an unexpected cruise through Alaska is sent by her dead father, she feels propelled to follow where it will lead, driven by something to be in a strange land for mysterious reasons.

On the first day of her journey, she discovers she'd have to face much more than she'd intended, but Morgan couldn't run from it any longer. Had to face it head on, come to terms with what happened to change her life. After years of turmoil over a guilt and blame she'd placed upon herself, she discovers peace and serenity in majestic land untouched by man. Feels but a miniscule speck on the grand scheme of things and it humbles her, opens her heart to begin healing from the years of pain she'd suffered.

The cruise served well to help her begin to let go of her past haunts, but she would also have to let go of her childhood dreams and her connection to a man that seemed at one time unbreakable. Afterwards, she would have to trust her still unsettled heart to where it wanted to lead her. Morgan discovered she would truly have to go home again before she could find real peace.

THE BEST MAN:

True dreams have a way of embedding themselves and never letting go, and a young woman lives with a childhood dream of what her future would be. Only to discover she would have to sacrifice it for love. Give up what would truly make her happy and take a safe road of solid footing. But her choices come into question when she finds herself in a tailspin of revenge after a failed wedding attempt, finds herself with a stranger on a Hawaiian honeymoon cruise who shows her possibility and hope of something different.

Taken away by a tropical ambiance that fills her senses, she's unaware of a bond of honor and loyalty that couldn't be broken. She's caught in the middle of a binding union, a connection that would prevent her from loving a man who had stolen her heart.

BEYOND THE HORIZON:

Maggie Pace wasn't looking for anything else in her life. Content and fulfilled to be alone after a string of unsuccessful relationships, she wasn't thinking of love and romance as she boarded a cruise ship for a week with friends. Friend's who suffered their own heartbreak and had come to the same conclusion as Maggie, banned the notion of needing a male companion to complicate things.

But surprises are found beyond a horizon that looked vast and empty. None of them expected the dreams that lay in the azure sea, the love they find amidst balmy tropical breezes. Relaxed and carefree among winds of the Caribbean, they left themselves vulnerable to its magic. Exposed and open to a pain they thought they'd left behind them, a pain that began new when a web of lies and deceit are discovered.

ONE LAST TIME:

Alana Gibbs is a happy, single mother until the death of her father throws her into a downhill spiral. She searches for the courage to fight a battle that threatens to drown her. As if reliving a childhood trauma, she suffocates alone and isolated in a struggle that must be overcome. If not, it would completely destroy her.

Taking the last chance she could possibly have to share the world with her son, they set off on a journey of adventure. Board a cruise ship bound for exotic wonder. A night of deception comes back to haunt her, but it leads to an escape of her painful reality. She immerses herself in tropical breezes of another world, finds the unexpected along shores of glorious splendor. But the truth must be faced, and she must risk it all to face it alone.

For more information write us at:

Travel Time Press
163 Mitchells Chance Rd. #212
Edgewater, MD 21037

Visit our website: www.TravelTimePress.com

Write us at the address above or email us from our website to join our mailing list and be the first to know of new releases and pre-release orders and to order books.

SEND US A REVIEW!
We'd love to hear from you. Send us a review at the address above or visit our website.

All titles are available at special quantity discounts for bulk purchases for sales promotion, premiums, fund-raising, education or institutional use.

Special customized printings can also be arranged for bulk purchasing, for details, write or email.